W9-AYD-201

Talon

Talon

J.P. Mercer

P.D. Publishing, Inc.
Clayton, North Carolina

Copyright © 2006 by J.P. Mercer

All rights reserved. No part of this publication may be reproduced, transmitted in any form or by any means, electronic or mechanical, including photocopy, recording, or any information storage and retrieval system, without permission in writing from the publisher. The characters herein are fictional and any resemblance to a real person, living or dead, is purely coincidental.

ISBN-13: 978-1-933720-03-6
ISBN-10: 1-933720-03-4

9 8 7 6 5 4 3 2 1

Cover art and design by Barb Coles
Edited by Day Petersen/Betty Anderson Harmon

Published by:

P.D. Publishing, Inc.
P.O. Box 70
Clayton, NC 27528

http://www.pdpublishing.com

Acknowledgements:

Lynne, you have my sincere thanks and my gratitude. Your skill and time is so very much appreciated.

Sue, you are as always, my friend, my rock.

My thanks go to PD Publishing and to the editors, Day Petersen and Betty Harmon.

DEDICATION

The house seems so quiet without you. Without fail for eighteen years you were there to greet me when I opened the door. Your chair and place beside me at night are heartbreakingly empty. I miss the special little ways you always showed that you loved me. I miss you following me from room to room and constantly being underfoot. Putting up a Christmas tree will never be the same without you. You were a big part of what made the season and putting up a tree so special.

The morning just before you crossed over Rainbow Bridge, as I held you and told you how much I loved you and appreciated all the happiness you had given me, I heard you struggle to purr your last goodbye. It broke my heart. I didn't want you to go. I didn't want to say goodbye to my best friend, but I promised you that you would never suffer.

Thank you, my beautiful Toadie, for toddling lost down the street so many years ago and finding your way into our lives. You keep watch across Rainbow Bridge, Toad. One day you'll see me and we'll never be parted again.

Chapter One

February 25, 1997
Dateline: Washington, CNN...8:32 PM EST

Con Air Flight 209 from Paris, carrying an estimated 500 passengers and crew, including more than 300 Americans, exploded over the Atlantic Ocean at 5:45 PM as it began its descent into JFK airport in New York City. Witnesses report that the plane erupted into a ball of fire as it appeared to collide with a streak of light that lit up the night sky. CNN correspondent Miles Tanner is on the scene and reports that thick fog and darkness are hampering rescue efforts. Early reports indicate that wreckage and remains have been strewn across miles of freezing water. Due to the force of the explosion and the location of the crash, there is little hope that there will be any survivors. Representatives of the FAA and NTSB say that it is too early in their investigation to speculate on what caused the downing of Con Air Flight 209.

Terrorist warnings have been numerous, and transportation facilities have been in an elevated state of alert since fundamentalist Islamic groups in the Middle East threatened a demonstration of force during Easter week. When asked if the crash was the result of terrorist activity, officials declined to comment, saying that an official statement would be issued after the investigation is complete and the plane's black boxes are recovered and examined. No terrorist group has claimed responsibility.

February 25, 1997
Dateline: Washington, CNN...11:48 PM EST

In an address to the nation moments ago, a grim-faced President Wade Kincaide announced that a known terrorist group has claimed responsibility for the destruction of Con Air Flight 209 from Paris that went down at 5:45 PM in the Atlantic Ocean. This same group, led by reputed terrorist, Ashraf Nusair, was responsible for the bombing in Dhahran, Saudi Arabia that targeted U.S. military personnel at the headquarters for the U.S. Air Force's 4404th Wing. The Con Air flight was carrying 485 passengers and crew, all of whom are presumed to be lost. The President's voice shook and he wept openly as he expressed his condolences to the nation, but he was resolute as he issued this warning:

"At this hour, a comprehensive team of experts is on its way to the crash site to conduct an investigation into this disaster. I vow to you, my fellow Americans, and to the world, the deaths on Flight 209, as well as those in the Khobar Tower bombing at King Abdul Aziz Air Base on June 25, 1996, will not go unpunished. I want this warning to be heard in every corner of the globe: any country that harbors the despicable terrorists who committed this heinous act, or any terrorists, will pay the price. Anyone involved in any way will be hunted down and brought to justice. This is my personal promise to the leader and to those responsible: you cannot hide. Look over your shoulder; look into the eyes of the person standing next to you. From this day on, uncertainty will rule your lives. Now, you are the hunted. I give my solemn word to the families of those who died today, and to all who have lost loved ones to an act of terrorism, these contemptible deeds will not go unavenged."

Late March 1997

Due to an accident at the FBI's practical problem training area at Hogan's Alley, Liberty arrived at her Defense Tactics class a few minutes late. She tried to slip into the gym unnoticed, but the instructor had eyes in the back of his head. From day one, it had been obvious to Liberty and to the other NATS, the new agents in training, that he didn't like Liberty. He went out of his way to single her out to harass and to deliberately make the training difficult for her. During the first week, the instructor's opinion that women didn't belong as field agents or at the FBI Academy, particularly women like her, was also obvious.

Liberty cringed when she heard his bellowing voice.

"All right, listen up NATS! I need a volunteer. Sheffer, you'll do. Agent Starr, front and center!"

Liberty made her way to the mat, ignoring the snickering that she heard coming from a few of the male agents. She could see the look of dread mixed with pity and anger on the faces of the other female agents. The best of the class in martial arts, Sheffer was homophobic and just plain mean. He was a stereotypical jock with the attitude that a woman was too weak and too emotional to be a good agent, and that any woman recruit took a spot at the Academy that a "good man" should have. He and some of his cronies had been giving Liberty and the other women a hard time since the beginning of the seventeen-week FBI training. With every step Liberty took toward the mat, she had a sickening feeling that she wasn't going to like the outcome of this exercise. *This ought to be interesting.*

She had barely completed the thought when Sheffer landed a kick that broke her nose and sprayed blood across the mat. A follow-up sweep landed her hard on her back. Dazed, she was trying to clear her head when she felt the boot to her side and heard the sound of ribs cracking. Swimming up through the fog in her mind, she heard a female voice.

"Hey! Wanna try me? Or does it make you feel more of a man to land a sucker punch, then kick an agent when she's down?"

Sheffer chuckled and winked at his buddies. He didn't recognize the woman as Yancy Bane, Special Agent in Charge of Training. Yancy had been absent from Quantico until that morning, and the agents in training had only heard the rumors about the infamous SAC who was as hard and as tough as nails. When Sheffer turned to see what woman was stupid enough to oppose him, he saw the fire in the confident eyes staring back at him. By the time he positioned his lead leg to throw an offensive kick, it was already all but over. Two swift moves from the lissome powerhouse — one, a kick to his kneecap and the second to his groin — had him face down. Howling in pain, with a knee pressing hard between his shoulder blades, his arm was pinned behind him. Everyone could hear the bone on bone sound of his shoulder dislocating.

The stolid redhead leaned over and whispered in his ear, "I never said I couldn't fight dirty. If you can dish it out, you'd better learn to take it, Agent Sheffer." With that, she removed her knee and released Sheffer's arm and stood up.

By this time, Liberty had made it to her knees and was numbly staring at Sheffer lying on the ground in front of her. She was trying to stop the flow of blood from her nose when she felt a cloth pressed against her shoulder and what sounded very much like an order.

"Pinch."

She grimaced as she pressed the cloth against her nose, then instinctively used her forearm to splint the pain she felt along her ribs on the left side. Before she could catch her breath, the redheaded agent knelt in front of her and steadied her head with one hand, while with the other she pushed her nose back in place. It happened so fast that all Liberty could do was gasp and bite her lip to keep from yelling out in pain as she tried to focus on a pair of sympathetic green eyes. Gritting her teeth, her shaking hand held the hanky to her nose. She managed to get to her feet without any help, but the pain in her ribs prevented her from straightening up. "Shouldn't you have let a doctor do that?" The minute the words came out of her mouth, she knew they sounded too harsh. This woman was the only one who had stepped up to stop what no doubt was meant to be a message that women couldn't cut it and weren't wanted.

The SAC turned and looked steadily into the eyes of each NAT, one at a time. "I will say this only once, so you all better listen up. I am a woman, and I am also a damn good agent. I won't go away, so get used to it." A few lowered their eyes in shame, but the Bubbas sneered and looked at her bold-faced. She turned to face the instructor with a look in her eyes that gave a new meaning to the epigram "hell has no fury". She went over to a writhing Sheffer, bent over, then asked with a hint of sarcasm, "Do you want me to put your shoulder back into place?"

Sheffer hissed, "Not on your life, bitch!"

"Suit yourself, but if I were you, if you plan on completing this training, I wouldn't be so damned insubordinate to the SAC. I might really lose my temper." Yancy straightened up and barked, "Get it taken care of, Agent Sheffer, before it swells and becomes more painful." The SAC turned to the instructor, who had paled. "I don't think that there is any point of continuing this exercise today. I will see you and Agent Sheffer in my office at 0600 tomorrow."

Liberty watched with her mouth agape as the dynamo of a woman took charge with few words. The SAC walked past the line of trainees that were now standing at attention, stopping when she reached Liberty.

"Come on, Agent. I'm taking you to the ER."

Chapter Two

The SAC debated whether to lend Liberty a hand getting out to her Jeep or let her save face by walking out under her own steam. The issue was quickly settled when Liberty clenched her jaw, straightened her shoulders as best she could, then followed Yancy out of the gym. Once they were through the door, Liberty leaned against the wall, gasping in short shallow breaths.

The SAC put her hand lightly on Liberty's shoulder. "Try to focus on taking in slow breaths. The hospital isn't that far." Then she said, "My Jeep is in the parking lot. Should I get some help?"

Liberty shook her head, grateful that the woman didn't insist.

"Wait here, I'll get the Jeep and pull up."

Liberty was convinced that the SAC was deliberately aiming the Jeep at every bump and pothole in the road. By the time they reached the hospital at Woodbridge, she was aching all over. Every move and breath was painful.

Yancy parked the Jeep in front of the ER entrance and hopped out. "Wait here," she ordered, then hurried through the automatic doors of the ER. After a few minutes, she returned pushing a wheelchair, and opened the door of the passenger side to help Liberty out of the vehicle. This time Liberty was grateful for the assistance, grimacing in pain as she eased herself into the chair.

A nurse met them at the ER entrance. "If you will give the admitting clerk the necessary information," she said to Yancy, "I'll get your friend into an exam room." Once inside the cubicle, the nurse attempted to assist her onto the exam table. Liberty was hesitant; she didn't want to move. Everything hurt, and the pain along her rib on the left side was making it difficult for her to breathe.

The nurse took one look at her battered, swollen face. "If I leave you in the chair while I go get an ice pack, will you promise not to pass out on me?" Liberty nodded and the nurse hurried out of the room then returned a few minutes later with a rubber glove filled with ice water. "This might help. Can you hold this to your face?" At the confused look that crossed Liberty's face, she clarified. "Lay it across the bridge of your nose. It won't hurt as much as an ice pack would." Liberty took the rubber glove and held it against the bridge of her nose and her forehead. "The doctor has already written orders for stat x-rays of your ribs and an MRI of your skull. She'll be in to see you and do a neurological exam," the nurse said.

"Neurological exam?"

The nurse handed Liberty a small pillow and showed her how to splint her side with it, then looked at the form on the clipboard that the admitting clerk had handed her. It included a brief description of Liberty's injuries, and how she had sustained them. "Says here you took quite a beating, kicked in the head and in the ribs. I'm sure the doctor wants to evaluate you for concussion and determine whether or not to keep you overnight for observation." The pretty but tired looking nurse gave Liberty a long look. "You might as well stay in the wheelchair until they come to take you to Radiology." She turned and took the gown off the exam table. You'll need to undress and put this on before they come. I'll help you if you want..."

"Uh...no, I can do it. Thanks."

The nurse placed the gown across Liberty's lap, then folded her arms across her chest and leaned against the counter. "Modest? It's nothing I haven't seen before."

Liberty's antenna picked up the signal. Under other circumstances, she might have welcomed it. Instead, all she could do was force a pained smile. "Thank you, but I think I can handle it." The nurse feigned a disappointed look, then responded to an overhead page and was out of the room before Liberty could ask the whereabouts of the woman who had brought her in.

Doctor Jacquelyn Biscayne stood in front of a series of lighted boxes, viewing the patient's films. Standing beside her was radiologist Ramesh Patel. "Nothing remarkable — no internal or cranial bleeding, no facial fracture. It's better than I anticipated from the history I read. Being kicked in the face with that much force could have done much more damage, but I think we can safely rule out traumatic brain injury. My understanding is that she never lost consciousness, and the agent that brought her in didn't notice any changes in her mental state."

Patel pointed to the eleventh and twelfth ribs on the left side. "Cracked and bruised, but there's no damage to the spleen or any other internal organs. She'll be plenty sore for a while. Are you going to admit her overnight for observation?"

"Hmm, I should do just that, to teach her a lesson about picking on someone bigger than she is." Doctor Biscayne shook her head thoughtfully. "Or for letting someone get the advantage over her like this. I'll collect her friend and go give her the good news."

Liberty lay on the uncomfortable exam table staring up at the florescent lights, trying to find a position that didn't hurt. She eased her legs up, then over the side, using one hand to close the flimsy gown in the back while pressing the small paper pillow into her side with the other. *Gee, this is miserable. They call this thing a pillow?* She was still trying to catch her breath when the curtain opened and two women stepped into the room, one being the SAC who had come to her rescue, and the other... "Jake?"

"Well, the good news is: your head is hard, no fracture. But you will have to be observed closely for the next twenty-four hours." Jake looked at the pillow Liberty was clenching white fisted to her side. "The bad news is: your ribs are cracked and bruised. More bad news, my friend — Extra Strength Tylenol will have to do you for pain for the next twenty-four hours."

Yancy looked curiously at Jake, then back to Liberty. "You two know each other?"

"Uh, Jake, what about my nose?" Liberty looked at the SAC, embarrassed that she had sounded doubtful, "I mean...um...she kinda..."

Jake chuckled and held out a hand to the redhead. "We haven't been introduced. Yes, we know each other. I'm Doctor Biscayne, Agent Jacquelyn Biscayne, and thank you for rescuing my roommate here." Jake shot a look at Liberty. "You did a good job on her nose. It would have been a whole lot more painful to do it now if you hadn't, and please call me Jake."

Yancy took Jake's hand, all the while wondering about the roommate comment. "I'm Yancy Bane, Special Agent in Charge of Training at Quantico. Seems Agent Starr got herself into a bit of a mess."

Embarrassed, Liberty's face turned beet red as she inwardly groaned. *Why me!*

Yancy winked at her and said to Jake, "I'm sure your roommate didn't think that reducing that break was a good idea at the time."

"Be that as it may, it was a job well done." Jake noted the looks Liberty was getting from Yancy that were obviously going over Liberty's head. Jake crossed her arms and looked teasingly at Liberty. "I should admit you overnight for observation." The look of protest on Liberty's face had Jake chuckling. "But I won't. You can—" An emergency page blared overhead and Jake shrugged. "Sorry." Then she hurried out of the exam room.

Yancy studied Liberty a moment before she asked, "Do you need a ride home, Agent Starr?"

Liberty eased herself off the exam table, trying to keep the back of her gown closed. "Thanks, but Jake will be off duty soon. I'll wait and ride home with her, but I...uh...want to thank you for your help today."

"No thanks needed. I can only apologize for the actions of a few. Take care, so you can resume your training." She handed Liberty a card with her phone number on it. "Call me if you need anything. You also have the option to file a complaint against Sheffer." With that, Yancy Bane turned and left the room.

Liberty moped around the apartment over the weekend, nursing her bruised body and her ego. Her thoughts had been on the confident SAC, more to the point, the woman that had taken Sheffer down. She was attractive, with copper colored hair and probing green eyes. Liberty wasn't ready to admit it, but she was attracted to the feisty agent. On Monday morning, against Jake's advice, she reported back to Quantico to resume training, opting not to make an issue out of it by filing charges. Two weeks went by and she hadn't seen the SAC. Several times she'd taken out the card with Yancy's phone number, debating whether she should call Agent Bane and thank her properly. She was driving Jake mad with her pacing and restlessness, and was just about to ask Jake again whether she thought she should call the Yancy when Jake put her hand up to stop her.

"I took the..." a big grin crossed Jake's face, "*liberty* of inviting the SAC to dinner tonight." Jake looked at her watch. "In about an hour."

Liberty stopped dead in her tracks. "You didn't! Tell me you didn't!"

"I'd say you have about fifty-five minutes to get out of those sweats, take a shower, and make yourself presentable, while I throw a salad together."

Liberty dashed down the hall toward her room, then stopped and ran back to the kitchen. "Is that all we have, salad? Shouldn't we...shall I...?"

"For God's sake, Liberty, go! I have it covered."

Liberty had just finished dressing when the doorbell rang. She was nervous, and that wasn't like her. She looked into the mirror, hoping that the image that reflected back was one that Yancy might be interested in, instead of the pitiful sight she must have been the last time Yancy had seen her — her face bloodied, her nose out of place, and her eyes blackened. As a rule, she could always tell if a woman was interested, but given the situation at the time, she had no clue if Yancy Bane was gay. *Well, I guess tonight I'll find out, one way or the other.*

The moment Liberty entered the front room and looked into

Yancy's eyes, there wasn't a doubt in her mind that she and Yancy would be lovers. And by the way Yancy's eyes feasted on her body, she knew the woman was thinking along those same lines.

Jake was amused at the ardent looks that passed between Liberty and Yancy during dinner. In the time that they had been roommates, Jake knew that many women had tried to catch Liberty's eye, but for Liberty it was all business and work and she had not found any woman interesting enough to ask out. Jake looked appraisingly at Yancy. It would take a strong woman to get Liberty's attention, and Yancy was definitely that — very confident and sure of herself, but not in an arrogant way. Yancy, like Liberty, was an attractive woman, but in contrast to Liberty's natural easiness, Jake observed that Yancy possessed a practiced ease. Yancy listened attentively, skillfully including both Jake and Liberty in the conversation. She seemed to be a woman who knew exactly what she wanted, and it was evident that she was interested in Liberty. Jake could see by Liberty's response that Yancy Bane was exactly the kind of woman that Liberty could lose her heart to.

After they'd eaten, the three women sat and relaxed in the living room, sharing conversation and a bottle of wine. Jake finished one glass, then decided it was time to leave the two women alone, in addition to which she was looking forward to a night when she could turn her beeper off and sleep in. "If you ladies will excuse me, I have an early day tomorrow." She shot a quick warning glance at Liberty, who knew that it was actually her day off, then turned to their guest. "Yancy, we will have to do this again soon." With a pointed look at Liberty, she left the room.

Each waited for the other to say something, then finally Yancy chuckled and got up from the sofa chair on which she was sitting and went to sit beside Liberty on the couch. Liberty's breath caught as Yancy laid cool fingers lightly on her forearm.

"How are your ribs?"

Liberty swallowed. Yancy smelled like she looked — provocative and spicy. Her closeness was affecting Liberty in ways that had her pulse racing; she definitely liked Yancy's touch. It excited and aroused her, sending shivers along her spine and down her legs. The woman was looking at her in a sensual way and Liberty felt her mouth go dry. "They're fine. Looks like I'll live."

Yancy's eyes never left Liberty's lips as her fingers continued to tease along Liberty's arm to the underside of her breast along her ribs. "Are they...too tender?"

"I don't know. Too tender for what?" Liberty rested a hand lightly on Yancy's shoulder.

Yancy swung her leg across Liberty's lap, positioning herself with her hands resting on either side of Liberty's head against the couch. Her voice lowered to a throaty whisper. "Well, let's see... Better yet, let me show you."

The moment Yancy's wet tongue traced her trembling lips, Liberty's world started to spin. She sank her fingers into Yancy's hair as her lips parted and hungrily took in what Yancy was offering, what her life had been missing. Yancy was the spark that ignited every fiber in her body, fueling desires she never knew existed. When they broke for air, Yancy's eyes held Liberty on the cusp of drowning helplessly in their wake. Yancy's words unleashed a passion in Liberty that superseded reason.

"Come home with me tonight. I could ask you out to dinner tomorrow, wine and dine you, take the time to court you, while all the while both of us would already know what we want. I leave on an important assignment in a few days and I don't want to waste a minute that I could be making love to you." Yancy leaned in and took Liberty's earlobe between her teeth, pressing her pelvis hard into Liberty's abdomen.

Liberty's breath caught when she felt the wetness of Yancy's tongue inside her ear and the heat permeating through her shirt against her belly. Her hands found Yancy's buttocks to pull her in tighter, twisting her body until Yancy was lying under her on the couch. "You're crazy, and you're making me crazy. This is insane, but I want you now, right here."

They made love on the couch, then half supported each other to Liberty's bedroom and made love until the light of dawn stole through the small spaces between the slats of the blinds. Liberty woke when the smell of coffee filtered through her exhaustion. She opened her eyes to see Yancy lying across her thighs, and thought briefly about trying to ease out from under the redhead without waking her, but the sight and feel of Yancy's warm, naked body riveted her in place. Her eyes drank in the firm body and soft curves she had gotten to know so well throughout the night. Her fingertips gently followed across the small of Yancy's back, then along the soft skin and shape of her hip.

Yancy's sleep-filled voice broke through the peaceful morning silence. "See or feel anything you like?"

"I see lots of things I like, and I sure do like what I feel. Come up here; I want to hold you."

Yancy crawled into Liberty's arms, her muscles feeling the workout she'd given them through the night. "Oh, and I thought I was in shape. Do you think we can bum a cup of that coffee I smell?"

Liberty chuckled, nibbling on Yancy's neck. "I think so, if Jake doesn't kill us both for keeping her awake all night."

A sexy smile crossed Yancy's face and her Irish eyes sparkled mischievously. "Were we that loud?"

"Well, you were. I seem to remember a few screams that might have shaken the pictures off the wall."

Yancy slid down Liberty's body taking a hardened nipple in her mouth, playfully teasing it with her teeth. "My screams? Just my screams, huh? We'll see about that."

Jake was pouring a cup when she heard the renewed sounds coming from Liberty's room. She looked at the clock on the kitchen wall and groaned, then chuckled. "It's going to be an interesting morning." She fleetingly thought about getting dressed and going in to the hospital, then shrugged and took her coffee and toast and headed to her bedroom. "I'm too tired. I'll be asleep before my head hits the pillow."

The following few days, Liberty and Yancy spent every moment they could together at Yancy's apartment, in bed making love, or just lying in each other's arms talking about nothing and everything. The time passed too quickly and the day came when Yancy was to leave on a special assignment. Liberty went to Yancy's office. They planned to have a special dinner before Yancy left, but the agent in the outer office told Liberty that Yancy had already left that morning, as planned. Liberty didn't see or hear from Yancy during the remainder of the training. It was the last day at Quantico, and Liberty planned to make an appearance at the traditional Academy celebration, then go to dinner with Jake, just the two of them. She was cleaning out her locker when an agent approached her. "SAC wants to see you, Starr. Would you come with me, please?"

Hurting from Yancy's apparent abandonment, Liberty grudgingly complied. *If Yancy is back, why send an agent to ask me to come to her office? And why didn't she get in touch or call?* When they reached the office, the agent excused himself and left the room. A few minutes later, Yancy entered with a man Liberty recognized as one of President Wade Kincaide's personal advisors, Brady Lawrence. He was the first to speak, as he handed her an envelope bearing the presidential seal.

"Thank you for coming, Agent Starr. Would you take a moment to read this letter?"

Liberty stared at the seal, her curiosity piqued and her heart beating more rapidly. She hoped the slight shaking of her hands was not noticeable as her fingers ran across the honored seal before breaking it and opening the letter. She looked up at Brady Lawrence, then to Yancy, before lowering her eyes to read.

Thank you, Agent Starr, for opening this letter. Brady Lawrence, the man who delivered it to you, represents me. I am sure you are aware of the hysteria that faces us as acts of terrorism increase in frequency around the world. Terrorism has wounded the heart of our country and has struck fear in the hearts of people of every nation. I have pledged to fight this pestilence and bring those responsible to justice. Mr. Lawrence will explain as much as he can to you at this time, then you will be faced with a decision. One that you will not make lightly and possibly the most difficult you will ever make in your life. We will speak soon, Agent Starr. Until then, I wish you well.

Wade Kincaide

Liberty looked up at Yancy and found the seriousness of what she'd just read on Yancy's face.

Brady Lawrence broke the moment. "Agent Starr, right now you must have many questions. I will explain to you what I can. I am going to ask you to leave today to participate in a special Delta Force training at Fort Bragg, in North Carolina. The individuals with whom you will be training have been carefully screened and chosen from groups such as the Rangers and Special Forces. Each trainee has an exemplary record and extraordinary special skills. The standard Delta Force training is no picnic, but the rigorous training you will undergo will be even more intense. If you are one of the few that make it through the training, you will be asked to make a decision. If you choose to decline this assignment, you will continue with the Bureau and your career. We would ask you never to speak of this meeting." Brady Lawrence exchanged a long look with Yancy, then quietly left the room.

Liberty sat looking at the letter she held in her hand. "You were involved in this before we met. Tell me, when did you decide to recruit me — before or after we slept together?"

Yancy took the letter out of Liberty's hand and looked her in the eye. "Yes, I was already involved with this assignment when we met, but that had nothing to do with us. I slept with you because I couldn't resist you, then I fell in love with you. Now, Agent Starr, if you choose to go to Fort Bragg, I suggest you get packed. We leave in an hour."

Wade Kincaide was admired and was one of the most respected presidents in the history of the country. He was known to be fair and just. His altruistic goal was to make a difference and to restore the American people's faith in their government. Kincaide had only been in office a short time when the level of terrorist activity around the world increased, threatening the security of the United States and world peace. Frustrated at the political stonewalls and the countries that encouraged and harbored terrorists, he formed a covert group called the Talons that would function in the shadows, beyond the law if necessary. Brady Lawrence, Kincaide's aide, was given the task of assembling the elite force from the many government agencies.

Liberty was the optimal candidate; she had no ties or family to miss her. She'd been abandoned when she was a few days old at an adobe mission church in the foothills of the Sangre de Cristo Mountains in New Mexico. Because El Santuario De Chimayó is a sacred place to the Native American as well as the Hispanic communities of New Mexico, she was kept and raised by the Pueblo who found her. She was treated no differently than any other child and her needs were met, but Liberty never felt that she fit in with her light colored eyes and blonde hair. What remained constant in her young life was her desire to learn and to excel in sports, which earned her a choice of scholarships to several prestigious colleges. She had chosen to study law enforcement and found her way into the FBI academy at Quantico, where Yancy had found her.

During the arduous training at Fort Bragg, Yancy didn't show Liberty any special consideration. If anything she seemed to push Liberty harder than the rest. They agreed that it would be best if they kept their distance from one another. Only the most resilient and toughest made it through the demanding training and each that did accepted the President's call and stood proud to be a Talon. When Liberty surpassed all expectations and successfully completed the training, she chose to join the Talons.

For the protection of the presidency and anonymity of the Talons, each agent who agreed to serve the President in that capacity was reported killed during an assignment or on a mission. Liberty Starr ceased to exist. The notice of her death was delivered to the only address on record for next of kin, the church of Chimayó, New Mexico. It read — To Whom It May Concern. So it was then that Liberty found herself standing in the rain at Arlington, watching the muddy dirt being shoveled onto her coffin.

Later, she sat alone in a hotel room, staring at her new identity spread out on the table before her. She had never felt as lonely as she did at that moment. When she heard the light knock on her door, Liberty crossed the room and opened the door to find Yancy standing in the rain, soaking wet.

They stared at each other for the longest time until Yancy said, "I couldn't stay away any longer. I've missed you."

Tears formed in Liberty's eyes as she held out a hand to Yancy and gently pulled her in out of the rain, into her arms. Kissing the drops of rain on Yancy face, she sobbed, "God, I've missed you, too. It's been torture seeing you every day and not being able to touch you. I agonized over the decision to join the Talons because I knew that if I did it would mean I would never again hold you or make love with you. If I didn't, I knew I would never see you again."

Yancy returned Liberty's kisses with equal passion, and with trembling fingers started to unbutton Liberty's shirt.

Liberty covered Yancy's fingers with her own. "Before we make love, tell me this is not a good-bye or just for one night. I couldn't stand it if it were. I would rather..." The look in Yancy's eyes and her fingers caressing along her cheek told Liberty everything that she needed to know.

At first, Liberty was assigned to infiltrate grass roots organizations and militant groups to obtain information regarding their loyalties to the United States government. No one was hurt or killed, and the information was used to monitor and avert the escalation of radical movements. It wasn't long before the assignments became more complex and demanding and her role changed.

Liberty and Yancy lived in a world of intrigue, of extreme solutions to a clear and present danger to the interests of the United States. They'd both vowed to do whatever it took to protect those interests, and they knew the risks and the rules. They'd talked about it briefly, the "what ifs", both knowing that each day they were able to be together could be the last, and that there was no road back. For obvious reasons, fraternization was frowned upon and discouraged, so was developing emotional ties amongst the team. As far as Liberty knew, she and Yancy were the only Talons that were lovers.

The only time the entire team had come together was in a clandestine gathering in the Adirondack Mountains. They met in a secret, de-commissioned, nuclear underground site that had been converted into a survival shelter for the President, his family, and a select group of his advisors in the event of nuclear or chemical attack. In her mind, she could see the cold dispassionate eyes of Brady Lawrence, and his words wrapped around her heart, squeezing the life out of it.

"It is rare that we will all be together in the same place. Some of your paths may cross on an assignment, and you may never see that agent again. Some of you will die serving your country. You will live your lives in the new identities we have provided, but don't get too comfortable with that personage because your identity will change often. The person you started out as has been buried with honors. Fingerprints, dental records, anything that could ID you as that person have been altered. If you are ever detained or apprehended, you will never be connected to any agency of the United States government. You will be identified as a rogue mercenary employed by a foreign interest, a political fanatic working alone or as a common criminal, depending on the circumstances. Never draw attention to yourself, and never ask questions about a fellow agent or events that might occur. Remember that the name and the person you know today will not exist tomorrow."

Liberty and Yancy took every precaution, determined to stay together between assignments. Willingly, they lived their lives in the shadows for the honor to serve their country and their President. Often, they'd talked about the new life and identities promised to them when the Talons had accomplished their mission of curtailing the acts of terrorism around the world by eliminating the leaders of each cell. Devoted to that goal, they knew that their sacrifices were necessary and that what they were doing took priority above their own personal dreams and desires.

President Kincaide was using the powers of his office to help in anyway he could, including diligently tracking the trail of money and cutting off the funds that were being filtered through various countries and banks that supported terrorist activities.

The day finally came when the Talons were ready to move on the terrorist, Ashraf Nusair. Liberty was the one chosen to go into Iran to eliminate Nusair, the most important assignment any Talon had been given. Taking out Nusair, was the ultimate goal of the Talons. Liberty felt honored that she'd been chosen. She had trained hard and she was ready.

Yancy was present in the room when Armanno Santini, the commander of the Talons, briefed Liberty on the assignment. Yancy showed no emotion, and when Liberty's gaze met Yancy's eyes it was like looking into an ice storm. In a few hours, Liberty was to depart for Iran. She wanted to say her goodbye to Yancy in private. They rode back to their apartment in silence; neither wanted to talk and neither mentioned the mission.

When they arrived at the parking garage, they walked to the elevator and rode up to the fifth floor, not touching, still in silence. Yancy unlocked the door and reached for the light, but Liberty's hand gently stopped her. She heard a sound like that of a wounded animal escape from deep in Yancy's throat and felt Yancy trembling as she pulled her into her arms. They stood in the dark, holding each other tightly. Yancy was first to speak. Her voice betrayed the turmoil and emotion she was feeling. "This mission is dangerous and I... It should be me going instead of you. When I learned that you were the one assigned to this mission, I asked Armanno to let me go. I'm more experienced than you and..."

Liberty tenderly pressed her finger to Yancy's lips. "Hush, I'll be back; I promise." Yancy's quivering lips found Liberty's neck and her hands fervently started to pull at Liberty's clothes. Liberty heard her own emotion filled voice repeating, "I'll be back. Believe me, I'll be back."

They slipped to the floor and Yancy started an urgent trail of sweet pleasure down Liberty's body, licking at the rivulets of passion that formed on her skin. Yancy's hands and tongue were everywhere — driving her wild. Her warm, moist tongue found a swollen nipple, then found and tasted the tender skin in the crook of her thighs. Yancy's fingers slid through her wetness and entered her. Frantic hips rose to meet fierce thrusts until she reached a place of no thought, just an overpowering awareness of the incredible feeling that was building, taking her to a place of delirious pleasure. Every nerve ending snapped and met head on at the same time, lighting up the darkness behind Liberty's closed eyes just as lightning across a night sky. Before the waves of orgasms had stopped, Yancy took her with her mouth until she begged her to stop.

Their lovemaking was always passionate and filled with desire, but this time it was so much more. The uncertainty of seeing each other again was tearing at both of them. Spent, they lay in the darkness, side by side on the cool tile floor of the apartment staring at the ceiling. When the warmth of Yancy's fingers found and gently wrapped around hers, Liberty turned, holding back a sob, and went into Yancy's arms. They needed to feel each other, to be close. Before Liberty left the apartment, they made love one more time, tender love. All the while she lovingly held Yancy and made love to her, she whispered over and over that she would be coming back.

March 1999, Tehran, Iran, before dawn

Clothed in the conservative shirt and loose pants of the Muslim male, the figure ghosted along the broken pavement of the narrow streets, merging into the darkened shadows of the crouched buildings of south Tehran. The impoverished, polluted heart of ancient Persia was far removed from the trendy, westernized high-rise buildings of modern Tehran. Lurking in the dark passageways and behind blackened windows, menacing, hostile eyes watched, eyes that sheltered and protected terrorists with the blind sanction of the government.

The piercing, melodious muezzin's cry broke through the silence, announcing Azan, the pre-dawn's call to prayer. The figure slowed then disappeared into the black recess of a doorway to wait. Intent ebon eyes followed the flow of Muslims on their trek to the domed mosque.

An awaited sound — the creaking of a door opening nearby in the darkness — then three men appeared out of a narrow alleyway. The shadowy figure silently stepped out behind the men, blending in unnoticed with others answering the call to prayer, following them across a courtyard and through a tiled archway. Each man stopped to ceremoniously remove his shoes before entering the male place of ablution to perform the wudu, the ritual cleansing before prayer.

As promised by the American President two years earlier, the time for retribution had come. Before the light of another day spread across Iran, the terrorists responsible for the deaths on Flight 209 and at Khobar Towers would feel the retribution of the Talon. For months, President Kincaide's elite counter-terrorist squad had doggedly tracked every move the terrorists had made, while Kincaide had appealed to the government of Iran to make arrests and to extradite the terrorists. Iran repeatedly and adamantly denied that they were harboring terrorists in their country. All the while the political posturing was taking place, the Talons were preparing to deliver the promised justice.

The figure waited, knowing that the three terrorists would be the last to leave the cleansing area prior to entering the cavernous place of prayer. When the three were alone, the figure moved inside unnoticed. A hand slid quickly inside a shirt, and a glint of light gleamed menacingly along a thin, razor sharp blade. A wraith moved silently, swiftly across the room. In a split second, the throat of one of the men was cut, his life's blood flowing onto the sacred ground. Before a cry of warning could be uttered, the second man met the same fate. Then the blade slid effortlessly into the base of the leader's skull while he was still bent washing his feet, killing him instantly. The acrid smell of death and the storm to come hung suspended in the air as the man slumped silently forward, the cleansing water of the ablution running blood red with retribution.

Airspace over Saudi Arabia, shortly after daybreak the same day

Safely back in the private jet, the lone Talon stood in front of the bathroom mirror and removed the dark contact lenses to reveal hazel eyes. Undressing and placing the bloody clothes in a plastic bag, she stepped into the shower and let the hot water run over a toned body and firm breasts. The water running down her tense body turned black as her short hair was restored to its natural dark blonde.

Liberty was committed to the cause and to the mission of the Talons, understanding well the need to eliminate the leaders of the brutal acts of terrorism that were increasing in frequency around the world. It wasn't her first mission or her first kill, but the immediate aftermath was always the same. Liberty's heightened senses and the adrenaline flowing through her veins pounded at her temples, keeping her strung tight and on edge to a point that demanded release. She retrieved a bottle of water from the small refrigerator and settled into a comfortable leather chair for the solitary trip back to the States then turned on the satellite-viewing screen to watch a news bulletin.

This morning before dawn in Tehran, Iran, the reputed terrorist leader Ashraf Nusair and two of his followers were assassinated as they prepared to worship. Nusair had claimed responsibility for the 1997 crash of Con Air Flight 209, which killed all 485 on board, the majority of whom were Americans. Nusair and his terrorist cell were also responsible for the 1996 Khobar Towers bombing and the rash of U.S. Embassy bombings in 1998. The Iranian government denies any knowledge of how Nusair entered Iran or that he was hiding in Tehran. United States intelligence sources have tracked funding and training for Nusair's terrorist cell to Osama Bin Laden. It is not known who was responsible for the assassinations, but officials of the Iranian government have protested the act of violence on their holy ground and pledge to launch a full investigation.

Liberty turned off the large screen and stared out the window. She was alone, suspended between two worlds. There would be no communication with another human being during the flight. She would never see the pilot, nor would the pilot see her. She thought about the mission and the objective of the Talons, and all the sacrifices that had been made to ensure success. The Talons had undergone stringent training and dedicated long hours to practice scenarios to bring to justice those who were responsible for the reign of terror that was holding the world hostage in a grip of fear.

The past two years had been the most difficult, and at the same time, the happiest years of Liberty's life. The one thing that had made everything bearable for her was Yancy. Soon she could be back with her lover. That thought pacified her and calmed the inner conflict that her conscious mind would not allow her to acknowledge. She leaned back and closed her eyes, remembering the day she'd met Yancy. Her memories took her all the way to when they were making love the night before she left.

Chapter Three

Liberty's thoughts about the past were interrupted by a disembodied voice that echoed through the otherwise empty plane, briefly announcing their impending landing. She reinserted the dark contacts over her hazel eyes and pulled on a dark, hooded sweatshirt, folded and tied a red bandanna gang style around her hair, and then slipped the hood up. When she looked into the mirror, she saw the effect she wanted: a young woman dressed in torn jeans that no one could describe with any accuracy.

As the plane taxied into an empty hangar, she slipped on a pair of latex gloves and took a car key from an envelope that had been left for her in the cabin. She exited the plane and walked a short distance to a plain, older sedan, then drove to the exit leading to the congested inner city. Keeping well within the speed limit, she blended into the early morning commuter traffic. Cautiously taking several exits along the route, she reentered the freeway, all the while keeping a watchful eye on the rear view mirror. She drove for two hours before she exited the freeway again. This time she pulled into a busy shopping center and parked in the crowded lot. She looked around for a few minutes watching to see if anyone pulled in after her. Satisfied that she wasn't being followed, she left the key in the ignition and walked toward the entrance, pulling off the gloves and depositing them in the nearest trashcan.

The schematic she'd memorized was exact; the rest rooms were right where it indicated they would be. Liberty entered the last stall, removed the hooded sweatshirt and bandanna, and combed her fingers through her short blonde hair. She retrieved a key from under the lid of the toilet paper dispenser and exited the shopping center through a door on the opposite end from where she had entered. As planned, another nondescript car was waiting. She drove to a more affluent part of the city to another shopping center where she carefully followed the plan to the letter. This time, dressed in a business suit that had been left in the previous car, she entered her own vehicle. She proceeded to drive home to the apartment that she shared with Yancy when they were both between assignments.

As Liberty drove, she thought about her lover and the surprise that she'd planned for Yancy when this mission was completed. When she'd left on assignment less than forty-eight hours before, Yancy was understandably nervous and on edge. She'd looked worried, and Liberty had the strangest feeling that it wasn't just about her going on this assignment. As Yancy made her promise one last time to be careful, she saw a look in Yancy's eyes that she had never seen before. Yancy kissed her as if for the last time, and her last words were that she loved her more than she ever thought possible. That was something she had never done before.

Driving toward the apartment they now shared, Liberty passed along the tree-lined street of well-kept homes and apartments with their sprawling manicured lawns. She was struck by the extreme contrast between the circumstances of a woman who lived in the U.S. and that of a woman in the Middle East. She was going home to her lover, a woman. Although there were undeniably still prejudices in the U.S., things were better here than in many Middle Eastern countries, where if a woman were to lay with another woman, it was punishable by death. In the United States, a woman could walk the streets alone, shake a man's hand and look him in the eye, and most certainly compete with him in love and business. She felt proud to be serving her country as part of a force that was doing something to safeguard the freedoms that so many took for granted.

As she turned the corner onto her street, Liberty's heart started to pound, just like it did every time she thought of coming home to Yancy. Smiling for the first time since she'd left on the mission, she thought about how beautiful Yancy looked after they'd made love the night before. Both hoped that when Liberty returned, they would have a few uninterrupted days before either one was sent out on another assignment. Liberty wondered how Yancy would react to the gift she planned to give to her tonight that she had hidden in her drawer. When she pulled into the building parking garage, she was surprised to see a car parked in her space. She also thought it odd that Yancy's Jeep wasn't in its spot next to hers. Disappointed, she feared that Yancy probably had been sent on assignment.

Liberty was constantly aware of everything around her; looking over her shoulder had become second nature, necessary to staying alive. Something didn't feel right. An uneasy feeling prickled down her spine. She hadn't seen Yancy's Jeep out in front of the building either, and it struck her as odd that the car in her space bore the identifying sticker of a resident, especially when there were vacant spaces available. Anxious to get up to the apartment, she parked in Yancy's empty space. She had a creepy feeling that she was being watched and she unconsciously unbuttoned her jacket and ran her fingers along the pistol in the holster clipped to her belt. The sense of unease grew stronger as she retrieved the apartment key from under the dashboard and got out of the car. Listening intently as she walked toward the elevator, her keen ear was aware that the only sound was of her own footstep echoing off the cement walls.

Liberty got off on the fifth floor and walked down the hall to apartment 523, telling herself that the uneasiness she felt was just the remnants of adrenaline from the mission. Wanting everything to be perfect, she regretted that she hadn't stopped for flowers and a special bottle of wine. Tonight she was going to give Yancy the ring she'd had specially designed — cascading diamonds and sapphires set in white gold, the stones of both their birthdays.

A foreboding sense that something was wrong was flashing a warning; her pulse raced as she stood outside the door fumbling to get her key into the lock. When it wouldn't fit, a feeling of panic gripped her. Frustrated, she tried it again, cursing under her breath. "Damn. What the hell?"

Instinctively, she examined the key, running her fingers along the edge, relieved that it was smooth and felt used. Her blood ran like ice water through her veins and her heart hammered as a fist tightened around her chest. She hadn't realized that she was leaning on the buzzer until the door was opened by an elderly, frightened looking woman wearing a robe.

"Can I help you? Is something wrong?"

Startled and confused, Liberty stammered, "I...I...was looking for...the woman who lives here. Is she home?"

"I'm sorry. My husband and I are the only ones who live here. Are you sure that you have the right apartment?"

Liberty struggled to maintain an outward calm, but inside that fist was squeezing the life out of her and her world was tumbling out of control. Her gut clenched and her mind raced frantically. *This can't be happening.* She wanted to scream Yancy's name and push her way into the apartment, instead, she stepped back away from the door. "I'm sorry; it's been a while. I was sure this was her apartment number. How long have you lived here?"

"Over three years, dear. Perhaps the manager could help you find your friend."

"Yes, perhaps, thank you. I'm sorry to have disturbed you."

"No harm done." With that, the woman smiled and closed the door.

Liberty was stunned. Struggling not to hyperventilate, she willed herself to walk back to the elevator. Her mind was reeling as she walked into the manager's office. The pretty receptionist who always flirted with them both greeted her as if she hadn't seen her for a long time, although it had been less than two days earlier. "Hello, Sarah, it's nice to have you back. You've been gone a while this time. Did you have a good trip?"

Liberty felt the hairs on the back of her neck standing on end; on full alert, every fiber in her body screamed for this game to end. Sarah Fletcher was the name Liberty had used since her death was faked and she'd moved into the apartment with Yancy. Her house of cards was tumbling down and Liberty felt as if she were walking through the Twilight Zone.

"What can I help you with today, Sarah?"

Liberty's thoughts were running rampant. It felt as if she was standing outside her body, watching a scene being played out over which she had no control. "Karen, I can't get my key to work. Could you open the apartment with your master key?"

"Sure, hold on while I get the keys and I'll go up with you. I wanted to check on Mrs. Bleaken's cat anyway. She's visiting her daughter for a few days and I told her I would make sure Tuff has food and water."

Liberty followed Karen into the elevator. Her knees felt weak as she watched Karen push the button for the sixth floor, not the fifth. *Why are we going to the sixth floor?* Karen led the way down the hall, stopping in front of apartment 623. The veins in Liberty's neck distended and her pulse pounded as she tried to hide the difficulty she was having taking in a breath. Instead of using her keys, Karen held out her hand.

"Let's try your key again, Sarah. If it doesn't work, I'll have a new one made."

The adrenaline was pumping through Liberty and everything around her seemed distorted, in slow motion, as she watched the key slide into the lock without a problem.

"It seems to be working fine now, Sarah."

Liberty fought the taste of bile and fear that was rising from her stomach. "Yes...I'm sorry. I should have tried it again before bothering you."

"Oh, no bother. I always like to see you when you're in town, Sarah. Is there anything else I can help you with?"

Karen was obviously part of whatever was going on, and Liberty knew she had to go along — for the moment. Inside she was raging, but she controlled her emotions and chose her words carefully. "Silly of me, but I seem to have forgotten my parking space number."

Karen laughed. "You have been working too hard. It's the same as your apartment number, 623."

"Of course, how could I've forgotten that?"

"Well, I'm off to the second floor to feed the cat. I hope to see more of you while you're home this time."

Liberty had deliberately avoided mentioning Yancy or the name

Yancy had been using, but she needed to judge Karen's reaction when she heard the name. "Thank you, Karen. Oh, before you go, my friend, Lee, the redhead, has she left any messages for me?"

"Lee? I don't remember her, Sarah, but I'll check and call you if you have any messages when I get back to the office."

She's good; I'll give her that. And she seems to be in a hurry to leave. What the hell is going on!

Liberty waited until Karen walked down the hall and got into the elevator before she drew her pistol, pushed open the door, and carefully entered the apartment. Everything looked the same as it had just forty-eight hours ago, except that it was the wrong apartment. Her eyes took in her sneakers alongside her favorite chair, and the newspaper that she had been reading still lay folded on the coffee table in the exact spot she'd left it. But where there had been two wineglasses that she'd rinsed and set on the sink, now there was only one. With every footstep she took toward the bedroom, the blood pounded painfully against her temples.

A paralyzing, cold fear washed over Liberty as she reached the door to the bedroom. She knew what she would find — emptiness. Yancy was gone. She'd awakened many a night in a cold sweat clinging to Yancy, as if she had a premonition, a forewarning this day would come. She pushed open the door. Everything was in its place, except that every trace of Yancy had been removed. She walked to the bureau and ran her finger along the frame that once held a picture of her with her arms around Yancy. Now it held only a picture of her. She opened the drawer, searching for the velvet ring box she'd hidden there just two days ago. It was gone. The room echoed her silent scream of denial at the realization that Yancy had vanished.

Liberty knew the rules — no questions, but her mind railed against it. None of this made any sense; she needed to get into the apartment downstairs. Maybe she could find something that would give her some answers. If Yancy had been sent on an assignment and wasn't coming back, why go to the elaborate ruse of changing apartments and removing everything that indicated that Yancy had ever been there?

Liberty waited until dark; then went down the rear stairwell of her building to scout out an empty apartment in the new building directly across the street. From there she could watch apartment 523 without being seen. The building was under construction and empty at night, except for a security guard, and he wouldn't be a problem. She hurried back to 623 and quickly gathered her gear. It wouldn't be difficult to bypass the security code to get into the building across the street or to slip by the security guard. A half-hour later she was in and set up. Apartment 523 was dark, and with the naked eye, Liberty couldn't see any movement. She adjusted the sensory equipment that would detect sound, then focused the night scope on the living room window. The apartment was empty, literally empty. No furniture, nothing. Liberty stumbled back over the equipment and fell to the floor. She cursed herself for losing control, then consciously slowed her breathing. When she got up, she packed her equipment and slipped out, leaving nothing behind to indicate that she'd been there.

It took Liberty a few seconds to pick the lock of 523, and a moment later she was inside with the door closed behind her. While her eyes were adjusting to the dark, her senses studied the room. She could smell fresh paint and new carpet, and something else that triggered a burst of fear in the back of her mind. Without a thought, she flipped on the lights and stood in the middle of the empty apartment where she and Yancy had spent what time they could together. The cold silence of the room sickened her. When she regained her balance, she studied the carpet that had been replaced in the hallway, then ran her fingers over the newly painted wall until she felt an irregularity. She took out a pocketknife and started to scrape away the paint. Using the tips of her fingers, she traced the outline of the small round holes that had been filled in. There was no doubt in her mind that they were bullet holes. She cut the edge of the carpet and pulled it back to find the reason for the pungent, coppery smell. The carpet had been hastily replaced to cover the bloodstains that had soaked into the wood beneath. Liberty leaned against the wall and sank to the floor. Was Yancy dead? Had she died while she herself was in Iran?

Liberty didn't go back to the apartment upstairs that night. There were no tears. She felt numb as she sat on the floor of the empty apartment until dawn. It was as if their life together never existed, Yancy never existed ... just as she didn't exist.

As each tormenting day passed and turned into weeks, Liberty began to lose hope that Yancy would return. She went through the motions and got through the days as she waited and prayed that Yancy would contact her to let her know she was still alive. In her heart, she believed that if Yancy were alive, she would somehow let her know. First fear, then anger took her through a kaleidoscope of emotions. She began to doubt, to ask herself the questions that lay quiescent behind the wall of her commitment to the Talons and to the President. After weeks of waiting, the phone rang and one word was spoken — "Ghost." She gathered what she would need and left, not bothering to lock the apartment, knowing that she would never return.

Within hours, Liberty was on a U.S. Air Force C-30 touching down in Arauca, Colombia, with Special Ops and a team of Green Berets. They had been assigned to protect the 480 mile oil pipeline that ran from Arauca to the Caribbean against sabotaging attacks by rebel terrorists. In the guise of a Green Beret, Liberty's true mission was to track down and eliminate the rebel leader. She was not aware that she would be eliminating one rebel so another more sympathetic to the concept of controlled growth of the lime-green cocoa bush could take his place. The U.S. government was of the mind the way to control the predictable distribution of its byproduct, cocaine, into the U.S. was to trade favors with the Colombians.

It took six months of tracking the rebels through the steaming jungle. When Liberty caught up with them, it was during the monsoon season. Camouflaged, she sat in the downpour of rain overlooking the rebel camp until nightfall on the third day when the rebel leader was finally alone. She crept on her belly through the rain and mud into the rebel camp. She slipped into his hut and took his life quickly by cutting his throat, then sliding a blade through his heart. After activating a homing device that signified that the job was completed, she was picked up by an RAH-66 Comanche Stealth Helicopter and was on the way back to the States before the rebel leader was discovered lying in his bunk in a pool of his own blood.

Each successful mission honed Liberty's skills. And with each mission she hardened. Preferring to work alone, she stayed on the move, never staying in one place long enough for anyone to take notice or to remember her. Occasionally she would be teamed with another faceless agent, who would look at her with the same cold eyes that reflected back at her in the mirror. Her reputation grew and soon the name whispered among the Talons themselves was Ghost.

As an FBI agent, Liberty had been trained in the art of self-defense; Delta Force had trained her to kill. She became the Talon's master in the art of assassination. After she'd taken out Nusair and Yancy disappeared, she'd struggled with the kind of assignments she was given, but she learned to justify them. It was easy to do when the targets were the terrorists responsible for the hijacking of a busload of international students and then demanded the release of political prisoners. Many were rescued, but several of the students were brutally slain before the President called upon the Talons to rescue those remaining and to take out the terrorists.

Other kills were not as easy to explain, and after a while, she stopped justifying and simply did as she was told. Then she would disappear into another identity until the next call came. She had chosen her destiny and there was no turning back. It was hard for Liberty to remember the idealistic reason why she'd joined the Talons. President Kincaide had taken the burden upon his own shoulders to counter the rash of terrorist attacks that held the nation and the world in a state of terror. The world was threatening to fulfill the prophecy of Armageddon and needed a champion, an uplifted sword of justice to destroy the evil and restore the amity. Liberty and the other Talons had willingly chosen to become paladins; instead they became worse than what they had vowed to destroy.

She seldom ruminated on her life anymore. It was self-inflicted pain, like the pain that came in the form of a dead face when she closed her eyes.

Liberty had idealistically answered the President's call, and had become entangled in a web of betrayal and deceit. The blood that spilled from each life she took stained Liberty's soul until the act itself defined her and who and what she had become — a killer, without a conscience. She was as the Talons had named her — a ghost with a heart of stone, that lurked in the dark shadows of humanity.

Chapter Four

Kayla busied herself serving the last of the stragglers who had braved the heavy snowfall to ski the last run of the day down Lone Mountain. This year's snowfall had packed the slopes. If Lone Mountain realized the Farmer's Almanac prediction of heavy snowfall for North Western Montana for the 2004/2005 winter season, her family could recoup the loss from the previous seasons' lack of snow. The ski resort and Kayla's Pub were nestled in Montana's rugged Rocky Mountains. It was Christmas Eve and the pub was typically quiet. Most of her usual customers were at the lodge waiting for the skiers to start down the mountain for the torchlight parade. Most would stay and attend the Christmas Eve mass afterward. She looked at the clock, remembering that she had reluctantly promised her brother Nathan that she would try to put in an appearance at the lodge after she'd closed the pub for the night. Her heart wasn't in it. She knew Nathan worried about her, and that it was out of love and concern that he frequently encouraged her to get out and meet other people. She cringed every time he used the word "socialize", when what he really meant was that she should put the past and memories away and begin to live again. Kayla couldn't say she had honestly tried to let go of the pain of her loss; her heart was too full of hate. Her memories were her reality, as was the face in her dreams. Both got her through the lonely nights and made her days bearable. When she'd first lost Addie, her guilt was the reason she'd reached for the bottle, now it was her memories of Addie that kept her sober.

Kayla stood in front of an expanse of windows facing Lone Mountain, watching the quiet beauty as the new snow fell, laying a serene blanket of white on the mountain. To any eyes but hers, it was a picturesque scene of a winter wonderland. For Kayla, the destruction behind the placid deception only fueled her anger toward the mountain. The longer she watched, the more anxious she became; the more anxious she became, the more the snow taunted her. Her eyes locked defiantly on the mountain, she unknowingly twisted the towel in her hands. She would never forgive the mountain for taking all that she loved.

The slender woman wearing the dark ski cap had been sitting in the pub most of the afternoon. With her back to the wall, she watched the entrance as if she were expecting someone. She'd finished her drink and sat staring into the bottom of the glass as if gazing into a crystal ball, waiting for it to tell her future. Each time a displacement of cold air disturbed the warmth, fanning the flames in the stone fireplace, her eyes darted toward the door. And each time, a subtle disappointment, or perhaps relief, etched her brow as she relaxed and sat back in the chair. The woman focused her attention on the barkeep, who was standing at the table next to hers staring out of the window at a strengthening winter snowstorm. The play of emotion on the brunette's face caused Liberty to hesitate, wondering if she should interrupt whatever it was out there that held the barkeep's attention. She'd seen the look before — every time she looked in the mirror. The words left her lips before she realized she'd spoken them. "You look at the mountain as if you hate it."

Kayla never diverted her eyes from the mountain, but the intruding voice drew her back to the present. It unnerved her somewhat that a stranger could read her thoughts so easily. After a moment, she turned to look at the woman and forced a smile. "I'm sorry. I was just thinking that with all the snow, the skiing tomorrow will be great for everyone." Kayla picked up the glasses and wiped the top of the table. "Can I get you a refill, or do you need to be somewhere before we are snowed in here?" Without waiting for an answer, she turned and walked back to the bar. *That was rude. Why did I say that? No cause to take my mood out on a customer.*

The guest looked at her glass and shrugged. "No one is expecting me, so, if you're not in a hurry to close for the night, I would like another, but make it a coffee, please."

"Coming right up."

The years of ascetic discipline required for survival taught Liberty to evaluate everything and everyone around her, every waking moment and then even in her sleep, so she watched intently as the barkeep discarded the dregs and set a fresh pot of coffee to brew.

As the snow continued to fall, fewer customers ventured into the pub, until only a handful of quiet die-hards remained. While the woman drank her coffee, Kayla busied herself behind the bar, cleaning up and going through her inventory for the private party she had booked for New Year's Eve. Occasionally she would glance up to look at the worsening storm outside the window and at her last two customers, one of them the woman in the ski cap. She didn't look like a woman that would spend Christmas Eve sitting alone in a bar. She wondered what the story was behind the empty look in her eyes. *Guess we all have a story. She isn't a regular on the mountain. I've never seen her before, but she looks as fit as any athlete — in a rugged sort of way.*

The only other customer was Mike. A grizzly bear of a man, he was Lone Mountain's year-round maintenance supervisor and the last one to leave at night after shutting down the lifts and the ski patrol swept the mountain, making sure all the skiers were in. He always stopped at the pub for a beer, and shared the stories of the skiers' escapades with Kayla before going home. Mike and his wife lived in a log cabin on the property adjacent to Lone Mountain on the other side of Glacier Creek. They always spent Christmas Eve with their son and his family in Kalispell, a town at the foot of the mountain. He slid off his stool and threw a bill on the top of the bar, professionally eyeing the snow that continued to fall, threatening to turn into an all out blizzard.

"Guess I'd better haul my carcass down around the mountain. They just might close the road if the weather doesn't clear and this snow piles up much more. The grandkids will be mighty disappointed if Santa hasn't shown up when they get up in the morning." Mike's broad smile was as big as his heart. "Merry Christmas, Kayla. Will we see you tomorrow evening at the lodge for the Christmas party?"

Every year since Augusta and Ethel Sinclair cleared the first run and built Lone Mountain Ski Resort, the lodge had held a Christmas Day celebration, handing out presents to the children of the employees and those who were spending the holidays as guests, skiing the mountain. After their parents retired and moved to Arizona, Kayla, Nathan, and their younger sister Cassie assumed the responsibilities of the lodge and continued the tradition.

Deliberately avoiding his question, Kayla reached under the counter and brought out two gift bags of presents and handed them to Mike. "Merry Christmas, Mike, and to your family. You'll be busy tonight getting all those toys put together for the grandkids."

Mike tugged the flaps of his hat down over his ears and buttoned up his parka. Before he opened the door, he caught Kayla's eye. "We miss you, Kayla; the kids miss you. We all hope to see you at the Christmas party tomorrow. The kids have a present for you."

"We'll see, Mike. Now, if you spend any more time jawing with me, you'll get caught in this storm and you won't get to spend Christmas Eve with those kids."

He looked to the woman who had moved to sit on a stool at the bar. "Merry Christmas to you, too, young lady." Then he stepped through the door and disappeared into the swirling snow.

Kayla stared at the door a moment in deep thought, then began to pick up the chairs and place them on the tables. She'd forgotten about the woman as she dimmed the lights and threw the bolt on the door.

"I have been locked out of a few places, but I can't recall ever being locked in. I'm sorry. I'd forgotten that it was Christmas Eve. I'll be going so you can close up and go home to your family." The woman swayed a little when she stood up from the stool.

Kayla knew it wasn't because the woman had had too much to drink. She'd nursed two drinks most of the afternoon, and yet she looked as if she might be unable to maneuver down around the twisted mountain road into Kalispell, especially in a blizzard. "I live upstairs over the pub, so I don't have far to go." Rubbing her hands together briskly to warm them, she offered a semblance of an apology. "Please, I really wasn't rushing you. I have a pot of tea simmering. Why don't you stay and have a cup with me while we see if this storm is going to ease up a bit?"

The woman stood up and straightened her shoulders, then leaned against the bar a moment for support before reaching for her gloves. Her face grew pale and she had a white-knuckled grip on the edge of the bar as she retrieved some money from her jacket pocket. "Thank you for your kindness, but I should get going. I've kept you long enough."

Kayla was summoning the courage to ask the woman if she was all right when the loud shrill of the emergency alert radio sounded, startling them both. She picked up the phone behind the bar, then suddenly the electricity went out, leaving the pub lit only by the light from the fireplace. "Well, the phone's dead, too. I suspect this heavy snowfall has taken down the lines, and the pass has probably been closed." She saw a barely detectable flicker of concern in the woman's eyes. "They'll bring in the snow removal equipment and should have the road open before morning. Are you staying at the lodge?"

The woman hesitated before she answered. "I really hadn't decided." She started to zip up her ski jacket and Kayla reached for the cell phone behind the bar, aware of the slight shiver and subtle look of distress behind the somber expression on the woman's face. "How about if I call over to the lodge and see if they can put you up for the night?"

"I'd appreciate that." *It would be nice to rest a while, maybe sleep a few hours before I move on.*

"While I light a lantern, why don't you sit by the fireplace and I'll bring you a hot cup of tea." Before the woman could refuse, Kayla led her to an overstuffed chair in front of the fire, then went to get the tea and call the desk at the lodge.

The woman closed her eyes to rest them a moment as she listened to the barkeep talking on the phone.

"Not a room, nothing? ... Yes, I know the services are tonight. ... A lot of people are stranded? Cassie, tell Nathan when he starts to fret, and he will, they'll probably have the road cleared by the time the skiers head up the mountain in the morning and he shouldn't worry. At the rate this stuff is coming down, it will be one of our best days of the season. The new powder will be great on top of the base we already have. They'll be lined up and anxious to try the new run down the south mountain. Oh, before I forget, Cassie, ask Nathan to have the ridge above the new run checked again. You never know with all this heavy snowfall. ... He did? When? ... Gill was sure it didn't need blasting and the ski patrol confirmed? I know I'm overly cautious, but to be on the safe side, please ask Gill to check it again early in the morning before Mike opens up the lifts to that run. Are you skiing in the torch light procession tonight? ... No, I don't think the patrol will cancel it. We've only cancelled it once that I can remember, and I'm sure that Nathan will only allow experienced skiers up on the mountain tonight. ... Good night, Cassie. Get some rest; tomorrow will be one busy day. ... Not to worry, she can stay in my extra room for the night. I'll be over early in the morning to open the ski shop." Before Kayla hung up, her voice softened. "Merry Christmas, little sister."

Kayla looked toward the fireplace where the woman sat with her legs curled up under her. She had taken off her boots and appeared to have fallen asleep in the chair. For an instant, in the flickering light of the fire, Kayla thought it could have been Addie sitting there. *Let it be, Kayla. It isn't Addie. Addie's gone.* She retrieved a throw to cover the woman with and reached behind the bar to fetch the emergency propane lantern. Upstairs, she built a fire in the guestroom, then returned to the pub's kitchen to brew the tea and fix a tray of sandwiches. She herself hadn't eaten since morning, and she knew her guest hadn't ordered anything to eat all afternoon. Kayla leaned against the counter, watching the fire create shadows across the wall. Every day without Addie was hard, but the ache in her heart around the holidays was an unbearable reminder that her lover was gone.

Kayla had left Lone Mountain on the day of Addie's services, and didn't return until she'd hit bottom. Somehow she'd found her way home, gone through recovery, and reopened the pub. Tonight she'd planned to close early and sit alone by the fire, remembering the Christmas Eves that she and Addie had spent together.

Every Christmas Eve since she was a young girl, she would get up before daybreak and wait anxiously until Addie arrived with her parents. Addie's parents were avid skiers, and every year they would come up from Kalispell to spend the holidays at the lodge. Kayla and Addie had the run of the entire place and they loved it. They would go sleigh riding and roll snowmen, and shake the presents under the tree when no one was looking while they waited for the party and for Santa to arrive. As they grew up, they both lived to be on the slopes, and then one Christmas Eve when Kayla was ten and Addy nine, they each received their first pair of competition skis. They were ecstatic, and couldn't wait to try them out on the slopes of Lone Mountain on Christmas morning. From that day on, Addie spent every moment she could on the mountain, training with Kayla. During the short Montana summer months, both kept in shape for the slopes by hiking the Rockies and working for the Forest Service. Kayla's dream was to qualify for the Olympic ski team, and Addie was determined to help make that dream come true.

When Addie finished high school, her parents insisted that she take the scholarship offer from a college back East. Kayla was offered a full academic scholarship at the University of Montana in Missoula. Addie couldn't bear the thought of being separated from Kayla, and at first she refused to go, causing a rift between her and her parents. Kayla eased the tensions between them by convincing Addie to go, telling her it was an opportunity she couldn't let pass. It was the first time they had been separated since before first grade, and it was difficult for them both. Each did a lot of soul searching the first two years away at college and both came to the same awakening: they loved each other more than just friends.

It was on a snowy Christmas Eve, when Addie was home for the holidays, that they first made love in front of the fire in Kayla's room, neither doubting that they were meant to be together as friends and as lovers in this lifetime. On Christmas morning, hand in hand, they faced both Kayla and Addie's parents, creating quite a stir when they told them that they were in love.

The last two years of college were hard being away from each other, and they looked forward to being together during every break and holiday. If Addie couldn't come home to Montana, Kayla would go to her. Now, there was nothing to look forward to. Kayla dreaded the season, and Christmas, and couldn't bring herself to put up a tree in the apartment upstairs. It hadn't always been that way.

After the '98 Olympics, when Kayla brought home the gold medal, she and Addie, in front of friends and family, had their joining ceremony on Christmas Eve. Traditionally, every Christmas Eve after that, they would start out cross-country skiing early in the morning to find the perfect tree, then spend the rest of the night decorating it and celebrate their anniversary by making love in front of the fireplace. Kayla smiled as Addie's beautiful face materialized in her mind and she could hear Addie's voice saying, "What do you think...should this go here...is it straight...are the lights on right..."

Other than the guests for whom she tended the bar, Kayla hadn't spent a Christmas Eve with anyone since Addie's death. She felt the emptiness and an unreasonable resentment toward the stranger sitting in Addie's chair. She busied herself slicing sausage and cheese to go along with the sandwiches. Occasionally, she would glance through the open half doors of the serving area to where the woman was resting. The reflection of light from the fire chased the shadows and played across the woman's face. She guessed the woman to be in her late thirties or early forties, but it was hard to say. There was a look of hardness about her face that remained even in rest. She had taken off her cap, and Kayla could see that the woman's hair was a dark blonde. At first glance, she just blended in, almost unnoticed by the patrons who had come and gone from the pub throughout the day. Looking at her more closely now, Kayla realized how attractive the woman was and wondered how she'd miss it earlier.

Kayla carried the tray of food out and set it down on the table next to the stranger, and went back to the kitchen for the tea and mugs. She sat by the fireplace across from the dozing woman and poured herself a cup of tea, then pushed back into the worn leather chair to get comfortable. As she wrapped her hands around the warm mug and stared into the fire, she felt an unexpected sense of comfort that the woman was there. Listening to the howling wind and the appeasing sound of the crackling fire, she dozed off. When she woke she was looking into a pair of tired hazel eyes. "Now it's my turn to be sorry." Kayla stretched and yawned. "Have you been awake long? Better yet, how long have I been asleep?"

A hint of a smile touched the corners of the woman's mouth. "Not too long. Actually, I just poured a cup of the tea and it's still warm. I've been eyeing the sandwiches. May I?"

"Please, that's why I made them." Kayla studied the gaunt, hollow-eyed look about the woman. "When was the last time you ate?"

The woman blinked her eyes as if she couldn't remember, "Yesterday sometime, I think."

"Well, then, you start on these while I make another pot of tea. You're shivering. Are you warm enough?"

"Yes, thanks. It's nice here in front of the fire. Thanks for the food; I am a bit hungry."

Kayla put another log on, picked up the teapot, and went into the kitchen for fresh tea leaves, then back to the fire to add hot water from the kettle warming on the swing arm. "I do have a back up generator, but I never use it unless the power goes out when the pub is open." Kayla looked at the kettle in her hand; her heart ached for Addie. "I have propane, but we always used to..." Kayla never finished what she was going to say, that it was tradition on Christmas

Eve for her and Addie to use the kettle on the side arm to heat water.

As Liberty ate the food Kayla prepared, she looked around the room, seeing it in a different light than she had earlier. Someone had put a lot of thought and special touches into making it appealing and homey. It was a perfect place to spend a while out of the cold and rest. "The pub, it's very comfortable." Kayla nodded but didn't answer. The woman could see a far away look in Kayla's eyes as she drank her tea and stared into the fire. It was apparent that the pub keeper would prefer to be alone. "I should be going. I've imposed on your hospitality long enough. Did you say you were going to call the lodge for a room?"

The woman's voice brought Kayla back from the past. "Oh, I'm sorry; you had dozed off. The lodge is full. There's not a room to be had tonight, and the closest place to stay is in Kalispell, but the road has been closed. You're more than welcome to stay the night here. I built a fire in my spare room. It's warm and the bed is fairly comfortable."

Liberty thought of refusing and going on, but she was exhausted and hurting. She needed to rest and take care of the wound in her side. The roads were closed, and spending the night in the car in a blizzard was not an option if she could avoid it. And, there would be less chance of her being spotted at the pub than at the lodge. "If you're sure, I accept your hospitality, and, thank you, again." An edgy smile crossed the woman's face. "You've been my savior tonight. If you don't mind, it's been a long day. I'd like to go out to my car and get my duffel and turn in."

Kayla had just finished checking the fire and making sure the screen was in place for the night, when she heard the bell tinkling above the door. The woman stood with her hair and shoulders covered with snow, an old military duffel bag in one hand.

"It's coming down something fierce out there. It doesn't look as if it's going to let up real soon."

Kayla noticed how pale the woman looked and...something more. It was the way the woman moved and held her body, much like an athlete with a keen readiness. She also seemed to be favoring her side. "Are you hurt? Is there something I can do?"

"No. I just pulled a muscle earlier today. But thank you."

Kayla picked up the lantern. "Shall I show you to your room? The mountain has its own natural hot spring and it supplies the water for the pub's water tanks that I heat with propane, so if you would like to bathe, there will be plenty of hot water. Everything you will need is in the cabinet as you go into the bath." Kayla led the way toward the stairs, then stopped. "I think names might be in order here. I'm Kayla, which you probably surmised from the name on the pub."

An odd look flitted across the woman's face as she extended her hand to Kayla. She hesitated a moment, then said, "My name is...Liberty...Liberty Starr."

Kayla accepted the offered hand, wondering why the woman seemed unsure, stumbling over her own name. Pushing the darkness out of the way with the soft light cast from the lantern, she led the way up the stairs and into a quaint room warmed by a crackling fire. A cranberry down comforter covered an antique sleigh bed, and a Victorian style black writing desk and chair sat in front of a corner window that looked out toward the ski slopes. Two comfortable chairs sat in front of the fireplace on an oval braided rug that covered the hardwood floor.

Kayla walked over and stood in front of the double French doors that led to a wrap around deck. She drew open the curtains, stopping a moment to listen. "Sounds like the storm might be letting up a bit." When she saw Liberty shiver, Kayla reached for a throw from the foot of the bed and wrapped it around the woman's shoulders, then she opened the doors to the deck. "Come look, they're starting down the mountain."

The simple gesture of kindness and Kayla's touch felt foreign and awkward to Liberty as she stood next to her on the balcony, watching the skiers with their lighted torches traversing down the mountain. Liberty stole a look at the face of the woman standing next to her. She had a natural beauty. Her dark hair curled around a strong face, but her blue eyes reflected an inner sadness. "It's quite inspiring, isn't it? Do they do this every year?"

"Yes, from the first year and the opening of the first run, the lodge has had the Christmas Eve torch procession. I could hardly wait until I was old enough to ski in it."

"How old were you?"

The expression on Kayla's face told of the sadness in her heart. "I'd just turned eight and my best friend was seven." Neither said anything for a few moments as they watched the skiers carrying their torches down the mountain. Kayla broke the silence. "My brother, my sister Cassie, Addie, and I grew up on the mountain. We cut our teeth on skis." Kayla's face softened. "The first time Addie and I were old enough to ski the mountain on Christmas Eve was a night much like this one. It was all we'd talked about that entire year. A snowstorm blew into a blizzard earlier that day, too, and our parents thought it would be too dangerous for us to participate. We were broken hearted."

"What happened?"

Kayla's reminiscence brought a look of longing and a slight catch in her voice. "We moped around the lodge all afternoon, begging our parents and praying it would clear up so we could ski."

Liberty wondered if she should ask how it turned out as she watched the play of emotion on Kayla's face and the moisture welling up in her eyes. "Did it stop snowing?"

Kayla kept her eyes on the mountain, "Yes...yes, it did."

Liberty turned toward the mountain, feeling an inexplicable sympathy for the woman beside her. Compassion of any kind unsettled her; she blamed it on feeling more tired and weary than she could ever remember. "Is your friend skiing the mountain tonight?"

Kayla's answer was a whisper, more to herself than to Liberty. "No, she...doesn't ski the mountain anymore."

Liberty followed Kayla back into the room and watched her light a second lantern on the mantle, then Kayla said good night and left. When Liberty heard Kayla's bedroom door close, she sagged against the mantle for support. She was tired, and the pain in her side was distracting her; the sensation of sticky wetness under her sweater added to her discomfort. Her hand shook slightly as she withdrew a leather case from her duffel. She picked up the lantern and made her way into the bathroom. She'd been lucky; the bullet had only grazed her side, but the flesh wound had bled a lot before she'd found a truck stop far enough away from Denver to pull over and tend to it. Before she pulled back onto the highway, she searched her memory for some place she could go. Her vast store of information pulled up the ski lodge in Montana, from an assignment when she had reentered the country from Canada by crossing the Canadian Rockies. The area was remote, and would be the perfect place to lie low for a while and heal.

Liberty unzipped her cargo pants and let them drop to the floor, took out a syringe and a vial of antibiotic, and injected the medicine into her thigh. She removed the rest of her clothing and peeled off the blood-soaked dressing she'd applied at the truck stop. Superficial wounds bleed, and Liberty knew that she needed to watch for infection, especially with a gunshot wound. She turned on the shower and let the warm water run over the wound and her tired body. More exhausted than she could ever remember, she struggled out of the shower and applied an antibiotic cream and a clean dressing over the injury. The whole time, she wracked her brain, wondering what had happened to blow her mission, and who had tried to kill her. She couldn't be certain that she had lost whoever might be following her, but if she had, she'd bought herself enough time to recuperate a while and to plan. She was dead tired; she needed to sleep. She stumbled back into the bedroom and slipped her 9-mm under the pillow before easing her bone-weary body down onto the feather bed.

The minute she closed her eyes, the scene in the hotel room in Denver started to replay in slow motion in her mind. The order, as usual, had come from Lawrence. She was to be in place and ready in the room in Denver the next day at a certain time. An assassination hit — no name or gender of the target. She would receive two calls. One would give her enough time to set up and calculate the shot, the second would identify the target as the target exited the building across the street. When the second call came, she was ready. The target's head was in her crosshairs. She took in a deep breath and began to squeeze the trigger when she recognized the woman as Ingrid Sheppard, Vice President Elect to President Elect Brady Lawrence.

Liberty sat straight up in the bed. "I remember now! I eased off the trigger. I had aborted the kill and was standing up when I saw the flash from an upper story window in the building directly across the way. Fuck, someone knew exactly where I'd be; I was to be the second target! What the hell is going on? Why would Kincaide and Lawrence want Ingrid Sheppard dead?"

Liberty lay back down, knowing that sleep would not come easily. Too many questions were running through her mind; too many Talons had been killed in unexplained accidents and botched missions.

Chapter Five

Kayla lay awake watching the fire die down and listening to the pub creak as the storm blew and howled outside. When she finally fell into a restless sleep, she was dreaming that she was entwined with Addie, who was snuggled into her favorite spot next to her. On a blustery winter night like this, Kayla's cold hands always found their way to the warmth and softness of Addie's back. She could actually feel the sensation of Addie's cold nose and her warm lips against her neck, and smell the hint of the apple and ginger soap that always lingered on Addie's skin. Kayla felt a smooth thigh slide across her leg and settle between her own as Addie nuzzled in against her as she slept.

Deep in the throes of the dream, she moaned as her fingers found Addie's warm wetness. Her memory echoed the soft whispers and her skin tingled as anxious hands pulled her closer. Kayla struggled to block out something that was hovering in the shadows, pulling her from her dreamscape, telling her to wake up. She held Addie closer, but Addie's voice was fading as it whispered, "I love you, Kayla." Frantically, Kayla slid her hand across the sheets to find nothing but the cold emptiness.

She was still half-asleep when a sound like a deep rumble registered a warning and the room started to shake. Kayla knew what it was before her eyes flew open and her feet hit the floor. When she reached the window, she looked past the lodge to the mountain. "Jesus, it's the ridge above the new run!" Confused, she looked at the clock, trying to clear her head. *Would anyone be up there this early? No, please, no! But I asked Cassie to have Gill check it out this morning.* She tried to shake the cobwebs from her head. "Think, Kayla, what did Cassie say?" She froze. "Oh, my God! She said she would go and meet the ski patrol to check out the ridge herself!"

In a state of near panic, Kayla quickly dressed, pulled on her boots, then ran down the stairs, grabbing her coat as she bolted out the back door of the pub. Her heart was hammering painfully against her chest and she could scarcely catch her breath as she slid the snowmobile to a stop in front of the lodge. Nathan and several others were already putting the last of the rescue equipment on their snowmobiles. The grim looks on their faces confirmed what she had feared. "Is it Cassie?" she screamed at her brother.

Nathan's voice trembled as he looked his sister in the eye. "She signed out this morning, an hour before she was to meet the ski patrol to check the south ridge above the new run. We've tried to raise her on the radio, but she hasn't responded."

Kayla went as pale as the new snow on the ground and her entire body stiffened. "Have you picked up a signal from her transmitter?"

Nathan's eyes reflected his fear, and he turned to tie down the rest of his equipment so Kayla couldn't see the worried look on his face. "Nothing yet, Sis. I'll let you know as soon as we do." Nathan scanned the somber faces of the rescue team as he swung his leg over the seat of the snowmobile and started up his engine.

Kayla stood motionless as the team followed his lead and started up their snowmobiles. She watched helplessly as they made their way toward the mountain.

Liberty was a light sleeper, and she'd felt the movement long before she heard the rumble and the whining sound of a snowmobile. She could also hear the wailing of an emergency siren as she stood at the window watching the snowmobiles head up the face of the mountain. She retrieved her duffel bag and pulled out a small satellite radio, tuning the dial to the emergency band. The road into Lone Mountain was still closed and the conditions on the mountain were unstable.

Liberty sighed, feeling that her luck was holding true — summing everything up in her mind: everything in the past forty-eight hours had gone wrong. She'd been betrayed, and as a result, she'd walked into an ambush in Denver. Liberty had aborted the assassination when she recognized Ingrid Sheppard as the target. But someone was lying in wait to kill her as soon as she had assassinated the target. If it hadn't been for a brief glint of light from the building across the street, she wouldn't have been able to avoid the sharpshooter's bullet seconds later. Wade Kincaide's involvement puzzled her, but she had the distinct feeling that Brady Lawrence wouldn't have been too disappointed to hear that she was dead. She had many questions, questions he wouldn't like, and she was determined to get the answers.

Liberty checked the dressing on her side. It was dry. She took a clean pair of jeans and a tee shirt from her duffel and dressed, then pulled a sweater over her head and went downstairs. The few hours of sleep she had gotten eased some of her weariness. She knew that she could ski cross-country around the blocked road and hitch a ride into Kalispell, where she could catch a plane or rent another car. As she walked toward the lodge to procure skis, it occurred to her that she had nowhere to run to.

When she arrived at the lodge, the lobby was chaotic; many of the guests were standing around, unsure of what to do. It was early, but most of them had been up and ready to take on the slopes to get in a full day of holiday skiing. A section of the dining area was cordoned off, and the ski patrol was setting up a command center. It was obvious to Liberty that Kayla was in charge of coordinating the second rescue response team to advance on the mountain.

Kayla stood stiffly in front of the windows, looking out at the mountain. She cursed Cassie for not waiting for the two members of the ski patrol before she went up on the mountain to check the ridge. Knowing Cassie, she probably thought she would take a look, and if everything was all right, save the patrol from going out so early on Christmas morning. Kayla keyed her radio. "Cabe, are the rescue dogs on the mountain? Anything?" She pinched the bridge of her nose and looked at her watch. "Follow procedure. Allow the dogs and the handlers to search each quadrant first, so they don't have to waste time ruling out surface human scent from the rescuers. The dogs and first responders are to probe and sweep a section. If they find anything, second line stays behind to dig while the dogs and the rest go on. Every second counts, Cabe." She turned and looked at the huge clock on the wall, then faced the hopeful eyes and serious faces of those who were standing vigil at the command center. "It's been ten minutes since the dogs arrived. The odds of finding her alive are reduced by every second she's buried. Those of you who are going out now, make sure your transceivers are set to search mode."

The scraping of chairs was the only sound in the room as the rescue team checked their transceivers, picked up their gear, and filed silently out of the room. Kayla turned back to face the mountain. "Damn it! Come on, Cassie, where the hell is your transceiver?"

Liberty filled two cups with coffee from the large urn the staff had set up and approached Kayla, who continued to glare out at the mountain. She could feel the fear and the anger radiating off the tall innkeeper. Kayla looked at her with eyes that were tormented and full of fear. It was as if she didn't recognize Liberty as she handed Kayla the steaming cup of coffee. "I thought you could use this."

Kayla's hand shook as she reached to take it, then she apologized and set the coffee on the table. "I'm sorry, uh...Liberty. I'd forgotten about you."

"That's okay." Liberty heard herself ask, "What can I do to help?"

Kayla ran her hand across her face. "Nothing. Unless you know the mountain and are an expert in avalanche rescue. Rescue is doing everything it can. All we can do is wait and hope they find her before..." Kayla couldn't finish the thought; it was too painful.

"No signal from her transceiver?"

Kayla's anger erupted and she pounded her fist on the table, sending the coffee spraying onto the floor. "No, damn it! She knows better, I've harped about it every time she's gone out on the mountain. Long before..." Kayla clenched her fists and mentally composed herself, while visualizing what was going on up on the mountain, hating the weakness that kept her from being out there leading the rescue attempt.

So cold, Cassie felt so cold. She was encased in a coffin of snow, curled on her side, vaguely aware of a perception of pain in her right arm, which was twisted behind her back. Her forehead was lying across her left arm, and she felt a heavy wetness pressing against her face. Her eyes were closed, and her nostrils and mouth were filled with moisture. Conscious awareness of what had happened forced her to focus, to attempt to control the threatening panic at the realization that she was trapped and buried alive in a snowy grave.

An image of Death standing next to a giant clock, his scythe the second hand, ticking away the seconds of her life, taunted and pounded in her skull. Bits and pieces of her survival training raced frantically through her mind. *How long? Please God, how long has it been?* Fifteen minutes had been disciplined into her — the window of surviving an avalanche was being found within fifteen minutes. Fear and a silent scream crept into her mind, gripping her psyche with a frozen hand. Frantically, she wondered if she had lost consciousness and how much time had passed.

Process, Cassie. Do what Kayla has drilled into you over and over. You're breathing, so you have an air pocket until the snow settles or you use up the oxygen. You weren't killed during the fall, so that's a positive. It feels like I'm wedged up against something solid. Think, Cassie! Think! You were crossing Colman's Ridge when you heard the fracture. I can't remember! Oh God, did I turn on my transceiver!

Halfway across the ridge, Cassie had sensed it, and knew she was in trouble before she felt the snow giving away under her skis.

They'll be looking for me on the south side of the mountain, in the main avalanche tract, but I remember forcing my body over the ridge on the opposite side when I heard the cracking.

Cassie tried, but was unable to move her legs, and the attempt sent excruciating pain throughout her body, speeding up her breathing. She gasped in a ragged breath and felt the weight of the snow constricting her chest. Snow was running down the back of her throat. Her whole body shuddered as she tried to will herself to slow her breaths. *Calm it down. Don't use up your air. Think of something else. Concentrate! Kayla will search; she'll find you.*

She forced herself to remember the day she'd sat on the massive deck of Lone Mountain Lodge, waiting with the rest of the members of the ski patrol for the new instructor to arrive. It was off-season, but the lodge was open year around, catering to summer hikers and tourists on their way into Canada. Many of their Canadian neighbors came across the border to enjoy the trails and to shop in Eureka and Kalispell.

Looking out toward the mountain at that time of year, Cassie could see crystalline blue sky and an array of brilliant colors from the wild flowers that blanketed the slopes. It was easy to understand why Montana was called Big Sky country. She walked around the deck to watch the rising sun catch the poetic skill of a lone fly fisherman as his line danced and played over the cold water of the river that fed the mountain lake. Cassie wondered what instructor would conduct the annual training and refresher course that was required for the up-coming ski season. She'd called the ski patrol that morning to see if Dan Olson needed anything for the class, but was told that Dan wouldn't be conducting the class that morning on Lone Mountain, he was down in Bozeman at the Big Sky Ski Resort; a replacement would fill in.

When she had come downstairs that morning for breakfast, Cassie had stopped, as she did every morning, in front of the glass display cases to admire the trophies and the gold medals. Her sister, Kayla Sinclair, was the best skier the mountain had ever seen, had once been on the threshold of being the best in the world. Cassie's heart grew sad. She missed her sister, and she worried about her. No one had heard from Kayla since she'd disappeared after Addie's accident. Nothing was the same after that. The family had hired investigators to try and find her. Some had picked up a trail, but none had ever gotten close to finding her.

Cassie felt herself drifting. It was getting harder to focus. If only she could sleep, just for a few minutes.

Chapter Six

Kayla paced back and forth, her eyes fixed on the clock. "What the hell are they doing up there? It's been fourteen minutes!"

A hush fell across the room. Liberty could feel the dread that hung in the air. It was on the faces and in the eyes of everyone in the command center. Kayla was on the edge, strung tight, and with good reason. Time was running out. If a skier didn't die from fatal injuries during the fall, the likelihood of rescue dropped critically after fifteen minutes. After thirty-five minutes, the victim usually didn't have a chance in hell of surviving, due to the effects of slow asphyxia and hypothermia.

Liberty spoke quietly. "Your rescue team, are they well trained?"

Needing someone to vent her anger and frustration on, Kayla snapped back at Liberty, "The Lone Mountain Ski Patrol and Rescue Team is well trained; they know what they're doing. There isn't any better, anywhere!" She closed her eyes and took a breath, then looked back at the mountain as if willing it to release its icy grasp on her sister. "I'm sorry, it's just..."

As she watched Kayla struggle with her emotions, Liberty felt a compassion she'd thought had died along with the idealistic young agent she used to be. Her calloused heart felt something else — a longing. She could feel the sense of family amongst those who had gathered to help with the rescue or to lend Kayla and Nathan their support. When she spoke again, Liberty hardly recognized the gentleness in her voice. "Then you know they are doing all they can."

Kayla nodded, then swallowed the lump in her throat. Her whisper was more to herself than to Liberty. "I know, but damn it, it doesn't help."

Inch by inch Cassie maneuvered her left hand closer to her mouth. All she wanted was to sleep, just for a minute. She gripped her glove between her teeth and worked it off so she could use her fingers to dig. They were cold and stiff at first, then painful. Finally, they were numb and she couldn't feel her fingers at all. She had no sense of direction as she kept poking and scratching at the snow. Cassie prayed that she was face up when she had landed against what she thought was a boulder. She forced down the panic that was threatening, the fear of not being found, of dying.

She thought back to that late summer day, when she stood on the deck of the lodge. She tried to imagine how warm the August sun felt on her face as she stood watching the morning sun glisten off the lake, turning it to gold. She remembered the feeling she had when she heard a familiar voice coming from inside the lodge. And how rubbery her legs felt as she hurried back inside, and stood toward the back of the room as the instructor introduced herself.

"Welcome, members of the National Ski Patrol. My name is Kayla Sinclair. I will be conducting the classroom portion of your training, and Dan Olson will certify you on the mountain. Everyone here today should already have their medical training requirements out of the way, including your Outdoor Emergency Care, CPR-BLS for Health Care Providers, and your CPR-BLS for the Professional Rescuer. I expect you all to work hard and to learn. One day, it may save a life."

A young ranch hand standing next to Cassie pushed his cowboy hat back on his head and whistled low under his breath, then said, "Doggone it! Do you know who that is? It's Kayla Sinclair. She's won more gold medals than any woman in the history of the Winter Olympics. She sure is a good lookin' woman."

Cassie's eyes filled with tears as she looked at her sister standing in front of the room. She knew that Kayla was uneasy, she could see it in the way that she shifted from one foot to the other. She always knew when Kayla was keyed up or on edge about a race because she would mentally prepare herself by making that very small move just before the starter gun went off. A smile as bright as the morning sun spread across Cassie's face when Kayla looked at her with that lopsided smile of hers. "She sure is. That's my big sister, and believe me, you're not her type!"

It was getting hard to concentrate. Cassie was so numb that she couldn't tell if her fingers were moving, but her will to live and her faith in Kayla drove her to keep trying to poke through the snow with each thought: *Don't give up...don't go to sleep...don't give up...don't go to sleep.*

The time elapsed hit the eighteen minute mark, and the ticking of the clock echoed through the silent lobby of the lodge. Kayla flinched with each passing second that pounded painfully in her ears, threatening to destroy what little control she was hanging on to. Kayla paled and her jaw worked nervously as she stared at the mountain, while her fist maintained its white-knuckle grip on the radio. Nathan's voice coming over the radio shattered through the silence.

"Rescue to base. Kayla, come in please."

She could hear it in his voice: the anger, laced with fear and loss of hope. "I'm here, Nathan."

"Kayla, the conditions are worsening and unstable. We can hardly see two feet in front of us. The initial slide was from the south side of the horseshoe. The north side is going to go, and when it does, the track of the avalanche will follow the same path. Damn it to hell, Kayla! The search team has to come off the mountain!"

Kayla felt the room begin to spin. "Nothing from the dogs, no signal?"

"Nothing. I know Cassie wouldn't have forgotten to turn her transceiver to transmit when she went out this morning. I just know it!"

Kayla's face was a mask of stone as she squeezed her eyes shut. Her voice sounded raw. "Nathan, we don't have a choice here. Pull everyone off the mountain before we lose anyone else." Kayla turned and gave the radio to the man standing next to her, avoiding making eye contact with the silent group waiting anxiously behind her. "Take over for me, Josh. Are my skis and equipment still in my locker?"

Josh wasn't surprised, but when he answered Kayla there was an edge of worry in his voice. "Everything is just as you left it. I've kept up the maintenance on all your equipment, Kayla, but..." Kayla was half way to the door. Josh didn't have to ask her what she was going to do, and he knew he couldn't stop her if he tried. "Damn it, Kayla!"

Liberty could see the distress written all over the man's face. "She's heading up on the mountain, isn't she?"

"Damn right, she is, and she isn't in any emotional shape to go up on the mountain in this weather, let alone under these circumstances. She hasn't been on a pair of skis in a long time."

Liberty surprised herself when she heard herself ask, "Can you fit me with boots and skis and do it quickly?"

Josh studied the woman's face. She had a look that didn't invite questions. "I can, but you'd have to be one hell of a skier, and know exactly what you're doing out there. The conditions on the mountain are treacherous; you could get yourself caught in another slide."

Liberty was blunt as her eyes bored into Josh. "I know the risks. We're wasting time we don't have."

Josh motioned for someone to man the radio, and Liberty followed him at a quick trot toward the ski shop. Before they reached the shop Josh knew Liberty's height, weight, and boot size. He had her outfitted and the skies loaded on his snowmobile within minutes. She was halfway up the trail, minutes behind Kayla, before Josh turned and hurried back into the lodge.

Kayla had gone as far as she could by snowmobile. She couldn't chance the noise and vibrations from the motor triggering another slide. She unloaded her gear and skis, then pushed her way against the storm toward the ridge. The pounding of her heart kept time with each second that ticked down in her head. She cursed when she felt the cramp in the calf of her left leg, but it wasn't going to stop her. Somehow she was going to find her sister before she died beneath the onslaught of snow.

An image flashed in Kayla's mind of Cassie's smiling face looking up at Addie adoringly. It was the day she and Addie had given Cassie her first pair of skis. Kayla always feared that her sister felt that she walked in her shadow, but it was Kayla's fear, not Cassie's. Cassie was one of the hardest working members of Lone Mountain Ski Patrol. She trained hard and was a hopeful for the next Olympic women's downhill team.

Kayla knew her sister and how she would react as well as she knew herself. There was a chance, a slim one, but a chance that Cassie had circled around to the back side of South Mountain, crossing over Colman's Ridge that morning. Rescue had found her snowmobile where the trail split; she had either gone up toward the new run along the tree line, or taken the trail that led to Colman's Ridge. The heavy snowfall had covered any tracks that Cassie had left. The ridge was quicker and would give Cassie a better view of the snow on the summit, but if the snow was unstable, it was the more dangerous. If she was right and Cassie was on the ridge when the avalanche started, she could have gone down into the narrow gorge on the opposite side from where the rescue teams and dogs had searched.

Given the same circumstances, with the new run scheduled to open in a matter of a few hours, Kayla would have made the choice to go across Coleman's Ridge. It was a long shot, and the fall into the ravine could have killed Cassie. The narrow ravine with its steep rocky terrain was treacherous, more so if a skier was out of control and the snow beneath was unstable. Kayla knew Cassie had the skill to make it, and if she was alive, she would know that they were searching.

Kayla's fingers trembled as she double-checked that her transceiver was on receive. A surge of adrenaline elevated her heart rate as she stood poised to jump off the edge of the cliff into the gorge. The blizzard made it hard to see and the wind was blowing furiously against her as she calculated the landing in her mind and prayed that she could make it without triggering another slide or hitting the rocks. She shifted from one leg to the other, trying to work out the cramp in her left calf. After going through the AA program, she'd resumed a routine of physical training and fitness, recovering her strength, but had not been on a pair of skies or on Lone Mountain since the day Addie died. Kayla was readying her jump when a movement and a patch of color, partially obscured by the blowing snow along the ridge, caused her to pause. A few seconds later, she could make out the form of a skier.

As Liberty pulled alongside Kayla and took off her goggles, Kayla lost it. "Are you fucking crazy? No one is supposed to be on the mountain. For Christ's sake, you could have started a slide! What in the hell are you doing up here?"

Liberty didn't look at Kayla, but down into the ravine, quickly surveying the area. She pointed as she shouted over the howling wind. "If she's down there, she'll be in that area. We can jump to the left of the rocks. The snow looks solid enough there; we'll have a better chance of avoiding a fresh slide."

The wind had picked up and was biting at their faces, pushing them toward the edge. Before Kayla could open her mouth to protest, Liberty slipped her goggles down and squared her body, then dug her poles in and pushed off down into the ravine. Dumbfounded, Kayla held her breath as Liberty sailed with athletic grace and perfect form toward the jagged cliff of rocks. She had competed against the most accomplished and seen the best jumpers in the world, and she couldn't help stare in awe. *Who in the hell is this Liberty Starr!*

Liberty landed with her skies hanging precariously onto the side of the mountain. She motioned to Kayla, then cautiously side stepped down the ravine, allowing enough room for Kayla to land. The wind was pelting a stinging sleet of ice against her face and body as she leaned against the wind to watch Kayla leap off the mountain. Her breath caught when the wind gusted and changed directions, causing Kayla to drift too far toward the rocky terrain. *Lift your skis! Face into the wind; you can do it!* A look of relief lifted the corners of Liberty's eyes as she watched Kayla, with the skill of the champion that she was, adjust her flight and land precisely on target.

The temperature had dropped drastically and the wind was now a deafening roar. The angry storm was issuing a challenge with a vengeance, daring them to take back what the mountain had claimed. Liberty lifted a thumb up, motioned to the transceiver on her wrist, and began to traverse carefully across and down the ravine with Kayla behind her, imitating her actions. The clock in Kayla's mind continued to tick, brutally reminding her that it had been over forty-five minutes since the avalanche had rumbled down the mountain. Odds were that Cassie was dead, but Kayla wouldn't accept that; she followed Liberty deeper into the ravine.

Cassie's mind had disassociated from her body; she didn't feel the cold or the pain, just the overwhelming desire to slip into a peaceful sleep. She was floating, passing through a shadowy tunnel toward a bright white light. She sensed she was nearing the end of her journey when a figure appeared and stood blocking her way. It was Addie; her beautiful face held a look of infinite sorrow. Cassie reached to touch her, to take away the sadness from Addie's eyes and tell her that everything would be all right. Cassie's voice was silent, but Cassie knew that Addie understood. She could hear Addie's voice:

You need to hang on, Cassie. Can you do that for just a little while longer?

I don't know. I'm so tired, Addie... Worried about Kayla... Never...the same without you.

Addie whispered into the wind, *Kayla, Hurry, my darling, hurry!*

Cassie, what if I lie down beside you and hold you? Remember, like I used to do when you were a little girl?

Cassie closed her eyes, slipping deeper into a merciful sleep.

Answer me, Cassie!

Cassie was barely breathing and her heart quivered feebly in her chest.

Yes...please hold me. I'm a little...afraid, Addie. Afraid of what this will do to Kayla.

Cassie stopped breathing just as Addie pulled her into her arms.

Liberty stopped abruptly, her body rigid. Suddenly, she had a signal and it was strong! She hit the quick release on her skies and fell to her knees, scraping at the layer of snow where the signal was the strongest, uncovering Cassie's frozen fingers. She knew Kayla was seconds behind her and would notify Rescue, so she frantically continued to dig.

The second she saw Liberty release her skis, Kayla reached for her radio. She knew that it could only mean one thing: she'd found Cassie! Nathan would be standing vigil with Kalispell Regional Medical Center's Air Rescue. She screamed over the raging wind into the radio. "Rescue, Rescue, come in please. Nathan, please come in!" Kayla's radio crackled to life.

"I'm here, Kayla!"

"We found her, Nathan! We found her! We're halfway down the ravine behind Colman's Ridge." Reaching the spot where Liberty was digging, Kayla threw down the radio, gasping when she saw the stiff, frozen fingers. She never faltered for a second as she kicked off her skis and began to claw at Cassie's snowy grave. Seconds later, when they uncovered Cassie's upper body, Kayla desperately reached for the radio. "Rescue, we have her out. She's not breathing! Oh God, Nathan, please hurry!"

Kayla watched in shock as Liberty's stiff fingers searched for a pulse. An eternity passed before she heard Liberty's voice shouting over the wailing protest of the storm, "I have a pulse, a weak pulse!" She felt helpless as Liberty swept the snow from Cassie's mouth, then lowered her own mouth to breathe life into the frigid body.

Nathan's voice cut through the howling wind as the mountain continued to throw everything it had at the rescuers. "Kayla, it will take too long to bring her down by snowmobile, and the helicopter could trigger another slide. It's risky, you all could be buried!"

Liberty looked into Kayla's pleading eyes and nodded.

"Nathan, we need less than two minutes to secure her into the stretcher and she can be at Kalispell Trauma Center in less than ten minutes. Her only chance is for Air Rescue to start treatment while they transport her!"

The radio was silent and Kayla held her breath until Nathan's voice boomed, "Air Rescue is on the way, Kayla! You should be seeing them coming over the mountain now!"

The Rescue chopper loomed into sight and landed just as the snow on the ridge above began to crack and shift. The sound of the fracture above them ripped through the hearts of the rescue crew as they rushed to strap Cassie onto the stretcher. The blades of the chopper thrashed against the storm, creating a near white out. An oxygen mask was slipped over Cassie's face as they lifted her into the chopper. The mountain was moving beneath them and the thundering roar of the advancing snow warned them that they were out of time.

The pilot could see that the avalanche was almost on top of them and signaled to the rest. If he didn't pull up now, they all would be buried beneath tons of snow and rock. The only two who weren't on board were Kayla and Liberty. The encroaching snow was too close; they would never outrun it on skis. He had no choice; he had to take a chance with the extra weight. He could feel the snow beginning to push against the front of the chopper as he yelled, "Grab on, now!" He fought to keep the nose of the chopper up. "Fuck, this always works in the movies! I have to pull up!"

Liberty's arm went around Kayla's waist, pulling the woman toward her. She laced her other arm around the runner of the helicopter and screamed into the air, "Take it up! Take it up!" Liberty wrapped her legs around Kayla and held on. When she felt the arms circling her waist, she gripped the runner with both arms just as they were engulfed in a blinding sea of white, pulling the chopper down into the path of the avalanche. A higher power must have been looking out for them as the pilot cursed a blue streak and rode out the initial onslaught, managing to keep the chopper in the air. When he flew out of the ravine, he hovered briefly so his two hanging passengers could drop safely to the ground. Seconds later, the chopper was racing toward the trauma center while the emergency team on board worked to save Cassie's life.

Both Kayla and Liberty were shivering from exhaustion as they lay on the snow-covered ground, trying to catch their breath. Liberty was the first to recover. Crawling over to Kayla, she wrapped her in her arms and used her body to shield her against the freezing wind. This unselfish act from a stranger, and the fact that Liberty had risked her life to help, broke through Kayla's numbness and she started to cry. *Were we too late? Is she alive?*

Liberty wrapped her arms tighter around Kayla and pulled her closer. She kept whispering, "She'll be all right. It'll be all right."

Both knew that they wouldn't last long out in the open in the storm before they froze to death. When they heard the buzzing sound of the snowmobiles, they struggled to get to their feet. Visibility was zero, and the wind was whipping against them trying to throw them to their knees. The snowmobiles pulled up directly in front of them and Nathan hopped off the nearest machine and rushed to Kayla, "Thank God you're all right!"

Kayla held on to Nathan as she yelled, "How did you find us so quickly in this white out?"

Nathan nodded and shot Liberty a grateful smile. "Your friend here managed to turn her transceiver to transmit just after you two found Cassie. "Hurry, get on! Gill has his chopper ready to take us to Kalispell Regional. Cassie will need us, and you both need to be checked for exposure."

During the flight, both women were given dry socks and clothing to change into. Liberty was already beginning to strip when, embarrassed, Nathan turned around, diverting his eyes while they changed. Kayla couldn't help but look. Liberty's body was magnificent; her muscles lean and toned, her physical conditioning, obvious. Her eyes were drawn to the bloody dressing on Liberty's side and the many scars on her back. "You're hurt?" Kayla moved toward Liberty, thinking that she could help or at least take a look, but Liberty quickly pulled the sweatshirt over her head and down over the wound. "It's nothing."

A fleeting thought about the mystery of the woman who had come into her life just yesterday passed through Kayla's mind as the helicopter landed at Kalispell Regional.

Chapter Seven

Kayla and Nathan paced back and forth in the waiting area outside the trauma room. Dr. Mican had sent word that she'd be out as soon as she could to update them on Cassie's condition. They knew Cassie had been alive when the rescue chopper brought her in, but in transit, her heart had gone into a critical arrhythmia and she was cardio-converted during the flight. Rescue had her stable, wrapped in a warming blanket, and was administering heated air to her lungs while infusing warm intravenous fluids. Now the immediate concern was to stabilize her core temperature to prevent her heart from going into another potentially fatal dysrhythmia.

Liberty watched the emotional turmoil of Kayla and her brother at not knowing whether their sister would survive. She saw the reassuring touches that passed between them. *I wonder how it feels to have a family and someone to care about you like that.* It had been a long time since she had felt the comforting touch of another human being.

While Kayla and Nathan waited to hear about Cassie, Liberty searched and found a locked exam room on another floor. Two seconds with a bent paper clip, and she was in. After the aerobatics with the helicopter and Kayla's weight hanging from her waist, her side was throbbing. The pain told her she needed to check her wound. The room was windowless, so she felt safe to turn on the overhead light. She lifted her shirt. The wound was an angry red and it had bled, but it was no worse, considering her recent exploits. She chided herself for the position she'd put herself in. *Damn it all to hell, it serves me right for not tending to my own business. Someone's trying to kill me, and I run off and play hero.*

It was ironic. So many years ago, the thought of helping someone was why Liberty had joined the FBI, now it was something that only slowed her down. The killing had conditioned her to think always of herself and her mission first, without emotion or conscience. Every action and course of direction was to successfully accomplish the objective, no matter the means or the cost. She knew all too well that she could not be compromised or put at risk of exposure for any reason. If she put herself in danger of being caught, no one would come to her rescue. She'd be vilified as a hired assassin.

Kayla's determination and courage to brave the mountain to find her sister had stirred something in Liberty. She saw in Kayla the same inner strength of the proud Pueblo who had raised her. Following Kayla up the mountain hadn't been a choice, but an imperative. It had been a lifetime since she'd felt an emotion so compelling as the need she'd felt to help the kind bartender. Kayla stirred feelings that Liberty questioned. Was it just the altruistic desire to help Kayla or was it something more? Masquerading in one identity or another to accomplish a mission, she had slept with many, men and women alike. But she had never felt desire with any of them, except Yancy. Her body had responded to a few, always a woman, but her mind and heart had never.

Such thoughts and feelings put Liberty on edge; she knew the distraction could make her careless. She pulled her shirt back down and rested for a few minutes, then turned out the light and left the room as she'd found it. When she returned to the waiting area, she was carrying two cups of hot coffee. After handing one to Nathan, she went over to stand beside Kayla, who stood looking at the falling snow through the frosted lacy pattern etched on the window of the waiting room.

"Coffee?"

Kayla shivered. The exhaustion was showing in her eyes as she reached for the cup. "Thanks."

"Have you heard anything more?"

Kayla took in a deep breath, her words jagged and broken from raw emotion. "Nothing yet. I just wish... It should be me in there instead of Cassie. If it wasn't for my..." Kayla didn't finish. Instead, she turned and continued to stare out of the window.

Liberty studied the intricate pattern on the frozen window. It was complex and mimicked life. *And you, sweet Kayla, what happened on that mountain that made you stop wanting to live?*

Just then Dr. Mican appeared in the doorway. She looked tired and concerned as she entered the room and walked over to where Kayla was standing at the window. Nathan quickly joined them.

"Kayla, it's nice to see you, just not under these circumstances." Mican reached her hand out to Nathan. "You, too, Nathan. It's been a while. Please, can we sit?"

Fear squeezed like a tight band around Kayla's chest as her eyes searched Mican's face. "Rue, is she..."

"She's alive."

The knot of tension in Kayla's stomach eased a bit.

"I had my doubts when they brought her in, but she's hanging in there — stubborn woman, like her sister."

Liberty caught the subtle look the doctor gave Kayla.

"She isn't awake yet, but her vital signs are stable. It's too early to know if the lack of oxygen has done any damage to her brain. We've stabilized her core temperature and her heart is in a normal sinus rhythm." Rue Mican paused a moment as her eyes went from Nathan to Kayla. "Doctor McKlosky is evaluating the frostbite. I know you'll both want this straight: it's possible she'll lose the fingers on her left hand, and we're not sure about the toes on her right foot. At this point, we'll have to wait and see."

There was a long silence, and then Nathan finally spoke, "Rue, thank you. Can we see her?"

"Just for a moment. She'll be transferred to ICU shortly, then I would like you both to go back to Lone Mountain and get some rest. Cassie will be out of it most of the day, and her body needs the sleep to begin to heal. I'll leave an order allowing unrestricted visiting for only the family in the morning." When Kayla opened her mouth to protest, Rue Mican held up a hand. "No argument, Kayla. She'll need both of you as she recuperates and that can start tomorrow. I won't change my mind on this. Now, let's go see her."

Nathan and Kayla began to follow the doctor, then Kayla stopped and looked back toward Liberty, who was standing watching them go down the hall. "Are you coming?"

Liberty shifted and looked uncomfortable. "The doctor said family."

Kayla looked at Nathan, who nodded, then she looked back at Liberty. "I think it will be all right for the person who saved her life."

The man sitting at the desk in front of the windows in the Oval Office spoke briefly into a telephone that encrypted everything he said. "Have you located the remaining Talons? ... Just one? Who? ... I can't say that surprises me." He listened for a few minutes, then hung up the phone and unlocked a drawer in his desk. Removing a folder, he opened it, then sat staring at the intense hazel eyes that bored through him from the picture that he held in his hands.

"You always were my favorite...from the day you were recruited. You were the most idealistic, the most loyal. Have you become the most deadly, and a traitor? If there was any other way... But there isn't, is there? I can't change what's been done, and I can't take the chance you aren't the one. I never meant for it to end this way, my dear Liberty. But if you're the rogue, you're a threat to the security of this office and to this country. You have survived longer than the rest. I do admire you for that." The buzz of the intercom cut short his solitary commiserating. "Yes, Olivia?"

"You have five minutes before the ambassador to Korea arrives, Mr. President."

Chapter Eight

As the helicopter approached Lone Mountain, the lights that adorned the lodge lit the night sky with a special glow. When Gill landed on the helipad and shut down the rotor, the crew could hear the sounds of carolers and Christmas music coming from inside the lodge. After they heard Cassie would recover, the staff pulled together and went on with the traditional Sinclair Christmas party.

Kayla and Liberty followed Nathan and Gill along a pathway lit by the glow of holiday luminaries. When they came to a fork that branched to either the lodge or to the pub, Nathan stopped a moment to listen. His eyes misted over as he pulled a haggard Kayla into his arms and hugged her. "Merry Christmas, Sis. We have a lot to be thankful for. You're home, we have Lone Mountain and good friends, and Cassie is going to be all right. This has turned out to be a very special Christmas. I'll call Mom and Dad in the morning and tell them what happened. No need for them to try to travel here during the winter months. They'll want to, but Dad is still not getting around too well after the stroke. When Cassie is up to it, she can call and ease their worry. Now, how about you and Liberty coming up and having something to eat?"

Kayla took her brother's larger hand in hers. "Nathan, I love you too, but I'm not up to talking to people right now. I just want to rest a bit and get back to the hospital as soon as I can." She looked at Liberty, but before she could say anything, Liberty spoke.

"I could stay at the lodge, if...if there is a room available tonight."

Kayla kissed Nathan on the cheek, then started down the path toward the pub, her voice trailing behind her. "Your things are at the pub. You're welcome to stay there if you'd like."

Nathan watched his sister walk down the trail toward the pub. "This has been real hard on her. Don't mind her if she seems distracted. You're more than welcome to stay at the lodge, Liberty. We can't thank you enough for—"

"I'd like to stay at the pub, but thanks for the offer, Nathan. Kayla might need... I'll say good night."

Nathan watched Liberty follow the same path his sister had, feeling guilty for the thoughts he was having. His time in the Marines had been spent as an MP, and he had run into a few hard-core soldiers. He'd learned how to spot them, and to avoid them. Liberty's eyes had the look of the spooks that came and went mysteriously at every base where he had served. Was she dangerous? More to the point, was she a danger to Kayla?

Kayla tried to ease the tension from the tight muscles in her neck by letting the hot water pound against the knot between her shoulders. Her mind felt as if it were trapped in a cobweb of confusion. She had the sensation that a thread was being pulled, unraveling her control and her sobriety. She kept reminding herself that Cassie was alive and that she was too tired to feel anger toward the mountain. She knew if she ever let go of her hatred, she would have to face herself and with that, the guilt that it was her fault that Addie died. It was her cockiness that led them to ski the virgin snow in an area off-piste that day. The area around the snow bridge was posted with the warning flags that indicated there was a high risk of avalanche.

Kayla turned the water pressure as high as she could get it, hoping the pounding hot water would chase away the tormenting memories, if only for a while. When she'd finished showering, she wrapped up in a robe and sat in front of the fireplace, looking into the flames. She struggled with the continual ache for Addie, and the strong desire to have a drink. After Addie's death, she'd subsisted in a drunken haze, wandering from one place to another, barely sober enough to know where she was — and it didn't matter, nothing did. Her goal was to drink enough to numb her mind, then fall into a dreamless sleep where Addie's trusting eyes didn't haunt her.

After two years of pickling her senses, she woke up one day in the Kalispell hospital and didn't remember how she'd gotten there or how she'd made it home to Montana. Bits and pieces of dreams, with images of snakes and spiders and crushing snow, clouded her mind. She was lying shivering in a cold sweat when Dr. Rue Mican walked into the room and pulled up a chair.

"Welcome back, Kayla. You've had a go of it this past week."

Kayla blinked her eyes, trying to focus. "A week? I've been here for a week?"

"It doesn't surprise me that you don't remember. You've been out of it. If you want the diagnosis, it's delirium tremens or the DTs. I'll come straight to the point, Kayla. You can keep drinking yourself to death, or you can ask for help, go into treatment, and rejoin the living. No one can make this decision for you. You have to want it more than you want a drink or anything else."

The doctor's words clawed at raw nerve endings. Kayla didn't want to hear it. Her whole body was screaming with the agonizing need for a drink. She threw every expletive she could think of at the annoying doctor until she ran out of breath.

Doctor Mican waited patiently, then handed Kayla a glass of water. "Finished?"

Kayla's chest heaved with the exertion; all she could do was glare.

"You don't remember me. I'm Dr. Rue Mican. I was on duty when you were brought in a week ago. I was also the doctor on duty when they brought you and Addie in, the day she died." Kayla paled and jerked as if she'd been struck. "I watched you ski in the 1994 Lillehammer Olympics, and also in Nagano in '98, bursting with pride right along with the rest of America, when you stood on that platform and accepted your gold medals. When you walked off the dais and presented them to Addie, announcing to the world that you were in love with her, I stood a whole lot taller. I'm out now, but I wasn't always. I haven't hidden my sexuality from that moment on. Anyone with eyes could see how much you and Addie adored each other."

Kayla flinched from the words. Her eyes were dark pits of unrelenting pain. She tried to get out of bed; she wanted to run, to get away from the words that were tearing at her heart.

"These words hurt, I know, but it is time you accept her death. If what you want is to kill yourself, there are easier ways to do it. I don't believe your Addie would have wanted you to join her, leaving this world as a drunk, wallowing in self-pity, in the bottom of a bottle. Not the woman I met in Nagano the morning you won the first gold."

Kayla's bloodshot eyes snapped to the doctor's face. "You knew Addie?"

"I met her just that one time. She was pacing the floor in the hotel coffee shop in Nagano, waiting for you to come downstairs. She said that she didn't want to make you nervous. I mentioned that I was from Kalispell and had skied Lone Mountain many times. We sat and had coffee. Addie talked about you and how happy you were together. She told me that the two of you were going to build the pub on Lone Mountain, and that you planned to start a family. The pride and love she had for you was in her every word. She was an exceptional, beautiful, caring young woman. If she could see what you're doing to yourself now, it would break her heart."

Doubled over in pain, Kayla mustered up enough strength to yell, "Get out. Get the hell out of my room!"

Dr. Mican stood up and rang for the nurse. "You have to want to dry out; you have to want to live. I won't sugar coat this, Kayla. It will be tough, but you don't have to do it cold turkey. There are medications we can give you to take the edge off. You're in withdrawal now and are probably feeling like you're coming out of your skin. Before it's over, you'll beg for a drink. But if Kayla Sinclair is still in there somewhere, she'll make it. It's up to you. When your mind clears a little and you can think straight, ask yourself if this is what Addie would have wanted for you. Your family has been looking for you for two years. You might want to think about letting them know you're alive."

Mican knew she was hitting Kayla hard below the belt, that she had overstepped the propriety of the patient/doctor relationship by saying the things she had, but until Kayla wanted to be helped, it wouldn't work. She'd found her way back to Montana for a reason, and Mican hoped it was because she wanted that help. She walked toward the door. "I'll have the nurse give you something to calm you, and I'll stop back and see you later."

Hatred plain in her eyes, Kayla stared at the woman, venting all her pain and anger on her. But Dr. Mican's every word penetrated through her sodden brain, ripped at her soul.

A hiss and the snap of an igniting piece of kindling in the fireplace jogged Kayla from her reminiscences. She picked up the phone and dialed the pager number she knew by heart. After a few minutes, her phone rang. "Thanks for returning my call, Rue. How is she?"

"She's doing well. Her vital signs are good and her kidney's are functioning. She's been awake off and on. I've medicated her for the pain; hopefully she'll sleep. The biggest concern now is her fingers and toes. The fingers on both hands and the toes of her right foot are red and painfully swollen. Dr. McKlosky is following that very closely. We'll just have to wait and see."

Kayla was silent trying to find the words. "Rue, I..."

"You don't need to say it, Kayla. It's what I do." Mican's voice softened, "I'm sorry this happened to Cassie. It has to have brought back many memories. Are you doing all right?"

Kayla felt her hands shaking. She hoped Rue couldn't hear the uncertainty in her voice. "I'm fine."

"You don't sound like you are. I'm worried about you, Kayla. Have you been going to your AA meetings?"

"We've been busy at the lodge, getting everything ready for the holiday skiing. I'm doing fine. I'll attend a meeting when I can."

"Make it soon. I miss you, Kayla. Can we get together for coffee and talk, maybe go to dinner?"

Kayla massaged her temple. "Rue, I promised you we would talk, but this isn't a good time."

Mican could hear the stress in Kayla's voice and didn't push. "Will you promise to call me if—"

"You needn't worry about that, Rue; I'm fine. I'll see you tomorrow at the hospital."

When Liberty reached the pub, a light was on in the kitchen and the door unlocked, but the bar was dark. *Kayla must have gone straight upstairs.* The chime from the clock in the bar struck 1 AM; Christmas day was over. It had been a long and trying day for Kayla and her family. Liberty leaned against the counter and debated whether she should fix Kayla something to eat and take it upstairs. She had gone to the cafeteria at the hospital and had a sandwich, then brought coffee and sandwiches back to Kayla and Nathan. Nathan ate, but Kayla hadn't eaten since they'd shared the sandwiches Kayla had prepared after the storm took out the power the night before. Unsure if Kayla would want to be disturbed, Liberty locked up and went up to her own room.

Removing the leather case from the bottom of her duffel, Liberty opened it and emptied the contents on the bed. She removed the false bottom to reveal several passports with matching credit cards and driver's licenses and a cache of money, strapped tightly in place. She picked up an identification card she'd used on one of her first assignments, a lifetime ago, wondering why she'd kept it when her orders were to destroy it. The face in the picture was so young, so naïve, and free from the telling lines of guilt and disillusionment. A long forgotten memory surfaced from the shadows of her mind, of the pride and honor she'd felt when she was chosen to join the elite Talons and serve President Kincaide and her country.

Liberty built a fire, then sat thinking about her next move. Warning signs had been red flagging the Talons for a long time, and she'd prepared to disappear, as had Peter and many of the remaining Talons. She had secretly accumulated IDs and credit cards that no one knew about and could not be traced to her. Still, she needed help, and her best option seemed to be to contact Armanno Santini.

Restless, Liberty decided to go down to the kitchen to fix something to eat. She was outside Kayla's bedroom door when she heard the muffled sounds of crying. She stood for a moment, raised her hand to knock, then turned to go downstairs, instead. When she heard the sound again, she knocked lightly, waited a minute, and when there wasn't any answer, she retreated a step, only to be stopped by Kayla's muffled voice.

"Come in."

Liberty pushed open the door. Kayla was sitting in the darkened room in front of the fireplace. "I...heard...I thought I heard you on the phone. Is Cassie all right?" Kayla nodded mutely and continued to stare into the fire. Liberty struggled with the words to comfort the woman, just as she struggled with the emotions this woman was evoking in her, emotions she thought had been buried long ago. She wanted to take this woman's pain, to absorb it, to add it to the bottomless black pit of her own lost soul.

A shiver shook Kayla's body, whether of emotion or fatigue, Liberty did not know, but her feet took her across the room before her mind could fathom why she was compelled to do so. She knelt beside Kayla, her arms heavy with the need to reach out to this woman she had known for less than twenty-four hours. Every instinct was telling her that Kayla needed the comfort of a human touch, but that was a problem. She wasn't human any more. Inept words tumbled through her mind. She couldn't find the words that usually came so naturally, words she so often relied upon to seduce, to deceive, and to steal the emotions and trust of the many who were pawns in the deadly game she always won. Maybe it was for the same unexplained reason that when Kayla had asked her name, she'd answered with the truth. "You need to rest, Kayla. Morning will come soon enough and you'll want to get back to the hospital to be with Cassie."

Kayla inhaled deeply and shook her head as if to clear her thoughts, the fatigue evident in her voice. "I need to find someone to tend the pub. ... Cassie always helped cover the holidays. ... I have deliveries coming today, and it's way too late to cancel the New Year's Eve party that's been booked."

Without a thought, Liberty heard herself say, "I'm a pretty good bartender. I can help out until you can find someone."

Kayla looked hesitant. "It would solve my problems, but...I couldn't ask you to do that. Of course, I would pay you..."

"You didn't ask, and, if you don't mind me staying here at the pub, I could work for room and board." Kayla looked uncertain and Liberty didn't press her. "I was just going downstairs to fix something to eat. You haven't eaten all day, Kayla. Your Doctor Mican was right — Cassie is going to need you to be healthy. Why don't I get something for you, too, and maybe a glass of wine? It might help you get some rest."

Kayla almost accepted the offer of the wine, but demurred. "I don't drink, but a cup of tea would be good, thanks."

"Tea it is. I'll be right back."

Liberty had reached the door when Kayla called her name. "Liberty, thank you...for everything. I can never repay you for...for all you've done."

Liberty nodded and went downstairs to fix the tea.

Chapter Nine

It was a little after six the next morning when Kayla called the hospital again and was relieved when the nurse held the phone so she could speak to Cassie for a few minutes. When she hung up, she called Nathan, then dressed quickly and walked quietly past the guest-room to go downstairs. The roads had been plowed and reopened, and Nathan was going to pick her up so they could drive into Kalispell. When Kayla reached the bottom of the steps, she could smell the aroma of fresh coffee, and curiously followed her nose into the kitchen. Her book of notes was open and laying on the counter. Coffee was brewing in the large coffee maker to accomodate the early morning skiers who stopped in for a caffeine wake up on the way to the slopes. And the pastries that were delivered every morning by the kitchen staff at the lodge were sorted and arranged in the server. Confused, she walked through the kitchen into the pub, where there was a fire roaring in the fireplace and the bar was set up. She was standing in wonderment when a voice from behind startled her.

"Good morning. Did you get any rest last night? I heard you on the phone a couple of times. How's your sister doing?"

Kayla turned to see Liberty with her arms full of wood for the fireplace. "You did all this?" Kayla was surprised to see how professionally the bar had been organized. "I'm sorry, did I keep you awake all night? I...uh...see you found the wood pile."

Liberty stacked the wood in the bin and put another log on the fire. "Your split wood outside is low. I would have cut more, but it was too early and I didn't want to wake you." Liberty hesitated a moment, feeling awkward when Kayla didn't answer.

Kayla was staring. She couldn't figure Liberty out or what it was she wanted. The hardness was there, along with a vacant unreadable look in her eyes, but there was more to Liberty Starr than she revealed, and Kayla wondered what it was. She had been concerned about how she was going to manage the pub. Now this woman she hardly knew was again coming to her aid by offering to help keep the pub open through the busy holiday season so she could be with Cassie at the hospital. Liberty was a mystery, a beautiful woman with many talents, but Kayla doubted her profession was that of a bartender.

"If I read your kitchen notes right, your menu looks simple enough — pizza and sandwiches with a soup of the day. Everything is prepared at the lodge and brought over about 10:30?"

Yes, much more than meets the eye. "Most of it is. The soup and pizza are made daily at the lodge. The soup is kept hot and I bake the pizza. Sandwiches are made as they're ordered, and I usually have one of the employees from the lodge come and lend a hand during the busy time. Someone will be here today to help you through the lunch rush." Kayla looked at her watch, impatient to get on the road to Kalispell. "You're sure about this?"

"Absolutely." Liberty could read the doubts in Kayla's eyes and knew what she was thinking. "Honestly, I have tended bar before; I can handle it. You don't have anything to worry about. You go and spend the time with your sister; she needs you. I'll take care of things here."

"I want to pay—" The sound of a horn honking outside interrupted.

"We'll talk about that later. I fixed a thermos for you to take with you." Liberty went to fetch the coffee while Kayla shrugged into her jacket, putting her thoughts about Liberty on hold.

Night was falling as Nathan stood by the window with his arms crossed over his chest while Kayla sat by the side of the bed watching Cassie drift in and out of sleep. Both siblings were grateful that the morphine was relieving Cassie's pain, allowing her the rest she needed to heal. Living in Montana, a state where the weather could get down to forty below, not counting the chill factor, both Doctor Mican and Doctor McKlosky were well familiar with frostbite and had treated many cases. Kayla and Nathan were confident that everything possible was being done to save Cassie's swollen digits. Just as the nurse finished repositioning Cassie onto her back, Doctor Mican came in. Cassie opened her eyes briefly and smiled at Rue, then went back to sleep.

Rue motioned for the two siblings to join her out in the hallway. Her eyes went from Nathan to Kayla. "I'm sorry that I missed you on rounds this morning. I had an early surgery. You both look exhausted. I can have a cot brought in and you can take turns resting."

"Thanks, Rue. We appreciate all you've done." Kayla ran her hand nervously through her dark hair. "Doctor McKlosky was in a little while ago. He said that it might be weeks before Cassie's frostbitten tissue could be declared viable, and that it was too early to say whether she would lose the fingers on her left hand and possibly the toes and a portion of her right foot."

Rue was concerned about the brittleness in Kayla's voice and the unmistakable signs that Kayla was having a hard time coping with Cassie's condition. When Kayla was alone, she would ask her if she needed something to help take the edge off. "Did Doctor McKlosky get Cassie to sign a permit to do surgery if needed?"

Kayla unconsciously clenched her fists; the thought of Cassie losing any part of her body made her sick to her stomach.

Nathan was also aware that Kayla was having a difficult time. He reached for her hand and held it as he answered Rue. "He did, and he explained that the only immediate surgical intervention would be if an incision were needed to relieve the swelling to restore circulation. He said the goal for now was to manage Cassie's pain and avoid complications, such as further tissue damage or infection. Do you agree with that?"

"Yes, I do. I don't want to give false hope, but Cassie is a fighter, and ultimately everything is in her favor. She's healthy with good circulation. I believe she will recover without complication. It will be a struggle, and the not knowing for weeks will be difficult," Rue looked directly at Kayla, "for you all."

Aware of the looks Rue was giving Kayla, Nathan decided to leave them alone. "Thanks for your honesty. I know we'll work through this together. If you'll excuse me, I'm going to go sit with Cassie. Kayla, why don't you take a little walk or go get some coffee."

Kayla leaned wearily against the wall. "I can give you something to relax you and take the edge off, Kayla. You could lie down a while and rest in my office if you'd like."

"Thanks, Rue, I appreciate the offer, but I don't need anything. I want to stay in the room with Cassie. I will take you up on having a cot brought in, though."

"I'll stop by the nurse's station on my way out and order it. If you need me, or anything, will you call me?"

Taking in a deep breath, Kayla pushed away from the wall. "You're a good friend, Rue. I promise I will. I'll talk to you tomorrow." She kissed Rue on the cheek and went back into Cassie's room.

Cassie dozed off and on, waking up at times with a jerk to see if Kayla was still there. The worry showed on Kayla's face as she stroked Cassie's forehead until she went back to sleep, just as she had when Cassie was a little girl and was having a bad dream. When Cassie was awake, Kayla helped her to eat a little from the tray that had been left, but Cassie became nauseated and could only hold down a few sips of tea. Kayla held Cassie in her arms as she slept; she felt a surge of panic as she thought of how very close they had come to losing her sister in the same way they had lost Addie. When Cassie drifted off again, Kayla motioned for Nathan to join her out into the hall.

"I'm going downstairs for a few minutes. Do you need anything from the cafeteria or the gift shop?"

"No, you go ahead, Sis. I'll take a walk when you get back."

"Sounds good. Think I'll get some fresh air, too. I'll be back in a bit."

It was freezing out, but the cold air felt good as Kayla walked along the street. The day after Christmas was usually quiet, so there weren't many people about and the traffic was light. The streetlights along Conway Drive were beginning to come on. She'd walked this same route on a few occasions after attending an AA meeting and she knew exactly where it would take her. When she reached the intersection, she stood in the falling snow watching the neon sign flickering off and on in the window of the tavern. She'd stood in the same spot before, thinking of all the reasons to go in, but she'd always managed to turn around. This time the ache she felt inside overruled her reason; she wanted a drink. The liquor would help her escape to a place where she felt nothing. She stomped her cold feet against the ground and hunched her shoulders against the wind. *I could go in and just get warm, maybe have a coffee before I head back to the hospital. What harm would there be in that?* Kayla had her hand on the door when it opened and a woman dressed in a nursing uniform bumped into her, almost knocking them both down the icy stoop. "Anne, is that you? It's me, Kayla."

The woman's words were slightly slurred as she squinted and looked at Kayla. "Kayla, Kayla Sinclair?"

"My gosh, Anne, I haven't seen you since college."

Before either could say anything more, a man came through the door and put his arm around Anne's waist, then started to hustle her off the step toward the cab that had just pulled up. "Come on, baby, let's go. It's cold out here. We were heading to my place, remember?"

"We were? No...I think I told you I could get myself home." Anne pointed to the cab that was waiting. "Listen, I don't go home with men I meet in a bar. As a matter of fact," she hiccuped, "I don't go home with men, period."

The fellow pulled Anne closer. "Well, maybe I'm just the guy who could change your mind."

It was clear that Anne was trying to get rid of the guy, so Kayla stepped toward Anne and took her arm. "Anne, do you mind if I ride with you? I need to get back to the hospital."

Anne linked her arm through Kayla's. "It would be my pleasure to share a cab with you, Sinclair."

They talked a little on the ride, and Anne seemed to sober up a bit. "Thanks for coming to my rescue back there. That jerk was hitting on me the entire time I was in there. He wouldn't take no for an answer." As a nurse who worked at the hospital, Anne knew that Cassie had been admitted, and she turned the conversation away from herself. "I stopped in to see Cassie this morning before I went on duty. I think she's doing pretty well, under the circumstances."

"We can only hope so. Dr. McKlosky pretty much says we have to wait and see."

The cab pulled up in front of Anne's house. "Do you want me to come in with you?" Kayla offered.

"No, but thank you. It's better that I go in by myself. Teddy and I had words this morning before I went to work, and she's probably pacing the floor worried sick about me." She squeezed Kayla's hand. "I never got to tell you how sorry I was about Addie."

Kayla nodded toward the front door of the house. She could see Teddy standing in the doorway. Anne kissed her on the cheek and got out of the cab.

"Well, I'd better face the music. Thanks again for helping me out back there. Cassie will be all right. Rue's a good doctor."

When the cab dropped Kayla off in front of the hospital, she didn't go straight up to Cassie's room. Instead, she went into the chapel and sat down. It had been a long time since she had asked God for anything. Her anger had turned her away from her faith. When she lost the person she loved most in the world, she needed someone to blame, anyone but herself. She'd blamed God, and still did. Kayla's hands were trembling as she folded them together and looked at the statue of Jesus, then she prayed for the first time since Addie's death.

"Why, why Cassie? Addie never believed that you were a vengeful God. You took her, isn't that enough? Don't punish Cassie for my lack of faith. What lesson is there in that? Addie believed in you and so does Cassie. I won't pretend; I'm not sure I do. If you are there and you're listening, then take your vengeance out on me and not Cassie."

The only sound in the room was the low burr of the machines as Nathan stood looking out the window at a snowplow clearing the streets. Kayla had been gone a long while and he was worried. Since she'd come home and reopened the pub, she'd held everything inside; they didn't talk like they use to.

Cassie's groggy voice interrupted his thoughts, most of which were about Kayla. "You don't both need to stay here, big brother. And we both know Kayla couldn't be pried out of here."

Nathan turned around to see Cassie awake and struggling to sit up in the bed. Without the use of her hands, it was awkward and frustrating for her. He crossed the room and put his arms around his sister and boosted her up, then raised the head of the bed.

Tears pooled in Cassie's eyes; the movement caused excruciating pain to radiate through her hands and feet. She clenched her teeth and shook her head when Nathan reached for the call button. "No, it's all right. I don't want them to turn up the morphine. It makes me too groggy and I want to get out of here as soon as I can. Besides I can give myself...what did the nurse call it...a bolus."

Kayla was outside the door, about to enter the room, when she heard the exchange between her sister and brother. She waited until she could control the emotions that threatened to unravel her. Her frustration and helplessness were feelings that were ones all too familiar. She straightened her shoulders, forced a smile onto her face and walked into the room. "Look at you! I brought your favorite — a chocolate marshmallow shake. Feel up to it?"

Kayla and Nathan exchanged looks and Nathan helped himself to a cup of the coffee she had in a carrying tray. "You two tackle that shake. I'm going out to the visitor room and call the lodge to tell them we're going to spend the night in town."

"Nathan, wait, please. Kayla is here with me and you're needed at the lodge. We sold out every room weeks in advance for the holiday, and the slopes tomorrow will be jammed with skiers coming up for the day from Kalispell and Whitefish. Besides, I'm scheduled for whirlpool therapy early in the morning, and all you'll both do here is sit around. We've all worked so hard to get ready for this season, Nathan. And we've invested so much in the new run. Gill will be pulling his hair out trying to manage it all. Please, go home."

Nathan looked at Kayla. "What do you think? I could come back late tomorrow and pick you up."

"Cassie is right. I'll stay here tonight, and tomorrow there's no night skiing, so you can pick me up after Mike closes the lifts. I promise if anything comes up, I'll call you."

Nathan hesitated a moment, then reached for his parka. "This is going to be one of our busiest seasons. If the weather cooperates and we continue to get the snow, we should be able to pay off the loan for the improvements we made last year and the new run this year. What about the pub, Sis? Shall I get someone to look after it tomorrow?"

"Liberty has offered to help out a while. I'll call her and tell her

I'm staying in town tonight. This morning she seemed to have it all under control."

Nathan bent to give Cassie a kiss on the forehead, then turned and, as he hugged Kayla, he whispered into her ear, "You doing okay?"

"I'll walk you to the elevator. Cassie, I'll be right back and we can start on that shake."

When Nathan and Kayla were far enough away from the room, Nathan stopped and took Kayla's hand. He was worried and it was evident in his words. "How about it, are you doing all right? Yesterday was the first time you've been on skis since...well since..."

"It's all right, Nathan, you don't need to avoid saying it — since Addie was killed in the avalanche."

"It's still hard for all of us, Kayla, so I know how you must be feeling. It had to be tough going up on the mountain alone yesterday. The jump you took off that ridge would have been impossible for an expert skier who was in top shape."

"I'm fine, Nathan, and I wasn't alone."

"You were both lucky."

"I was lucky, Nathan. Liberty saved both Cassie's life and mine. She's an extraordinary athlete."

The worried look returned to Nathan's face. "That woman has a look about her. What do you know about her? Did you meet her when you were skiing on the Olympic team?"

"No, I'd never met her before she walked into the pub on Christmas Eve. When the pass closed and the lodge was full, I offered her my spare bedroom for the night. Whatever brought her to Lone Mountain, we can only be grateful. The way she handled herself on the mountain yesterday was pure skill, like second nature to her, as if she'd been conditioned to respond the way she did. There was never a time that I saw fear or doubt in her eyes, not once. I don't know why she came up on that mountain to help me find Cassie, but she did, and she did it for a stranger. I owe her and I won't ask her questions, Nathan. Besides, I have a feeling she's the kind that doesn't stay in one place very long."

The elevator door opened and Nathan got in. Just before the door closed he looked into Kayla's pale eyes. "We both owe her. Just you be careful, Kayla, hear me?"

Chapter Ten

Cassie had gone to the whirlpool, and Kayla was edgy, pacing the floor. The past forty-eight hours had dredged up too many memories and they tormented her. In her mind's eye she could see a five-year-old Addie in the blue dress she wore on the first day of school. Even then Kayla had thought Addie was the cutest girl she'd ever seen. Kayla took the school bus from Lone Mountain to Kalispell, and come rain or shine, Addie would be waiting for her. Addie's mother made her wear long brown stockings, and no matter how much Addie begged and cried that none of the other girls had to wear them, her mother wouldn't relent. Addie would tell Kayla to stand guard while she took the stockings off and stuffed them into her lunch pail, then she made Kayla swear she'd never tell.

They were the best of friends and when one was seen, there was the other. Growing up in the wide-open spaces of rural Montana, their lives revolved around skiing and they both loved the outdoors. That they had become lovers during their college years was as natural as the sun rising. Addie spent every moment she could with her on the mountain and Addie's face was the only one Kayla looked for in the crowd when she won the gold medal at Lillehammer in '94 and again at Nagano in '98. She recalled how unsettled she was as quakes shook the earth and snow and sleet pummeled Nagano every day, causing countless delays. The rescheduling got so bad that organizers had to cram the men's super G, women's downhill, and the women's combined downhill into one day — the first tripleheader in Olympic Alpine history. It was a trying few days. The weather was brutal and the earthquakes made the conditions on the mountain dangerous. Kayla could always depend on Addie's gentle smile and calm voice to settle her and give her the encouragement to chance the moving mountain at the breakneck speeds that the downhill skiers reached.

Kayla remembered waiting, poised at the gate to start her last run of the slalom. Visibility was poor and the pelting sleet stung her face. She felt the earth moving under her skis as another aftershock shook Nagano. She lowered her goggles and looked through the blinding snow at the barely visible marker flag that was whipping in the wind at the first turn. When the pistol sounded, Kayla jumped out with one thought on her mind: *This one is for you, my love.*

The weather had made the hill icy and extremely dangerous, and it took all her skill and strength to control her turns and keep them tight around the flags. One hundredth of a second could determine whether a skier won or lost. When she crossed the finish line, Addie was the first to reach Kayla. She jumped into her arms, wrapped her legs around Kayla's waist, and screamed her time into the wind. Kayla had won the gold!

In Kayla's mind's eye she could see that day as the American flag stretched its Stars and Stripes proudly over Nagano, Japan. She stepped down from the platform and went to stand in front of Addie. In Addie's shining eyes, she found her soul, and the inextricable threads of love wound around her heart. Cameras flashed all around them as Kayla removed the gold medal from her neck and placed it around Addie's, then kissed her on the mouth. She didn't care what her coaches or the world thought; the medal belonged to Addie as much as it did to her. Addie had been by her side every step of the way. They had made the decision together: they weren't going to hide the fact that they were lovers from the camera any longer. Those who loved them supported them, and that's what mattered. Addie just smiled and wrapped her arms around Kayla's waist as they both waved and faced the cheering crowds — and the world. When they came home from Japan, with support and love from both families, they built the pub and moved in together.

Cassie dozed as Kayla sat in the dark watching the green lights blink on the infusion pumps. Kayla's thoughts were still in the past and one particular crisp winter morning. She was in training for the 2002 Olympic Games in Salt Lake City. It seemed as if she was always in training, ever since she'd won her first skiing competition when she was nine years old. It had snowed the night before, and she could hardly wait to get out on the slopes. It was one of those perfect mornings. Kayla was on top of the world and touted to be the skier who would bring home several gold medals for the USA women's team in 2002. She was in love, and Addie loved her back. Kayla's world was complete. Kayla's share of the lodge and the income from the pub provided them with a good life, and Kayla planned to retire from competitive skiing after the 2002 Olympics so they could start a family.

Kayla had gotten up at the crack of dawn and showered and was toweling off when she saw Addie's reflection in the steam-covered mirror. Addie was leaning against the doorframe, watching her. Kayla recognized the look in Addie's eyes, and deliberately kept her back to her as she ran the towel slowly over her taut body, then bent slightly to dry long legs and firm thighs. When Addie shook her head and smiled that "I know what you're doing, Kayla Sinclair" look and bit her lower lip, Kayla asked, "See something you like — or maybe want?"

Addie grabbed the wet towel from Kayla and snapped it across her buttocks. "You're a devil, Kayla Sinclair." Kayla laughed, turned around, and pulled Addie into her arms. The desire was bright in Addie's eyes as her hands covered Kayla's breasts. "Don't you dare play dumb. You saw me watching you and you decided to put on a little show for me."

Kayla untied Addie's robe and slipped her arms around her waist, pulling their naked bodies closer together. Then, sliding her hands across the curves of Addie's buttocks, she pulled her pelvis tight against her own. "Did it work?"

Addie moaned as her mouth found Kayla's and she nipped along Kayla's bottom lip. Before Addie's tongue slipped into Kayla's mouth, she groaned, "Wise guy. Doesn't it always?"

The robe fell to the floor as Kayla lifted Addie onto the top of the vanity. Spreading Addie's legs, she dropped to her knees. Addie braced her hands on the cool marble behind her as Kayla nibbled and kissed along her inner thighs, sending cascading tremors and searing heat along her nerve endings, to the ball of fire in her belly. Addie had been ready from the moment she'd seen Kayla standing naked with the water dripping off her lean, toned body. She knew she wasn't going to last long. Gasping, her words came in between spasms of pure pleasure. "Baby, don't stop. Just don't stop!"

Kayla tasted Addie's desire as her tongue licked and teased her swollen clit until Addie's body tightened and formed a beautiful pose of release. Addie trembled as her arms lost strength and she draped them over Kayla's shoulders and fell into her arms. As she held Addie, Kayla knew that nothing or no one could make her feel as Addie did. Addie was her world.

Breathless, Addie asked, "My God, sweetheart, what turned you on this morning?"

Kayla ran her fingers along the feminine curves and muscles of Addie's back and thighs. "You need to ask? You're beautiful, Addie, in every way. Not only your body and your smile, but your passionate and gentle nature. You have a loving heart, my love. And if that isn't answer enough, you're sexy as hell." Kayla slapped Addie playfully on the ass. "Now, go get dressed. Let's go skiing!"

Kayla thrived on the unrelenting challenge of the mountain and she wanted to ski off-piste that day, in an area where the snow was deeper and undisturbed. The area was accessible only by traversing a narrow natural bridge. They had crossed the bridge many times before, and Kayla went first to check it out, then crossed back. It was late in the season and the snowpack was a multi-layered history of the season's storms. There was no way to know that the deeply buried layers were unpredictable as a result of the changes in temperature, which created uncertain conditions hidden below. The entire snowpack above was unstable.

Kayla crossed the bridge again and was waiting for Addie to cross when she felt the tremor moving through her skies and up her poles. She stiffened seconds before she heard the deafening echo of the sound of the snow fracturing between the peaks and saw a large slab of snow breaking away. Addie's name was frozen on her lips when the bridge gave way, plummeting Addie into the deep gorge.

The look in Addie's eyes tore Kayla's breath, and her life, away. Addie knew that she was going to die. They say in the split second before death, your entire life flashes before your eyes. In that split second before Addie disappeared into the rage of the avalanche, her eyes met Kayla's, Addie's hand went out, then she was gone forever.

The snow was moving beneath her skis and Kayla's survival training instinctively triggered as she used her strength and conditioning to keep her body in front of the avalanche. She knew it would cost her life if she faltered and fell. She outran the slide and made it to the bottom of the mountain without a scratch, then stood helpless for the first time in her life as she looked back. The powerful force of nature had changed the face of the mountain, ripping up trees and boulders in its path. Kayla's mind was numb. Where the bridge had been was a gaping space between the two ridges. She released her skis and tried to run back toward the mountain, but the deep snow held her legs. She screamed Addie's name over and over. Just before everything went black, she felt her heart stop beating, as if she'd willed it to do so.

Kayla didn't remember the memorial for Addie, or much of the two years that followed. She was a hollow shell that felt nothing, pickled in booze that deadened any memory or emotion. She cursed the day when she was sober enough to realize that another day had passed. She drifted from one city to another, one job after another, bartending, anything that would buy her another drink. When she was too gone on the booze to work, she drifted from soup lines to homeless shelters, anyplace she could fall into a drunken, unconscious stupor. Her last recollection was swamping for drinks and a cot in the back room in a dive in Barstow, California. She woke up one night in the hospital in Kalispell, back home in Montana, not knowing how she'd gotten there. She was staring into a woman's face, listening to her introduce herself as Doctor Rue Mican. Kayla could hear Mican's words as if it were yesterday.

"Welcome back, Kayla. Are you through beating yourself up and ready to rejoin the living?"

When the night nurse entered the room and woke Cassie to take her vital signs Kayla got up to stretch. "Don't suppose I could talk my big sister into going to McDonald's and getting me a chocolate shake now, could I?"

Kayla's sleep deprived face brightened into a smile. If Cassie was hungry, that was a good sign. "Well, I dunno now. Is my little sister hungry?"

"Your little sister is famished."

"Well then, I'm on my way to a twenty-four hour McDonald's. I'll be back before they finish changing the bed."

Chapter Eleven

Earlier that month, December

Wisps of smoke drifted from the chimney of the log cabin and circled aimlessly through the tall sentinels that blocked the warmth of the winter sun. Their shadows fell across a landscape haunted for centuries by myths and legends. A squirrel scrambled diligently along a branch, carrying its treasure to store away for the long winter months ahead. The muted sound of a twig breaking went unheard as a man, cutting firewood, repeatedly swung an ax against a log.

Peter Koch had fled to southwestern Germany after his last assignment. Botched missions, fatal accidents, and the questionable deaths of fellow Talon agents had unnerved him, and he'd decided that it was time to disappear. He'd purchased the property deep in the woodland of the Black Forest and built the cabin secretly, meticulously covering his trail and any tracks that could lead to him. When he made his move and vanished, no one would ever find him. He'd taken every precaution: never entering Germany through the same port, always alternating the country of entrance; at times, hiking for days across the Alps from Switzerland to avoid establishing a pattern. After his last assignment, he did what a Talon did best and staged his own accident and death. The cell phone embedded with the tracking GPS chip that each member of the Talons carried went up in the flames along with the unrecognizable body of the man that was carrying his phony identification.

As the sound of the splitting wood echoed through the forest, Peter thought about the upcoming presidential inauguration. He thought of Wade Kincaide and the last time he'd spoken to the President. On occasion, an agent would receive a phone call from Kincaide, expressing his appreciation for a job that was well done. With each call, the President never failed to emphasize the importance of their mission and the difference the Talons were making in the war against terrorism and in balancing the scales of justice. The agents were willing to give their lives for President Kincaide, and each had sworn never to reveal or speak his name in connection with the Talons.

The calls from the President stopped toward the end of his first term in office, after Brady Lawrence was appointed Vice President to replace Vice President Galbraith Fitzgerald, who had been assassinated while on a diplomatic mission. From then on, the only communication or contact the Talons ever had was directly with

Lawrence. After September 11, 2001, the world was in shock and the Talons waited anxiously for direction.

On October 8, 2001 the President signed an executive order creating the new Homeland Security Office, then addressed the nation saying that the United States had begun military operations to destroy terrorist training camps and military installations of the Taliban government. The next day, Armanno Santini had tried to contact Peter and left a message, but before Peter could get in touch with him, Armanno's son was killed and his daughter seriously injured in an accident. Peter wished he had contacted Armanno when he first suspected that Brady Lawrence was selling out the Talons.

Even in the dead of winter, the forest was filled with the sounds of life if one listened closely enough. As Peter swung the ax over his head, the forest grew silent. Something had changed. The razor sharp blade of the ax landed dangerously close to his boot as a chill ran from the raised hairs on the nape of his neck to the base of his spine. There was an intruder in the forest — a messenger of death. A deer that had been grazing unperturbed in a clearing raised his head and took flight. An owl, eyes wide with a knowing expression, sat as silent witness. Peter had been the hand of death; now the messenger of death had come to claim him. It was justice. He knew that it was futile to struggle; the day of reckoning had come. He buried the ax in the log and filled his lungs with the scent of burning wood. Then, in the last moments of his life, he sat down on the snow-covered log. His callused fingers reached into his shirt pocket to touch a worn picture of his mother and father and siblings, who thought he'd died a hero's death many years before. He straightened his shoulders and looked toward the rays of sunlight filtering through the tall trees. He had made his peace a long time ago. He was not afraid to die.

Same Day Camp David, Maryland

Wade Kincaide stood with fists clenched, his knuckles white, looking out the window of Aspen Lodge in the Catoctin Mountains of Maryland. The boyish face the country had grown to love over his two terms in office had aged and was drawn and rigid.

"Are you absolutely sure? Without any doubt?"

"Yes, Mr. President. The order to assassinate Vice President Fitzgerald came from Lawrence."

"And you have connected him to a group called the Talons?"

"Yes, sir."

Kincaide kept his back to his brother, the Attorney General, and wearily asked, "Tell me what you know, Mack."

"Bits and pieces of information that are unsubstantiated, but the name has surfaced many times over the past several years. Officially, we know that they are a highly trained group of government agents that were recruited to covertly counteract terrorism, most likely under orders from someone higher up who had the connections and the power to sanction the Talons' activities. From what our intelligence has gathered, Brady Lawrence was the go between, the one that dealt directly with the Talons. After your first term in office, Lawrence was appointed Vice President and things changed. The Talons' services were sold to the highest bidders, and they were being used to further Brady's political career and interests. They are as deadly as any terrorist group and the perfect assassins. When the Talons began to question their assignments, one by one, they started to die."

Mack's words struck the President like an arrow through the heart. "How many Talons have been killed?"

"We believe most of them are gone. There is no way of knowing how many for certain, because we don't know how many there were to begin with. An intricate maze of identities was created, and changed so often, they're impossible to trace."

Wade Kincaide turned and sat at his desk, then Mack handed the President a picture of a corpse lying on a slab. "We identified this man as a Talon. He was going by the name of Peter Koch. He was found dead in Germany with bullets through his head and heart. He hadn't been dead long when our people located him. Every time we get close to one of the Talons, they turn up dead. We believe the assassin to be a Talon who operates under direct orders from Lawrence, and whoever it is has been one step ahead of us all the way."

President Kincaide looked at his brother. "Could this rogue Talon be a woman?"

"It's possible, but it could be any one of the Talons."

Wade Kincaide's hand shook as he looked at the picture of a man lying on a morgue slab. It was John Peter Kochner, a decorated soldier who had served in Desert Shield and Desert Storm and whom he had personally selected to join the Talons. He knew his next words would not come as a surprise to his brother. "His name is Peter Kochner, and he was a good man, one of the best of the Talons. There were only two better, and one is dead. The one left, if she is alive, is the only person who could have gotten close enough to kill him." Kincaide stared at the picture. "Everything indicates that a Talon is responsible for the death of the others?"

"Everything we have points to it, Wade."

"Who actually killed the Vice President?"

"We're not absolutely certain," Mack pointed to the picture, "but it could have been this man. We don't know if the assassin knew that the target was the Vice President. When you asked Fitzgerald to go to the Middle East, you knew that American unpopularity and the upheaval made it dangerous for him. As you directed, his trip was unannounced. He was keeping a low profile and was checked into the hotel under another name. What our intelligence has been able to put together is that Brady directed the assassin to take out the person in the room at an hour when Fitzgerald would normally be sleeping and alone. Unfortunately, an all night session preparing notes for an important meeting the next morning put Fitzgerald's secretary in the room when the assassin successfully gained entrance to the room. Brady was also the one who had the rumor leaked to the press that the assassination was ordered by a government in the Middle East."

Several minutes went by before Wade Kincaide's somber eyes focused on his brother. "Your intelligence and thoroughness do not surprise me, Mack. You know most of it, so I'm sure you know that the Talons were recruited and gathered under my orders. What you couldn't know is that I ordered Lawrence to disband and retire the Talons before my first term in office was up. Each agent was to have a permanent identity and the economic means to live anywhere of their choosing. After Fitzgerald was assassinated, Lawrence seemed to be the best choice for the Vice President. A few months later, he said he had been investigating a rash of political assassinations around the world and that he had linked them to the Talons. He led me to believe a few had turned mercenary and were responsible for the cold-blooded murders around the world. He also said an agent that I admired and trusted was their leader. Her name is Liberty Starr."

Kincaide got up from his desk and walked to the window. His voice shook as he gazed out at the bleak winter day. "As God is my witness, I was not aware of what Lawrence was doing. After his appointment, when the assassinations continued, I began to have questions. That's when I asked you to investigate personally. I knew you would find out about my involvement, but I needed to know what was going on. He's used the Talons and turned an agent to do his dirty work, Mack. My guess is that Peter was the last Talon besides the assassin. If it is Liberty Starr, she's lethal. If she's the rogue, no one can stop her if she comes to remove the last remaining witness to Brady Lawrence's treason, and that's me. Liberty Starr is the only person besides myself who can testify to what Lawrence has done. He will be sworn in to the office of the President in three weeks; we can't let that happen. We need to find her, and we need her alive."

"If we take her alive, Wade, and she testifies, you'll be implicated."

"I know, and I will have to face the consequences of my actions when the time comes. I know that this will affect your career and our family. Many will judge you guilty simply because you're my brother. Some will forget the honest man you are and all the good you have done while in office. I'm sorry for that, Mack."

Mack Kincaide looked at his brother and knew that he felt he had no other choice. "I'll find her, Wade. I promise you — Brady Lawrence will never be sworn in." *Even if I have to kill him myself.*

Chapter Twelve

Liberty drew two glasses of draft and looked at the clock. *Fifteen minutes to closing.* It had been a steady pace most of the day, busier when the lifts closed after the last run and the skiers stopped at the pub to eat before heading down the mountain to their homes. She'd managed to keep up with the orders and the bartending, but was grateful that with everything else on her mind, Kayla had arranged to have one of the employees from the lodge to come in and help out during the busy time. She set the mugs in front of the last two customers. "On the house. We'll be closing in a few."

"Thanks. We heard about Cassie. Do you know how she's doing? Must be hard on Kayla, especially after losing Addie to the mountain."

Liberty had known there was something haunting Kayla; she could see it in her eyes that first night when she stood looking out at the mountain. "Cassie was doing fine the last I heard. Addie...another sister?"

The skier shot a quick look toward his friend. "Well, it's not something Kayla has ever hidden. Addie was her partner. They'd been together most of their lives. Built this pub after Kayla won the gold in the '98 Olympics. It was the winter before the 2002 Olympics. They were up on the mountain skiing when an avalanche took Addie. Kayla had a real tough time after that, even went away for a while. We all miss Addie, and Kayla just hasn't been the same. Then with this thing happening to Cassie, we've all been kinda worried about her."

Liberty had seen a picture in Kayla's office of Kayla with her arms around an attractive woman about her own age. She looked happy in the picture. There was a light in her eyes that wasn't there anymore. Now Liberty knew why.

When the last patron had finished his drink and left, Liberty locked the door of the pub and cleaned up before finding her way into Kayla's small office. She sat down at the computer and scrolled through the obituaries in the Washington Times. When the Talons began to turn up dead, Peter Koch tracked the remaining agents by using the GPS in their phones. After speaking with Peter, the agents ditched their phones and agreed to call a number once a week that connected to a remote computer program that was impossible to trace. If the program hadn't received a message after two weeks from an agent, it would run an obituary using the agent's code name. The following months, the obituaries mounted up, and many of the agents went into hiding. All but Peter and Liberty had turned up dead.

Liberty's eyes froze on the computer screen; the last thing she wanted to see was Peter's obituary. That left her. After Peter had contacted her, she'd considered that he could be the assassin, and that his call was a ploy. She thought the same thing now. It could be a diversion to make her think that he was dead. But, that could be the scenario with any of the agents that had died. Her gut instinct told her Peter would have never sold out his fellow agents, taking their lives so callously and in such a calculated manner. They all had worked as a team once, for the good of the nation, depending on each other to survive. All that changed when the assignments had turned to cold-blooded murder.

Liberty never doubted that her moment of hesitation at the last second in Denver, when she aborted her mission and stood up, saved her life. Someone that knew her every move was waiting to take her out as soon as she had taken out her target. When the bullet grazed her instead, knocking her to the floor, it wasn't fear she felt as she lay on her back in the empty room bleeding, but a strange sense of regret that the bullet hadn't hit its mark. Any one of the Talons could have made the shot. The question was — who had targeted the Talons, and to what end?

Liberty didn't want to believe that President Kincaide had ordered their deaths, but why hadn't he protected them? As she stared at the computer screen and the obituary, her gut instinct screamed that it had Brady Lawrence's imprint all over it. There was no point now in sending a message; she was the last Talon. She sent a virus to wipe out the program and turned off the computer, then shut off the light and walked wearily up the stairs.

Nathan drove south along Highway 93 toward Kalispell. He usually helped Mike shut down the lifts, but tonight he wanted to get into town before the snow got any heavier and made the roads worse. He wanted to have some time to visit with Cassie before he and Kayla started home. When he arrived at the hospital, Kayla was helping Cassie brush her teeth and get ready for the night. Always the big sister, Kayla looked out for both Cassie and him, hovering as a mother hen when they were growing up, but she was always more protective of Cassie. The three siblings visited a while, and when Cassie's eyes began to droop, Kayla pulled up the covers, tucked Cassie in, and kissed her on the cheek.

"The bolus of morphine the nurse gave you is starting to work. Nathan and I are going to head home, but I'll be back in the morning to help you with breakfast. Do you need anything before we go?"

Cassie looked at her big sister, hoping she couldn't see the fear she felt inside. She hadn't wanted to take the morphine, but both Kayla and Dr. Mican had insisted. She was deathly afraid to close her eyes. Every time she did, she had the sensation of falling and being buried alive. She could feel herself clawing at the smothering snow and screaming, but no one could hear her. Just knowing Kayla was there made her feel safer.

Concerned when Cassie hesitated, Kayla asked. "Honey, do you want me to stay tonight?"

Cassie reached for her sister's hand, but the pain stopped her, reminding her all too acutely that she might lose her fingers. "No, honestly. I am tired and the morphine will put me to sleep. I'll see you in the morning, but you don't have to be here at the crack of dawn either, ya know. The nurses here are great and very helpful."

"Not as helpful as I can be, so never you mind trying to get rid of me. I'll be here early. You sleep well."

After Kayla and Nathan left, Cassie struggled to stay awake, but the pain medicine was doing its job. She remembered that she'd wanted to ask Kayla about Liberty. She'd been in and out of consciousness the day before and only vaguely remembered meeting the woman. Kayla had told her how Liberty had helped to save her life, and she wanted to thank her.

Nathan followed along behind the snowplow, concentrating on the road. He stole a look toward Kayla, who was staring straight ahead at the snow falling in the beam of the highlights. "Cassie seems to be doing okay. Has Rue or McKlosky said when she can come home?"

Kayla pressed her fingers to her temples and rubbed. Her voice was tight as she answered. "Nothing for certain, right now, Nathan. We'll know more in the next few days."

The strain of the past few days was telling on Kayla, Nathan could see the deep lines of tension on her face. "You haven't had one of those headaches in a long time, Kayla. Maybe you should talk to Doctor Mican about it tomorrow."

"I don't need to talk to Mican about it, Nathan. For Pete's sake, it's just a headache." The minute the words came out of her mouth, Kayla was sorry she'd snapped at her brother. "I'm sorry, Nathan. I know you're concerned, and I know why. If I run into Rue tomorrow, if it isn't any better, I'll ask her for something."

"Promise me you will, Kayla."

Kayla didn't offer a promise and Nathan decided not push it, but all the signs were there and it worried him. When they arrived home,

Nathan let Kayla out in front of the pub. "Try and get some rest. I'll call you in the morning." Then he drove down the snow packed road toward the lodge.

Winter clouds draped a crescent moon as Kayla stood in the fleeting shadows and pulled her coat closer to ward off the cold and the blowing snow that chilled her to the bone. She thought about the omnipotence of the mountain that had seduced her — handing her the world, then abasing her by destroying what was most precious to her. Her gut tightened as the bitter taste of bile caused her jaw to clench. She had gone through the motions of putting her life back together, but she was on the edge, and that edge was starting to crumble. The avalanche had reopened the painful wounds that had pushed her over the top and led her down a road of self-destruction. The ache inside was still there. Addie would always be there when she looked at the mountain, whether the mountain was covered with snow or with the flowers of spring. As much as she hated the mountain, she hated herself for being the one that was left behind.

Liberty watched from the darkness of the bedroom window. She sensed Kayla was at a hard place, trying to deal with her sister's accident. It puzzled her to feel the empathy she did for this woman. There was something more she felt as her eyes scanned the darkness, a sense of someone watching from the shadows. It was the same premonition that she'd had in Denver, just before she aborted her mission, when she had her target dead center and her finger on the trigger.

Liberty pulled the pistol from the back of her waistband and ejected the clip, checked the mechanism, then reinserted the clip and slipped the gun back into the waistband of her jeans as she watch Kayla walk toward the pub. When she heard the pub door close, she opened the balcony door and walked out. She stood as the clouds passed and the silvery light of the full moon exposed her like a ghost. She brazenly dared whoever was out there to come and get her.

Who are you? I can feel you. Can you read my thoughts? I'm waiting.

Liberty was sitting in front of the fireplace in her room. Kayla hadn't come up the stairs, and Liberty could hear her moving about downstairs in the pub. She was just getting up to go downstairs to check on Kayla when she heard the sound of breaking glass coming from the pub downstairs. Liberty retrieved the pistol she had set on the table next to the bed and shoved it back into her waistband. Then she crossed the room, opened the door to the balcony, and was over the railing and down to the ground within seconds. In her bare feet, she stood motionless, listening. She'd left a lamp on for Kayla in the bar before she went upstairs, and the low light reflected from the window of the pub.

Liberty merged into the shadows close to the building and crept toward the window. When she reached it, she could see Kayla sitting at the bar staring at a bottle of Jack Daniel's. Relieved, she leaned her head against the siding and took a deep breath. When she looked back, she could see Kayla's shaking hands and the internal battle playing on her face as she reached for the bottle. She had surmised that Kayla had a drinking problem after her partner died, and it appeared that tonight Kayla was facing the devil again. She also knew that she was getting in way too deep, that every minute she stayed on Lone Mountain, her emotional evolvement with Kayla was growing stronger. It would only make her weak and vulnerable. In the back of her mind she feared that she was putting Kayla and her family in danger by staying and using the pub as a place to lay low. That thought made her realize that the attraction she felt toward Kayla was dangerous, for everyone. If she was to stay alive while she figured out what was happening, she had to have a plan and she had to keep Kayla at a distance.

Liberty knew that she was being stalked, hunted in the same way she had hunted her prey many times. She also knew, whoever it was out there was enjoying the game and would not hesitate to eliminate or use anyone to get to her. The time for running was over, the psychological game had begun; the feeling wrapped around her and heightened her senses.

As she watched Kayla bury her face in her hands, Liberty felt an unwelcome tug at her heart that she hadn't felt in a long time. At that moment, the desire to go to Kayla tore at her, and she swore that President Kincaide and Brady Lawrence would feel the wrath and the revenge of the Talons they'd created, then betrayed. Liberty felt the bite of the frozen ground under her bare feet. She looked up toward the balcony and decided to reenter through the kitchen door. She doubted Kayla would even hear her. The forlorn howl of a coyote drew her eyes toward the darkened tree line. A prickling sensation ran down her spine, raising the hair on her arms. She held her breath as she stared into the darkness. For a moment, her thoughts connected with an equal force of an unseen entity, then she lost it and slipped quietly into the kitchen. She had every intention of avoiding Kayla until she heard what sounded like a glass breaking against the stone fireplace. She walked through the kitchen and leaned against the doorway to the pub. Kayla's shaky hand was pouring whisky into another glass. When she brought the glass to her lips, Liberty said,

"Old Number 7. Mind pouring me a shot of that?"

Kayla lowered the glass as she jerked her head toward Liberty. "This is a private party. I'm sorry if I woke you."

Liberty walked behind the bar and flipped over a shot glass. She shoved the shot glass down the bar toward Kayla, and then walked around the bar to stand next to her. "That will cure what's bothering you, for sure. At least for tonight."

Kayla's eyes flashed with anger as she went on the defensive. "I appreciate what you did on the mountain and how you're helping out here, but this," she raised the glass, "is none of your business."

"You're right; it's not, so pour. If we're going to drown our misery and get shit faced drunk, let's get started."

Kayla eyed Liberty suspiciously. She wasn't sure what to expect, but it wasn't a drinking partner. "I'm not up to company."

Liberty reached for the bottle and poured herself a drink, then downed it and poured another. "What do they say? Misery loves company. Well, they're wrong. Misery loves itself, loves to wallow in its own grief."

Kayla slammed her glass down on the bar, spattering whisky on the countertop. "What the hell do you know about it? What the hell do you know about loss, a loss so devastating that your heart has been ripped from your chest?"

Liberty's eyes frosted over like minute crystals of ice. Her expression was devoid of any warmth or emotion. "You're right. As you said, it's none of my business." She threw down the last of her whiskey and set the glass quietly on the bar. She had turned to go when Kayla's hand on her forearm stopped her.

"I'm sorry. I just..."

Something about Kayla trespassed across the wall of emotional detachment that was essential in Liberty's profession if she was to survive. Each time she looked into Kayla's eyes, her every instinct warned her to move on. Kayla's closeness and the touch on her arm threatened Liberty's resolve not to get involved. Her hardened heart softened as she looked into the eyes of the woman who had managed to worm through a small chink in her armor. "Hey, it's all right. You don't owe me an explanation." Impulsively, Liberty's fingers were drawn to Kayla's cheek. It had been a long time since she had touched a woman, or anyone else, with true emotion. She had played many roles, cloaked like a chameleon in another identity, pretending to care. The softness of Kayla's skin jolted her. She struggled with her reaction and the aching, burning need growing in the pit of her stomach. It was easier to hide, to be someone else, than to be Liberty Starr.

Kayla closed her eyes as Liberty's fingers touched her face, then moved across her trembling lips. When Kayla moaned and the tip of her tongue touched Liberty's fingers, Liberty slid her arm around her waist. With her eyes still closed, Kayla leaned into Liberty and her arms went around her neck. It was what Kayla needed to chase away the maddening ache. It was only for the moment, a crutch to get her through the next second, the next minute. Kayla's breathing quickened when she felt the blood pulsing through Liberty's veins as she pressed her lips against the hollow of her throat. The surge of heat beneath Liberty's skin ignited a desperate need in Kayla.

Liberty's hands threaded through Kayla's hair, easing her face up so she could look into her eyes. Neither said a word; none were needed. Passion raged inside both women as Liberty lowered her lips to Kayla's. When she felt Kayla's body responding, her hands found their way under Kayla's sweater, pulling it over her head. Her mouth followed, finding a taut nipple through the fabric of Kayla's bra. She swiped the bar clear of glasses and the bottle of Jack Daniel's, then reached for the button on Kayla's slacks. She didn't need to ask what Kayla wanted; she could see it in her desperate eyes. Liberty pushed Kayla's slacks down off her hips then went to her knees to lower Kayla's underpants down her thigh. She tossed them both to the floor before lifting Kayla up on the bar. Kayla's legs wrapped around Liberty's waist and, with a whimper, hungrily sought Liberty's mouth. It was what they both wanted and needed — the physical and emotional abandon to touch and feel the warmth of another body, and for a little while, drive away the memories and the ghosts of the tormenting past.

Kayla's hips surged forward as Liberty entered her. She tightened her legs around the back of Liberty's upper thighs and moved frantically against her hand. With every fiber of her body, with every thrust, she concentrated only on the feel of Liberty inside her as the pressure built to a frenzied eruption of pent up anger and resentment that sent sparks of white light shooting behind her eye lids. Spent, Kayla collapsed into Liberty's arms; the tears finally came. Tears for her lost love, and tears for Cassie.

Liberty was shaking when she lifted Kayla off the bar and helped her put her slacks on, then she took her hand and led her toward the stairs. She'd built a fire in the fireplace in Kayla's room after Kayla's phone call to tell her that she was coming home. She helped Kayla undress and get into bed, but before she could pull up the covers, Kayla's hand found hers.

"Please stay, Liberty. Just for tonight."

Kayla's words shredded Liberty's last reserve of detachment. She nodded, took off her clothes, and lay down on the cool sheets next to Kayla's naked body. When Kayla slid on top of her and rested between her legs, forgotten memories of how it felt to be with someone you cared for fought to surface. The blood pumping through Liberty's body echoed painfully in her ears as Kayla's fingertips and tongue gently traced the scars on her body. The forgiveness of Kayla's touch penetrated the unseen scars of her tortured soul, and Liberty lost herself in every breath and beat of Kayla's heart pounding against her chest, until the demons no longer screamed in her mind and all she could hear or feel was Kayla.

Chapter Thirteen

Kayla woke up alone in bed with the light of morning just beginning to creep over Lone Mountain into her room. The embers in the fireplace had been stoked with more wood, chasing away the chill of the December night. When she rolled to her back, she felt the telling soreness in places that bluntly reminded her she'd had sex with Liberty. It was the first time she had knowingly been with anyone since Addie died. There had been times when she was drinking that she blacked out from the booze and woke up in undesirable places, but she didn't remember much about those episodes. If she'd been with someone, she didn't remember.

Kayla thought about Rue Mican. Rue had been extremely supportive when she came home to Montana. After she'd gone through detox and made it through the worst of it, and she was no longer a patient of Rue's, they had gone to dinner a few times. Rue often came up to Lone Mountain to ski, and in the summer would drive up to the pub to visit Kayla and have lunch. The attractive doctor had told Kayla that she was interested in seeing her on a personal level, but although she cared about Rue, she hadn't allowed herself to consider loving anyone but Addie.

The lonely, vulnerable part of her regretted waking up alone, but the impenetrable armor around her heart quickly reduced the feeling to a fleeting thought. She convinced herself that she was relieved that Liberty had left before she woke. She reached for the phone and dialed the number to the hospital, asking for the nurse's station to inquire about Cassie.

"Your sister is awake, Ms. Sinclair. I can go into her room and position the phone so that you can talk to her."

"No, don't disturb her. I can..." The nurse had already put her on hold and a few seconds later she was transferred to Cassie. In spite of the cheerfulness Cassie put on, Kayla could hear an edge in her sister's voice.

"Hey, Sis. How's the base for the weekend? The news said that it snowed all night, should be great skiing. You're up too early. Thought I told you to sleep in."

"You're up early, too. How did you sleep?"

Fighting back the pain in her hands and feet from the range of motion exercises the therapist had put her through just before Kayla called, Cassie forced a laugh. "Hasn't anyone told you, there is no sleeping in a hospital? The activity around here starts before the sun comes up. I just finished with the physical therapist."

"Right. How could I forget that?" She knew by the sound of Cassie's voice that the therapy session had been an ordeal and that Cassie needed to rest. It tore her apart to know her sister was in so much pain. "Cassie, please try and rest. I'll call the desk to ask them to hold your breakfast, and I'll help you eat when I get there."

Cassie had been given her pain medication just before the therapy session, and her eyelids were beginning to grow heavy. "I think I will. Don't speed coming off the mountain, okay?"

"Don't worry, I'll take it easy. I'm going to hang up now, Cassie. I'll be there before you wake up."

Kayla slipped into her robe and went out onto the deck to let the cold air clear her head. As she watched the gray storm clouds catch the winter light of the rising sun, she could smell the aroma of coffee drifting up from the kitchen. *Well, I guess I didn't chase her off entirely.* Kayla pulled the robe tighter around her and thought about Liberty and the lovemaking they'd shared the night before. It had been intense and edgy. Both had given and both had taken several times over during the night, and each time Liberty's hands and mouth quieted her raging heart. Kayla thought about the understanding and the tenderness she'd felt in Liberty's touch. It was as if Liberty knew what she needed and what lines not to cross. She felt guilty, as if she had been unfaithful to Addie, and she wasn't prepared to deal with that. Going back inside, Kayla dressed, then slipped quietly out of the pub without going into the kitchen.

Liberty heard the Jeep start up and went to stand in front of the window in time to see it pull away and head down the snowy road toward Kalispell. She'd heard Kayla come down and stop at the foot of the stairs for a moment before she left. Raising the steaming cup of coffee to her lips, she analyzed the part of her consciousness that wanted to reach out to Kayla and not ignore what happened between them the night before. All the while, the dominant part of her conscious mind reminded her of who and what she was, and that desire and sentiment were dangerous. Liberty realized that going to Kayla's bed had been a mistake, that she was putting Kayla in grave danger. She knew it was time to leave, before her heart wouldn't let her. She crossed the room and placed her empty coffee cup in the sink behind the bar, then started to prepare for the onslaught of patrons that would be coming up the mountain, anxious to lay their skis to the new snow.

Liberty looked at the clock; it was just past nine. It had been a busy morning, but now the pub was empty. It had snowed the night before and Mother Nature had graced the slopes with several inches of new powder. After stopping at the pub for their morning coffee and one of Kayla's famous cinnamon rolls, the skiers were eager to be first in line when the lifts opened, assuring that they would be the first to lay skis to the new powder. It was time to close up and go. With Cassie in the hospital, no one would question the pub closing after the morning rush. Liberty was anxious to put the few miles to Kalispell behind her then head to Missoula. She was just putting the Closed sign in the window of the pub when she heard a noise coming from the kitchen behind her. She stood still and listened. When she heard the noise again, she pulled the pistol from where it was tucked in her waistband, under her shirt, and chambered a round, then mentally checked the pressure against her ankle for her back up and the extra clip tucked into her boot. She moved to a more advantageous position so that she had a clear view of both the front and back entrances, and flattened herself against the wall. She could see a figure moving in the kitchen doorway. She eased her finger onto the trigger of the SIG just as the figure straightened and pulled a dolly loaded with several cases of liquor through the door.

Liberty instinctively began to assess the situation, leaving nothing to chance. If this was an attempt to get to her, it was crude and amateurish. It could be a cunning diversion, or just what it looked like — a delivery. She positioned herself behind the bar and slid the gun under a towel and waited. A moment later, a man dressed in jeans and a shirt with a liquor store logo pushed his load through the kitchen doorway, then through the door of the pub toward the storage room under the stairs. When he saw Liberty behind the bar, he stopped, stomped the snow from his boots on the wooden floor, and pulled off his gloves. Grinning, he rubbed his hands together and headed toward the side bar where a pot of coffee was still on the warmer and poured a cup.

"Howdy. You must be that woman they're all talkin' about, the one who helped Kayla find Cassie. Joe, over at the feed and tack, was tellin' me how you was hangin' from the helicopter with another slide breathing down your neck and Kayla hangin' on to you for dear life. Joe's on the search and rescue team, and he said he'd never seen anything like it, 'cept in the movies." The man wrapped both of his big hands around the cup. "The temperature sure is droppin'. It's goin' to be a cold one tonight. Sorry, if I scared ya. I usually let myself in and unload and stack the delivery in the storage room for Kayla. With New Year's Eve just a couple days away, this is a big delivery. Glad to see Kayla has some help here."

Liberty eased her hand off the gun and out from under the towel. "You from around here, Mister...?"

The man's face broke into a wider grin and he stepped forward offering his large hand. "Sure am. Born and raised on a little ranch this side of Whitefish. Worked nigh on to twenty years now for Montana State Liquor. Name's Caleb, and I'm mighty proud to meet you."

"Well, Caleb, why don't you stand by the fire and thaw out some? I'll warm you a cinnamon roll to go with that coffee."

"Why, thank you kindly. Think I'll do just that. Say there, what can I call you?"

A hint of a sad smile crossed Liberty's face. "You can call me Liberty." After a few minutes, Liberty returned and set a fresh cup of coffee and two rolls topped with melting butter on the bar. "Tell me, Caleb, how long has Kayla owned the pub?"

Caleb was standing in front of the fireplace, warming his hands. He rubbed his chin, crossed to the bar, and sat on a stool. He took off his hat and scratched his head. "Well, now, I remember, it was in '98. Kayla and Addie built it when they came back from Japan. Hell, anyone with half a brain and eyes could see the two of them loved each other. Had since they were kids. Kayla took it plenty hard when Addie died. It was a hard time in her life. Most thought she would never make it back, but she did. Now with Cassie gettin' hurt and all... The last couple years with the lack of snow have been a tough go here on the mountain. Kayla and Nathan borrowed all they could from the Kalispell bank. They put up the pub and the lodge as collateral, counting on a good season, then put in a whole lot of money upgradin' the lifts and puttin' in the new run this year. They sure as hell didn't expect that slide the day they were opening the new run. No one did. My brother-in-law Harold works at the bank, and he says that they could lose it all if they don't have a good year. Kayla needs the business from the New Year's Eve party just to stay afloat. We're all sure glad you're here lending her a hand, Liberty."

Having run out of topic, Caleb finished his coffee, stored the liquor away, and left Liberty alone in the quiet pub. She knew that she would be running out on Kayla, but if she stayed, it would put Kayla, and everyone on the mountain, in danger.

Making sure that everything was in order, Liberty turned on the light over the bar so the pub wouldn't be dark when Kayla got home. As she pulled her duffel out from under the bar and locked up, she wondered why she cared if Kayla came home to an empty and dark pub. She threw the duffel in the rented 4x4 and sat behind the wheel for a long moment before she started down the road toward Highway 93 and Kalispell. A sense of loss saddened her heart as she watched Lone Mountain and Kayla's pub disappear in the rearview mirror.

"Kayla, hold up a minute. I want to talk to you."

Kayla turned to stand face to face with Rue Mican, her face turning pale. "Is it Cassie? Is she all right?"

"No, this isn't about Cassie. It's about you. Come with me for a moment, please." Not giving Kayla a chance to refuse, Rue turned and walked toward her office. Kayla hesitated, then followed the doctor down the hall. Once in the office, Rue closed the door and pointed to the leather couch. "Sit down, please," she said, then sat down beside her. "Kayla, you know that you can talk to me about how you're feeling. Nathan called this morning and asked if I would talk to you about the headaches you've been having. He's concerned that you're holding everything in and that's why the headaches have returned. Have you given some thought to attending an AA meeting?"

Kayla's first response was to be mad at Nathan for calling Rue, her second thought was to get up and leave. She controlled her anger because she knew they both cared about her. "Rue, I'm fine. I will attend a meeting soon, but right now I want to spend as much time as I can with Cassie, and I have the New Year's Eve party to prepare for at the pub. Besides, the headache is better today." She felt a rush of heat warming her face as she thought of how she and Liberty had spent the intervening night. "I promise I will find a meeting as soon as I get through New Year's Eve and bring Cassie home."

Mican ran her hand along Kayla's arm. "Good. If you need help at the pub or someone to go with you to a meeting, I'm available. You know that you can call anytime. I miss you and I would like to see you, but more immediately, I want you to be okay."

Kayla cupped the doctor's face between her hands and kissed her softly on the cheek. "I care very much for you, Rue, you've been a good friend, but right now is not a good time to talk about this. Can it wait until Cassie is out of the woods — please?"

The doctor's intercom buzzed and her secretary's voice announced that she had a call from the hospital administrator on line two. Rue got up and went to take the call. "Of course, it can wait. I'm sorry, I need to take this call. Maybe we can get together for coffee later?" Rue picked up the phone and Kayla mouthed that she was leaving.

Chapter Fourteen

Cassie's day didn't start out well. The edema in her hands and feet had gotten worse, and so had the pain. The slightest movement hurt, and when Rue stopped in on rounds, she ordered the dose of morphine and bolus lock out increased. "Don't worry. This increase in the pain meds won't delay your recovery at all," she promised as Kayla hovered close to Cassie. "In fact, Doctor McKlosky and I both think that taking a dose of the medication just before you go to physical therapy will help your participation by allowing you to tolerate the therapy better."

All day long, Kayla stayed near her sister, encouraging her to rest and not to worry. After dinner, Kayla saw an improvement in Cassie's pain level and comfort, and helped her bathe and settle in for the night. Kayla read her to sleep, and it was well after visiting hours were over when Kayla was satisfied that Cassie was going to stay asleep. She decided to go home to Lone Mountain. Fatigue slowed her steps as she trudged through the newly fallen snow to where she'd parked her SUV early that morning. She was also worried about everything that still needed to be done to ready the pub for the New Year's Eve party.

It was late, and Kayla was exhausted as she drove along the icy, twisting mountain road toward home. The road had been plowed, but the brief appearance of the afternoon sun had begun to melt the packed snow, and when the sun went down, it left the road a treacherous sheet of ice. Snow clouds obscured the light from the moon, and her headlights didn't penetrate far through the gusts of snow that were blowing across the road. It was hard to see more than a few feet in front of the vehicle. The warmth from the heater was making her sleepy when she needed to be alert. The area was posted with signs warning of deer crossing, and Kayla knew that one could jump out, be startled by her headlights, and stop dead in front of her. It had happened before.

She was bone tired, but that didn't stop the thoughts of Liberty that hovered in the back of her mind, disquieting thoughts she hadn't allowed herself to dwell on all day. The woman was an enigma. Kayla remembered tracing along the scars on Liberty's back, scars that held mystery and untold secrets and silently spoke of violence. Liberty had stood beside her and challenged the mountain. She was grateful, but that was a rationalization and not the reason she had shared the passion of her rage and her bed with Liberty. Nor was it the reason she kept pushing from her mind how she'd responded to Liberty's touch, or her raw, desperate need for release, a blessed respite from the memories that were killing her soul. Each time Liberty pushed her over the edge, her body woke with abandon, until she wasn't chasing memories, but was lost in the passion of Liberty's touch.

When she pulled into her parking space behind the pub and didn't see Liberty's SUV, Kayla felt a subtle tightening in her chest. Her eyes went to the guestroom on the upper floor and found it dark. She sat for a long time looking at a pale moon cradled in the icy fingers of winter storm clouds that reflected the cold and forlorn feeling in her heart. She thought how silly she was to allow Liberty's leaving to affect her the way it was; she'd half expected her to be gone. A chill settled deep into her bones as the moisture in her breath turn to frost on the inside of the car window. A kindred loneliness touched her soul as she got out of the car and stood looking at a barren tree, its branches suspended and frozen, waiting for the healing season and the breath of spring.

Kayla let herself into the pub and went about making a fire to help keep the downstairs warm for the night. The ashes in the fireplace were cold, and she thought that Liberty had most likely left right after she closed the pub up that afternoon. The chime of the clock on the stone mantle finished striking midnight. It was officially New Year's Eve day, and she regretted that she wouldn't have time to go to the hospital in the morning to help Cassie because of the party booked for that night. Wearily, she climbed the stairs to her bedroom, thinking that she would have to call the lodge early and line up more help.

Kayla had just stripped off her clothes and was heading into the bathroom to shower when her eyes caught a flickering light reflecting through the glass doors to the enclosed part of the deck where the Jacuzzi was located. She crossed the room to look, and her breath caught and a surge of heat permeated through her at what she saw. Arousal bombarded her senses at the sight illuminated by the underwater light of the hot tub. Liberty was lying in the Jacuzzi, her body shrouded in steam, her naked shoulders glistening through the mustard colored mist. The swirling water dipped low enough to expose the top of her breasts and a hint of a nipple. Kayla felt her stomach clench, and a not unpleasant sensation prickled along her spine. She felt like a voyeur, but she was unable to turn her eyes away as she watched Liberty's lips part slightly as she tilted her head back and closed her eyes. Kayla's gaze followed along the lines of Liberty's face, over the wide set eyes and prominent cheekbones to the delicate line of her jaw. As if sensing her presence, Liberty opened her eyes and looked toward where she stood in the darkness. Her penetrating stare seemed to expose Kayla's naked need. For a brief moment, something passed between them in the dark, then Liberty leaned her head back and closed her eyes.

Kayla forced herself to back away from the window until she felt the bed behind her shaky knees. Trying to calm her pounding heart, she sat, knowing that her legs would never hold her up long enough to get into the shower. Instead, she crawled under the bedcovers unable to get the sight of Liberty out of her mind. Her reaction to Liberty jolted her. It was intense, and she couldn't deny her arousal. She didn't know anything about this woman for whom she was feeling such a compelling attraction. When she closed her eyes, she could still see the seductive way Liberty looked at her through the darkness, and she could feel fingers of heat gripping her loins.

Liberty had heard Kayla drive up, and every instinct told her that Kayla was watching her. When she opened her eyes, she could see the outline of Kayla's naked body standing in the doorway. The feel of Kayla's eyes on her body swept over her like a lover's caress, evoking a kaleidoscope of images. Erotic images of Kayla lying naked between her thighs morphed into an image of her lying on top of Kayla with her fingers buried deep inside of her. Threads of different colors joined, creating a brilliant tapestry that burst into a myriad of feelings of warmth and passion. She sensed the heat of Kayla's thoughts, and her heart raced. Always the master of control, not even a kill could raise a bead of sweat, but this woman did. It was taking all of her self-discipline to resist going to Kayla and exposing her well concealed flaw, the need for a human touch — Kayla's touch. Perhaps that is what brought her back to Lone Mountain.

Her plan that morning had been to get as far away from Montana, and Kayla, as possible. She needed an ally, someone with contacts, who had access to information she needed, information that would lead her to whomever was behind the betrayal of the Talons. She'd decided to take a chance with the one person she felt she could count on, the one person who could be trusted — Armanno Santini. He had been her mentor and the Talon's Chief of Special Ops from their conception until shortly before Kincaide was elected to his second term in office. Waiting to be airlifted out after a mission, they had spent a night together deep in the jungle off the Ivory Coast of Africa. Armanno had alluded to something that was bothering him concerning the missions, and said that he was looking into it. Shortly afterwards, Armanno's son was killed in an accident, and he himself retired, surrounding himself with people he could trust.

As she considered possible ways to contact Armanno, Liberty had driven as far as Big Fork at Flathead Lake when she knew she had to go back. What she had to do would wait. Kayla needed her help getting through the New Year's Eve party, and maybe even until Cassie was out of the woods and able to return home. Before she could supply that help, she first needed to throw off whoever was stalking her and lead them away from the mountain, and from Kayla and her family.

Liberty made good time and was in Missoula before noon. After checking into a motel, she retrieved her laptop and went online. She made half a dozen additional motel reservations in Missoula as well as purchased tickets on several flights that were leaving out of the Missoula International Airport over the next few days. To muddle the trail even further, she arranged for a rental car at each destination. When she finished, she turned on the TV, left a light on, put out the Do Not Disturb sign, and went out the bathroom window. She walked a few blocks to a bar, where she caught a cab that took her to the airport where she rented another vehicle. Having done what she could to protect the Sinclairs, and herself, she drove back to Lone Mountain, taking Route 83 through Seeley Lake and Big Fork on the west side of Flathead Lake instead of Highway 93.

When she pulled into the crowded parking lot of the lodge, a comforting feeling settled over her. She got out of the car and made her way on foot down the back road to the pub. When she'd gone part way, she slipped off the road into the trees and waited for a while to see if anyone had followed her. Then she stealthily continued on to the pub and went straight upstairs.

Her muscles felt tight and sore. It had been days since she'd worked out. She went upstairs to the guestroom and stretched by performing a series of T'ai Chi forms that helped center her mind and energize her body. Afterward, she stripped off her clothes, turned on the heated Jacuzzi on the deck, and got in. She had her eyes closed, sorting through her thoughts, when she felt Kayla's presence.

Morning came and Kayla hadn't slept. She couldn't tune out her thoughts or the images of Liberty that kept running through her head, images of smooth shoulders and smoldering eyes that saw deep into her soul. She tossed and turned most of the night, but in spite of her weariness, she had to get up. Food had to be prepared, the bar stocked, and the pub decorated. She finally managed to make it into the shower, letting the hot water beat against her tired body. She ached all over, holding the tension and stress of the past few days in the muscles of her neck and shoulders. She stepped out of the shower and was trying to stretch to ease the tightness in her neck muscles, when the connecting door from bathroom to guestroom opened. Liberty stood naked in the doorway, her toiletries in her hand and a towel slung over her shoulder. Liberty's expression never changed as her eyes moved slowly over Kayla's body, following the rivulets of water that fell from Kayla's hair, down her breasts, and over her now hardened nipples. She could feel the heat of Liberty's body. *What a comforting thing, the warmth of a woman's body.*

Kayla's whole body shivered, but she did not move to cover her nakedness. For a moment she thought Liberty was going to take her into her arms. *God help me, I want her to.* Instead, Liberty reached for a towel and handed it to her, then turned and went back into the guestroom and closed the door. Kayla's knees were weak and her heart pounded. A shiver ran down her legs and goosebumps pebbled her skin. Her wobbly legs barely got her back into her room.

Chapter Fifteen

Kayla finished putting up the last of the decorations, then went into the kitchen to check on the food and give last minute instructions to the staff. She'd managed to avoid having a conversation with Liberty, who had busied herself all morning with checking the liquor and setting up the bar. Friends had been popping in and out most of the day to wish Kayla a Happy New Year and to ask about Cassie, so she was never alone with Liberty. By late afternoon, the tension between them was palpable and each would watch the other when she wasn't looking.

Kayla had just put the "Closed for Private Party" sign in the window when a shadow blocked the fading light. She looked up to see a figure standing outside. Smiling, she pointed to the sign and mouthed, "We're closed," briefly making eye contact with the person. A hard chill ran down her spine, as if an icy hand had reached in and touched her. A noise behind her caused her to divert her eyes for a split second. When she looked back, the stranger was gone, but the eerie, uneasy feeling remained. She was still staring out the window when she felt a touch on her shoulder that made her jump. Liberty stood next to her with a concerned look on her face.

"I'm sorry, I didn't mean to scare you. You look pale, are you all right?"

"Just jumpy, I guess. I thought I saw someone looking in, but now I'm not sure. Maybe it was just my imagination." Kayla's uneasy feeling was quickly forgotten by the nearness of Liberty and her lingering hand on her arm.

"You didn't know this person?"

"I'm pretty sure I didn't, but it was difficult to make out the features in this light." Kayla's breath caught as Liberty moved closer to her. She was about to ask if they could talk when the first of the partygoers pushed through the door.

"Happy New Year, Kayla!"

Josh Henderson and his group greeted Liberty, then he hugged Kayla. "We're all so happy that you found Cassie and brought her in. How's she doing?"

While Kayla was bringing Josh and the others up to date on Cassie's progress, Liberty returned to the bar and began to mix drinks. Before long, the pub was hopping and the party was in full swing; everyone was celebrating and having a good time. Some of Nathan's workers, Anna, Susan, and Allie, had come over from the lodge to help out. Liberty and Anna were handling the bar and the others were busy keeping up with the appetizers, while Kayla prepared the food to be set out for the buffet to be served at eleven o'clock.

Several times throughout the day, Liberty had noticed how tired Kayla looked, so when she hadn't seen Kayla in a while that evening, she asked one of the staff to help Anna cover the bar and she went to look for her. She found Kayla in the kitchen, as white as a ghost, holding on to the counter. Liberty crossed the room in two strides and caught Kayla just as she was about to lose her balance, then helped her into a chair. "What is it, Kayla? What's wrong?"

"I...I just feel...lightheaded. I guess I..."

Before Kayla could finish what she was going to say, Liberty put her arm around Kayla's waist and helped her up off the chair. "I'm taking you upstairs to rest a while. Susan can handle the kitchen until I get back."

Kayla was too exhausted to protest as she rested her weight against Liberty. They made their way up the stairs to Kayla's bedroom, where Liberty helped Kayla to sit on the bed. She was worried. "Do you need a doctor, Kayla? Or I can take you down to the hospital in Kalispell."

"A few times during competition, I'd feel this way, usually when my stress level was high and I hadn't eaten." Feeling embarrassed, she started to get up, but immediately got dizzy and sat back down, then blurted, "I'm all right. I...it's just that... My blood sugar is probably low. I just need to eat something."

"And you're exhausted." Liberty picked up the phone, dialed the downstairs number, and waited for someone to answer. "Allie, would you please bring up a large glass of orange juice and a couple of those small sandwiches?"

Allie delivered the food and stayed long enough to make sure that Kayla was all right before going back downstairs. After she'd finished the juice and a part of a sandwich, Kayla was still shaky; she looked washed out. She tried to get up, but her wobbly legs wouldn't hold her.

Liberty's voice was firm. "You need something more to eat and some rest. I'm going to go and fix some proper food for you. Finish your sandwich, then lie down. And please stay put until I get back."

Seeing that the directive was not negotiable, Kayla nodded. Relieved, she lay back on the bed, rested her head on the pillow, and closed her eyes. She hadn't slept well in days, and she did feel exhausted.

Liberty fixed a tray and checked on Anna and Allie, who were handling the bar without a problem. Susan had the kitchen well under control. When she took the tray upstairs, she found that Kayla had fallen asleep. She debated the merits of nourishment versus rest, and decided to let Kayla sleep a while longer. Setting the tray on the nightstand, she took a throw off the foot of the bed and gently covered Kayla before she went back downstairs to the bar.

It was close to midnight and the party was gearing up for the countdown to the New Year when Liberty slipped back upstairs to check on Kayla. A bit of the food was gone off the tray, and Kayla was sleeping. Liberty stood next to the bed just looking at Kayla's face. With the lines of stress and worry eased by sleep, Kayla was truly a beautiful woman. She walked over to the window and looked out at the snow that had been falling all day on the mountain. Of all the places in the world she had been, Montana was one of the most beautiful, untouched in its splendor and its isolation. Tonight, she felt an emotional pain that wormed its way into her anesthetized existence. She remembered how it felt when Yancy had been taken from her and knew what Kayla must feel every time she looked at the mountain — the impetus that fueled her anger and her despair.

Liberty put another log on the fire and sat in the chair by Kayla's bedside, staring into the flames. As the Ghost, Liberty found New Year's an optimal window of opportunity to plan an accident that would avoid suspicion of foul play. She tried to remember all the places and faces of the nameless people she'd used and killed through the years. She had spent many a New Year's Eve masquerading in another identity, stalking her prey or executing a kill. She lived in the shadows, far removed from the human frailty of emotion, immune to the deep ache of loneliness that she now felt as she thought about Kayla and sharing her bed two nights before. She wondered what her life could have been like if she had stayed with the Bureau and not joined the Talons. Maybe if Yancy had lived, they might have had a chance and maybe, just maybe, she would have had a chance with someone like Kayla. Instead, the blood that stained her hands was a constant reminder of what she'd become.

Kayla woke to the crackling of wood burning in the fireplace and the jovial sounds of the party drifting up the stairs from the pub. She lay quietly without moving, studying Liberty's thoughtful face as she stared into the fire. The pain she saw reflected the depth of those thoughts, and Liberty's eyes held an age-old look of sadness. Kayla's impulse was to reach out and run her fingers over the lines of regret that the light of the flames exposed on Liberty's face. The voices from downstairs started the countdown to the New Year, and Liberty turned her head and looked into Kayla's eyes. The lost, forsaken part of her soul was searching, asking for absolution and forgiveness.

"You're awake. I...I fixed you a tray. Do you..." Liberty's voice trailed off when Kayla held out her hand. She slowly closed the distance between them and took the offered hand in her own.

"Happy New Year, Liberty."

The softness and acceptance in Kayla's voice reached across the distance and slipped quietly past the barriers and into Liberty's heart. Liberty felt exposed and vulnerable, unsure of how to respond. Kayla tugged her down onto the bed and kissed her softly on the lips. Liberty moaned when the tip of Kayla's tongue found, then pressed against, the pounding pulse of her throat. When Kayla reached for the buttons on her shirt, Liberty's fingers closed over Kayla's hand.

"As much as I...I could easily...this isn't a good idea. Being with me isn't a good idea, Kayla."

Kayla put her fingers gently against Liberty's lips. "I've already been with you. Tonight I don't want to have sex with you; I want us to make love. I'm not asking for tomorrow, or to know about your past. Just us, just tonight."

When Kayla reached for the buttons of her shirt again, Liberty didn't stop her, and her hands tangled in the dark hair that was brushing against her cheek. The past was forgotten as each undressed the other. Liberty's heart pounded against her chest as Kayla's bare thighs straddled her hips, and she felt Kayla's wetness on her abdomen. Lips and tongue kissed and caressed along her naked skin and Kayla's palms lightly grazed the nipples of each breast, then her fingertips gently traced the line of Liberty's collarbone. There was no urgency. Each touch was unhurried and gave Liberty agonizing pleasure. Kayla's hair brushed against her aching breasts and the tip of her tongue teased around each nipple before she laid a trail of wet kisses down along Liberty's ribs and belly to the softness of each inner thigh, then back up to take a nipple gently between her teeth. A strangled cry escaped from deep inside Liberty.

She moaned Kayla's name, the pleasure Kayla was bestowing passing from her hardened nipples to her throbbing clit. At that moment, as the blood raged through her veins and her body surged toward Kayla's mouth, there were no boundaries to her desire for Kayla. The heat of her passion torched and consumed her every thought. Kayla's fingers tangled in her pubic hair, eliciting another strangled moan when they found their way between Liberty's swollen folds into her wetness. Liberty reached for Kayla's fingers and guided them to where she needed them the most. Her hips moved in time with Kayla's rhythm and her climax came hard, exploding along her nerve endings, opening her soul to the memories and the feelings that had been chipped away with each life she had taken. Relentlessly, Kayla didn't let up until she brought Liberty to orgasm again, then yet again. When each was exhausted and couldn't move, Kayla rested her head on Liberty's thigh. Liberty's hand trembled as she touched Kayla's damp hair, and the tears so long unshed fell down her face, bitter tears that held the horrors of unspeakable things. She felt Kayla's soft breasts and lips against her skin and gently eased Kayla up so she could look into her eyes. She rolled Kayla over, putting Kayla beneath her. With every feeling she had forgotten, she wanted to make love to this woman.

Chapter Sixteen

President-Elect Brady Lawrence sat in his den in the brick Colonial townhouse in Georgetown. His glazed eyes stared into the bottom of the brandy snifter he held in his hand. The taste of victory was sweet, just as sweet as the rich, mellow taste of the fifty-year-old Cape brandy that pleased his palate. He knew he deserved it. It was the culmination of eight years of planning and machination. In the beginning, in order to strengthen his political aspirations, he'd seized the opportunity to use the skills of the Talons for an assassination in a Third World country or an untimely accident that was financially favorable to his personal bank account.

At first, it was easy to deceive the Talons. President Kincaide trusted him and was oblivious to what was occurring on a day-to-day basis, seeing only the diminishing number of acts of terrorism around the world. Armanno Santini wasn't as easy to dupe. It became harder to convince Santini that all the targets were justified, figures associated with terrorist groups. Santini began to ask questions, and Lawrence learned that Santini had begun to investigate. Lawrence had to do something about that. And he did — by arranging an unfortunate accident for Santini that had missed him, but killed his only son and paralyzed his daughter. The accident had a devastating effect on Santini and he retired. At least it had taken him out of the game.

Lawrence gently turned the snifter. The light from the fireplace reflected off the golden liquid as the aroma of the Cognac fueled the intoxicating feeling of power. He raised the glass in a toast. "To a profitable eight years in the White House, and to our continued friendship."

The sound of two glasses meeting echoed across the room and a baleful smile crossed the face of Lawrence's guest. "Yes. To a very profitable eight years."

Lawrence took a drink, then set the snifter on the side table. "I don't think I need to remind you that Liberty Starr threatens everything." The statement was met with a warning glare from his guest. A bead of sweat broke out above Lawrence's upper lip as his guest leaned forward, pinning him with eyes that were as hard and cold as death itself.

"You don't need to remind me of anything, Brady."

Lawrence gathered his composure and huffed, "She could put it all together, especially since the botched attempt you made to kill her in Denver. She has to have figured out that she was set up to die that day."

"Liberty is not stupid, of course she knows, and it's a sure bet she has figured out that either you or Kincaide are involved. My guess is that she won't discriminate. She'll come for you *and* for Kincaide, because she doesn't know which one of you is responsible, or if you both are. It won't matter; she'll take you both out and neither of you will see it coming."

Brady's face grew red and the veins in his neck were distended. His voice rose as an icy hand of fear clutched his gut. "She'll never get by the Secret Service. I've made sure of that. And if you are stupid enough to think she won't figure out who you are, you're a fool."

His bluster was met by a feral grin. "I think you know, Lawrence, that I'm no fool, and neither is Liberty. Liberty is the best of the Talons. Your Secret Service won't even get wind of her before you're both dead."

"Then for Christ's sake, what are you waiting for? The inauguration is less than three weeks away! Am I supposed to cower under my bed waiting for her to kill me?"

The guest slowly took a last drink, savoring the taste of the brandy, then got up and walked toward the door and opened it. The assassin turned, eyes devoid of emotion, and smiled coldly. "There is no place you can hide, 'Mister President'. If Liberty gets by me, you're a dead man. We created her, and you know that no one but me can stop her."

Brady stared as his guest laughed, walked through the door, and closed it, shutting him inside alone. His hands were shaking when he pushed a buzzer and a man hurriedly entered the room. "Make sure your people do not lose the person who just left my home. Tell them to report to me directly. And be sure everyone knows that no one is to make a move until I personally give the word. Is that understood?"

"Yes, Sir. We have our best agents on it."

Lawrence was shaking. He didn't know which one he feared most — Liberty Starr or his own assassin. Unraveling, he threw the brandy snifter against the fireplace. "Your best is nowhere near good enough! Get out!"

Across town at 1600 Pennsylvania Avenue, President Wade Kincaide sat in the Oval Office across from his brother. "Have you located Starr yet, Mack?"

"Not yet, but we have a pretty good idea where she is. There was an incident in Denver, and we feel that she might have been involved." Mack took a deep breath; his words were straight to the point. "We might not be able to take her alive, Wade."

The emotions playing across Wade Kincaide's face showed the depth of his concern. "You do what you have to do, but please try to give her every chance. I've given this a lot of thought. Everything I know about Liberty Starr is telling me she's not Brady's turncoat."

The President's shoulders sagged and his eyes expressed the sorrow in his heart. "How many good men and women of the Talons died thinking I betrayed them? If Liberty is not the one, I want her protected. We can't stop Lawrence from being sworn in; the legal process has to follow its due course. The evidence has to be turned over to the Justice Department and presented before the Senate. I can testify before a grand jury. All of that will take time, Mack. With the evidence we have, Brady will unquestionably be impeached. I hate like hell to see him get away with what he's done, but common knowledge of all this would throw the country into turmoil." Wade paused, what he was about to say nauseated him. "We may have to offer him a deal. If he knows that I am willing to go public and expose him, he might resign. I'll offer my silence, and you'll put all of the evidence in your confidential files with back up copies where his people can't find them. We can make sure he never steps foot in Washington again. Get a federal court order to seize the bank accounts in the states you've traced to Lawrence, and I'll do what I can to make sure the money he has stashed in other counties disappears. We can send him a message by stopping him from using his blood money, at least for now."

Mack Kincaide pounded his fist on the desk. "By God, Wade, if I had my way, he'd never leave Washington, unless it was in a pine box!"

Cassie sat in a wheelchair while Kayla stood behind her and brushed her hair. "Are you getting tired? I can call the nurse and we can help you back to bed."

"No, it feels good to be up and to have my hair washed. Thanks."

"You look better today, Cassie. When I spoke to Doctor Mc-Klosky and Rue, they both agreed that you could go home in a few days and continue your therapy as an out patient."

"I know; I can hardly wait to get out of here. Try to push them a little, Kayla. Use your influence to get Mican to discharge me tomorrow."

"I'll do no such thing, missy. You'll stay until they say you're healed enough to go home."

"But..."

"No buts. Now, how about lunch? I'm willing to go and get you a chocolate shake. Rue told me that you need all the protein you can get. It will help you with the healing process."

Cassie looked at Kayla's reflection in the mirror of the bedside table that was positioned across her lap. There was something different about her today. "You know, Rue is still interested in you. Every time you're around, she looks at you with those puppy dog eyes. I think she'd like to start seeing you again."

"It didn't work out the last time. I made her miserable."

Cassie turned her head to look at her sister. "You were recovering from the loss of Addie and the alcohol. You're better now. Maybe you should give her a second chance."

"Cassie, once an alcoholic, always an alcoholic. You're never cured. You just learn to control it, one day at a time. I wouldn't wish me on anyone."

"Rue is a big girl, Kayla.. You should let her make that decision. Besides, I happen to think you'd be worth the effort."

Kayla smiled. "When did you get to be so wise, little sister?"

Cassie smiled back, "I had a good teacher. Hey, how was the party last night? I'm sorry I wasn't there to help out."

"Well, the bank will get its mortgage payment, and you're not to worry. I had plenty of help."

"Who's minding the pub while you're here?" Cassie thought there was a hint of a blush on her sister's cheeks when she deliberately diverted her eyes and stumbled over her explanation.

"Uh, well, Liberty. She said she would stay...maybe...a few more days just to help out until you're home, so I can come into town."

Cassie started to giggle. "Come around here so I can see you." Kayla self-consciously tried to pull her sweater up higher on her neck. "Oh...my...you slept with her, didn't you? I know that look, Kayla Sinclair. Sit, tell me all about it."

Flustered and embarrassed, Kayla shushed her sister. "Cassie! For Pete's sake, what kind of talk is that? Keep it down. Do you want the entire hospital to hear you?"

"I knew that was a hickey on your neck; I just knew it!" Before Kayla could answer, Rue Mican walked into the room.

"Hey, sounds like someone is feeling pretty good today." Rue's eyes never left Kayla's neck. From the look on her face, it was apparent that the doctor had heard what Cassie had said about the hickey.

Cassie tried to divert Rue's attention away from Kayla. "When can I go home, Rue? I'm feeling pretty good and I can do everything at home that I am doing here. Remember, Kayla put in a whirlpool at the lodge to treat athletic injuries, and she has one at the pub."

Rue turned to Cassie and forced a smile, but the tone of her voice made it obvious what she was thinking. "It's possible; that could work. We could schedule a home care therapist for a while and see how it goes. Let me think about it. You are doing well, Cassie, and I promise that I'll talk to Doctor McKlosky today and see what he thinks." After an awkward silence, the doctor excused herself and left to finish her rounds.

"I think she heard me. I'm sorry, Kayla. She is a good woman and she cares about you."

Kayla exhaled the breath she'd been holding. "I think she did, too. Rue helped me through a tough time and I know she cares. I could see the hurt in her eyes. I need to go and talk to her."

Kayla softly tapped on the door of Rue's office, then stepped in. The doctor was standing by the window, looking out at the cars slipping around on the icy streets. Rue glanced at Kayla, then continued to stare out the window. "Rue, I..."

"You don't owe me any explanation, Kayla. Who you sleep with is your business."

Kayla closed the door quietly and went to stand beside Rue. She gently touched the doctor's arm. "Rue, please, it wasn't... I...I can't explain this to you. It has nothing to do with you. It's just... It's not what you think."

Rue turned angrily and faced Kayla, holding back her tears. "Not what I think? How do you know what I think, Kayla? You're too busy running from everything, including me, to stick around and find out. You slept with her; it's as simple as that."

"I'm sorry, Rue. I'm sorry you're hurt. I value your friendship; I don't want this to ruin that."

"But you don't love me, and you would rather give yourself to a stranger than to someone who loves you, is that it?"

"I think we'd better stop this conversation before one of us says something we can't take back."

"Can you take back fucking another woman?"

Kayla flinched; Rue's words were like a slap across her face.

Rue had wanted to hurt Kayla as badly as she was hurting, but she immediately regretted the words that had come out of her mouth. "Oh, Kayla, I'm sorry. I shouldn't have said that." Kayla had gotten as far as the door when Rue caught her and took hold of her hand. She wiped at the tears that were in Kayla's eyes. "Please, I'm sorry. You've had enough this past week without this too. Forgive me, please?"

"There's nothing to forgive. I can understand how you feel, Rue. It just happened. I can't explain it, but I'm not apologizing for it either."

Rue's arm went around her waist as she pushed the door closed and pulled Kayla into her arms and kissed her. "I've wanted to do that for so long, Kayla. If you needed someone, why didn't you come to me?"

Kayla touched the doctor's cheek. "Sometimes things just happen, and there is no explanation for it. I never meant to lead you on or to disregard your feelings. I'm just not in a good place right now and starting a relationship deserves more than I can give it. Please try to understand."

Rue rested her forehead against Kayla's. "You're right. This isn't the time."

"Rue, I need to get back to Cassie. Can we can talk later?"

Rue watched as Kayla disappeared down the hall. She'd loved Kayla from the moment she'd seen her in Lillehammer, streaking down the mountain. And the first time Kayla had broken her heart was the day Kayla announced to the world that she was in love with Addie.

Chapter Seventeen

Armanno Santini's frozen expression was an impenetrable mask as he read the report that the head of his security team had delivered to him. His large hands never faltered as he turned each page; his only response was the slight narrowing of his dark eyes and the barely detectable movement of his upper lip. When he finished, he slowly placed the report on the desk in front of him and closed his eyes. After a few moments, he got up and walked the length of the house to the wing of the villa that had been converted into a physical therapy center that included state-of-the-art therapy and lap pools. Before opening the door, Armanno pulled an old watch from his vest pocket where it was attached by a gold chain, then flipped open the cover to read the time. His face softened as he entered the room. His granddaughter Tiana was practicing in the lap pool, and his daughter Maggie was working in the whirlpool with her therapist.

Excited to see her grandfather, Tiana splashed over to the side of the pool. "Grandfather! Come join us!"

The icy grip that held Armanno Santini's heart eased a bit, and his handsome face broke into a smile as he knelt by the edge of the pool and looked at his beautiful granddaughter. "Tiana, you are swimming so well. You are like a fish in the water."

Tiana loved the sound of her grandfather's voice with its soft Italian accent. He always smelled of sweet pipe tobacco and spice. Many nights after the accident when her Uncle Robert was killed and her mother injured, it was her grandfather's voice and scent that soothed her to sleep and chased away the boogey man and the bad dreams. "Mama is doing well today, Grandfather. Lynne says she is getting stronger every day. Did you know Mama can get in and out of the pool all by herself? Aren't you excited, Grandfather?"

The love and optimism in his granddaughter's eyes and words tugged at Armanno's heart. "That is very good news, Tiana." Armanno placed his index finger under Tiana's chin. "Little one, have I told you today that I love you and your mama so very much?"

"You're so silly, Grandfather. Of course you have; you tell us every day. We love you, too."

"Tiana, I have something I have to do. Take care of your mama and tell her I will be back in time to have dinner with my two favorite ladies." Armanno watched proudly as Tiana showed off her skills as she swam the length of the lap pool into the open area where her mother was working with Lynne. Tiana was so much like her mother.

She had the natural grace and strength in the water that Maggie had had before the accident. Maggie smiled, raising her hand to wave.

Armanno retrieved a palm sized cell phone from his breast pocket and walked across the sunroom. He stood looking out the fern-shrouded expanse of bulletproof glass that enclosed the area. He loved this part of the villa. He'd had it designed especially to bring the outdoors into a protected environment for Maggie and his granddaughter. With plants and trees, it was bright and cheery, and the sounds of birds filled the air. He'd had boulders imported from the red rocks of Sedona and placed to create a natural setting with a waterfall and pond.

Armanno's cell rang. It was the call he had been waiting for. His mien was cold and emotionless as he listened to his head of his security. When he spoke, his voice reflected the grave seriousness of the order he was giving. "Marcello, triple the security around the vineyards and put eyes and ears along the coastline from south of Santa Barbara to Arroyo Grande. I'm putting the safety of my family in your hands until this thing is finished. I am leaving right now. Keep them alive until I get there."

Armanno drove his Jeep along the dirt road to a remote wine cellar on the property, his mind going over the report he'd read earlier. His suspicions had been right all along — it had not been an accident that killed his son and crippled Maggie, but rather a cold-blooded attempt to stop his investigation into the government's use of the Talons. He had been the target, but the outcome had accomplished its objective just the same, neutralizing him and aborting his inquiries.

It should have eased his anger to know that it had been Brady Lawrence's doing and not Wade Kincaide's, but the taste for vengeance was too bitter. Armanno, who prided himself on his keen intuition and judging of character, had never believed Wade Kincaide was a man who would resort to murder for money or power. Kincaide's assemblage of the Talons was altruistic, an unselfish act in an effort to protect the world from terrorism. Brady Lawrence's personal agenda and greed had corrupted the dream and the Talons, and now Lawrence was about to assume the office and powers of President of the United States.

Armanno Santini was a hard man — he had lived a life embroiled in espionage and black ops — but he was also a patriot. He'd served his country and had followed orders. He believed in the cause, even when the line of right and wrong blurred and became invisible. But when his son died in the prime of his life and the use of Maggie's legs was taken from her, it left a burning desire in Armanno's soul for revenge. Brady Lawrence would soon suffer his wrath. Armanno would also find out who had staged the accident that killed Robert and, if Liberty Starr was the Talons' Judas, God have mercy on her soul.

He stepped out of his Jeep and looked toward the sky. Storm clouds hung low over the mountains, pushing the fog deeper into the valley. He thought it an appropriate day for what he had to do, and as an omen of the storm that was to come.

Marcello roughly grabbed the slumped man's hair and twisted his head so that the man could look up into the face of Armanno Santini. The captive's eyes were mere slits in his bloodied, swollen face. Marcello leaned in closer to the man's ear. "Your partner is dead. You will listen to what Mr. Santini is going to ask you. He will only ask you once. Answer his questions and you will be released from your pain and allowed to die, to end your suffering. Do you understand?"

Blood gurgled in the man's throat as he tried to answer, then he weakly nodded. The metallic smell of blood and death mingled with the sweet smell of the oak wine barrels.

"Good." Marcello looked at Santini as Santini's strong voice echoed through the wine cellar.

"You are sure that Wade Kincaide was not involved in the death of my son?"

The man struggled, his answer a whisper, "Yes...I'm sure."

"The order came from Brady Lawrence?"

"Yes."

"You were sent here today by Lawrence to kill me and my family?" Again the man nodded. "Answer this last question, and you will be allowed to die. Who is the traitor, the Talon that is working for Lawrence?"

Blood trickled from the man's mouth and nose as he struggled with each word. "I don't...know..."

Armanno bent his head down close enough to smell the stench of death coming off the captive. "Was it Liberty Starr?"

Gurgling sounds came from the man's throat. Too weak to answer, he stared blankly at Armanno Santini as he choked on his own blood. Marcello released the man's head and it fell forward.

Armanno held out his hand, but Marcello quickly pleaded, "Mr. Santini, let me do this."

Armanno's eyes never left the face of the informant. "It is my place. He answered my questions; his suffering will end. Hand me your pistol, my friend."

Marcello directed his men to leave the room, then drew his weapon and placed it in Armanno's hand. He exited the cellar into a gray, somber day, and stood in the rain, waiting. The sky rumbled and grew darker as a shot rang out and hung suspended in the fog. A few moments later, a grim Armanno Santini exited the cellar and handed the pistol back to Marcello. "Give them both a proper burial at sea."

Chapter Eighteen

Liberty felt the cold hand of winter reach deep inside as she stood on top of Cougar's Peak, looking down at the rugged terrain below. A foreboding chill gripped her as a single dark cloud passed in front of the sun, casting a shadow across her path. She closed her eyes and thought about Kayla and the sweet touch that had embraced her petrified heart. The honesty of Kayla's desire tore the soft cries of passion from her lost soul, and her heart ached for what could have been and what she had to do. She had killed for her country, and she would kill again — both President Kincaide and President-Elect Lawrence. There was no other way. The country would emerge stronger from the chaos that would follow and be better for the vanquishing of the evil. She would avenge the honor of the Talons and the blood of all the innocent souls who had died because of the price that was put on their heads. Liberty knew her name would be written in the history books with the same tainted pen as Lee Harvey Oswald and James Earl Ray. She cared only about what one person would think of her, and that was Kayla. It pained her to her very core to think that all Kayla would ever know of Liberty Starr was that she was an assassin.

The wind shifted and Liberty sensed something disturbingly familiar. She knew the risk she was taking by being out in the open, becoming the perfect target to draw out the assassin. She'd calculated the distance from the tree line; the assassin would have to take her down with a body shot. If the sniper used armor-piercing ammo, the Kevlar vest under her sweater would provide very little protection. If she went down, the shooter couldn't take a chance that she would survive. A second shot would be necessary to be sure. That's when she would take the traitor down and then go after Kincaide and Lawrence.

Liberty bent to check her bindings. When she did, she saw a figure skiing out of the sun into the open along the ridge toward her, directly into the line of fire. For a moment she panicked, thinking that it could be Kayla. The area was off piste and in a black zone, and only an expert skier would attempt it. As the skier drew nearer, she could see that the movement was not as fluid as Kayla's would be, and that it was a man. When he was within a few feet of her, he pushed up his goggles and reached into his jacket pocket. As he pulled his hand out, a shot rang out and he jerked violently. Pieces of flesh and brain matter hit Liberty and splattered her clothes. The man fell like a rag doll, staining the white landscape a crimson red. It happened so fast that there was nothing Liberty could do. There was no question he was dead. The second the bullet had shattered his skull. The distance the shot was taken from was impossible, even for the best of marksmen.

Instinctively, Liberty went into a crouch to become as small as she could. Her hand grasped the object that had fallen out of the man's hand and she quickly shoved it into her pocket before she bolted down the face of the mountain. The sniper was a dead shot; Liberty knew that her only hope was to make herself a moving target. She had offered herself up as bait to lure the assassin out, but she had underestimated her enemy and put herself in a defenseless situation with her back against a wall and only one way out —straight down the rugged face of the mountain. If she didn't pile up on the rocks and break her legs, she might have a ghost of a chance to outrun a bullet with her name on it.

Liberty used every fiber of strength and conditioning she had to increase her speed. She could see that she was coming up to the edge of a cliff with a steep drop off. If she made the jump, she would have the cover she needed. She was in the air with her body stretched out over her skis as far as she could, when she heard the crack of the high-powered rifle a split second before she felt a bullet hiss past her ear. Ten more feet and she would clear the outcropping. Her skis scraped across the top of the jagged rocks as a bullet ricocheted off of them, spraying splinters of stone and ice into the air. When she touched ground, she was out of the sight of the shooter and able to ski out onto a well-populated downhill run and directly to the lodge. She debated whether to alert the ski patrol and the authorities to the body on the mountain, but there would be too many questions that she couldn't answer. For all she knew, the man had been sent to kill her.

Liberty didn't waste any time making her way back to the pub. Deception had become a cloak, a necessary weapon amongst her arsenal of many, but she couldn't lie to Kayla. And she couldn't tell her the truth. Doing that would be signing Kayla's death warrant. She had no choice but to leave Lone Mountain before Kayla arrived home from the hospital. Her presence had already put Kayla's life in danger. If whoever wanted her dead thought Kayla knew anything, they would come after her. It might already be too late. She couldn't wait any longer. It was time to contact Armanno Santini, to ask for his help. Liberty knew that he could help her to put a plan in place that would assure Kayla's safety.

Liberty stuck her skis in the snow and unbuckled her boots, then entered the pub through the kitchen door and hurried up the stairs to her room. It was New Year's Day and the pub was open until after the lunch crowd was served. Everyone wanted to get in that last early day of skiing before the kids went back to school.

She hurried and changed out of the bloody clothing, then threw her things together and stuffed everything into her duffel. She started to go downstairs, but stopped at the slightly open door to Kayla's room. Kayla had left before her that morning and the bed was still unmade, as Liberty had left it when she went out on the mountain. The heady smell of sweat and the passion of their fevered night of lovemaking still lingered in the room, and Liberty felt her abdomen clench with longing. Not wanting the night to end, she'd been awake a long time that morning before Kayla. When Kayla woke, the mere touch of her fingers on Liberty's face set her body on fire again. Kayla kissed her eyelids, then her mouth, and made the gentlest, most passionate love to her. They had touched and explored one another's body with desire and a shared need to bring comfort. The pain in Liberty's heart was unbearable as she slowly closed the door and headed down the stairs.

Susan and Allie had just closed the pub and were ready to leave when Allie saw Liberty with the duffel in her hand. Allie figured Liberty as someone who was hard to get to know. Maybe she wasn't overly friendly, but she'd helped Kayla to find Cassie and was helping to keep the pub open. She'd seen Kayla watching Liberty when they were setting up for the party yesterday, and there was definite interest in Kayla's eyes. Allie decided that she would take a chance and talk to Liberty, knowing quite well that she was meddling in something that was none of her business. "Susan, you go on ahead to the lodge. I'll catch up to you." When Susan had left, Allie turned to Liberty. "I hear that Cassie might get to come home this week. That's good news."

After a few moments of awkward silence during which Liberty didn't answer, Allie decided to skip the small talk and say what was on her mind. "Look, I'm going to be real blunt here. We all love Kayla, and she seems to have taken a liking to you. She has a vulnerable heart and...well, we just don't want to see her hurt again." Allie glanced down at the duffel in Liberty's hand. "And it looks like you're leaving, without saying goodbye."

Liberty swung the duffel over her shoulder and was reaching for the doorknob when the door opened and Kayla walked in. Kayla looked at the duffel, then at Liberty and Allie, and walked past them, through the pub and into the kitchen, without saying a word. Allie shrugged and edged her way out the door. "I'd better be going."

Liberty stood in the open doorway for a long while. *Damn, this isn't the time. What can I say to her?* She leaned her head against the doorframe. Every moment she remained put Kayla in more danger. She was about to leave when she heard Kayla's voice.

"I poured some tea. Do you want to talk?"

Liberty turned to see Kayla already climbing the stairs with the tray in her hands. She didn't turn around when she reached the top of the stairs, but simply said, "Close the door, Liberty. You're letting all the cold air in. Whatever it is you're running from can wait a little while longer."

Kayla was sitting in front of the fireplace when Liberty entered the bedroom. "Sit down, Liberty. Do you want to tell me what's going on? And please don't tell me you're a one-night stand kind of woman and afraid of commitment, because I wouldn't believe you. That's not why you're running from me or from yourself. You're one of the finest athletes I've ever seen, and you've had extensive training...military, I suspect. That first night I noticed the bloodstain on your sweater, and how you hesitated telling me your name. It was odd, like you weren't used to saying it, and, judging from the scars on your body, what you do is dangerous."

It didn't surprise Liberty that Kayla had summed it up in a few short words. What Kayla hadn't figured out was the danger she had brought with her. Liberty pulled the object that she'd picked up on the mountain from her pocket and set it on the table between them. It was a 1921 silver Peace Dollar.

"The year President Kincaide took office, I was a NAT at the FBI training facilities at Quantico. I met an agent, a woman, who recruited me for a covert antiterrorist group." Not leaving anything out, she told Kayla all of it, about the killing, and how someone had tried to kill her the day she made her way to Lone Mountain. When she was finished, she picked up the silver dollar. "President Kincaide gave each of the fourteen Talon agents a silver dollar with a different date, one for each of the fifteen years the Peace Dollar was minted, from 1921 to 1935. The Peace Dollar was to serve as a token of the Talons and their commitment, but also as a potential message. If a Talon was ever in a desperate situation with no way out, the agent was to send the dollar to the President. He would know who it was from the date, and move heaven and earth to help. Kincaide himself kept the first of the fifteen dollars, the one dated 1921. If he needed the help of a Talon, he too would send the Peace Dollar. This Peace Dollar."

Liberty turned the silver dollar between her fingers, slowly rubbing her thumb over the face of the coin. "This could be a trick to get me out in the open. I don't know who to trust. I am the last of the Talons. Whoever is behind the corruption and the deaths of the Talons, Kincaide or Lawrence, knows I will come for him. I can't take the risk that one of them is not involved. The only way to be sure is to eliminate them both."

Kayla was stunned. Her mind reeled as she tried to absorb all that Liberty had told her. It was an incredible story; one that was impossible to believe. And yet, oddly, she didn't feel afraid of this woman who had just told her that she was going to assassinate the President of the United States and President-Elect Brady Lawrence. If what Liberty had just told her was true, her life, as well as that of all the Talons, had been stolen. The country would be in grave danger if Lawrence were allowed to be sworn in as President. Kayla's heart went out to this woman she had made love with, but could she believe an assassin? When she finally found her voice, she asked, "Why did you tell me all this, Liberty? How could you trust that I would not turn you in or warn the authorities?"

Liberty picked up the poker and knelt to stoke the fire. The flames exposed an incredible sadness in her eyes. "It probably wasn't the smartest thing I could've done. My being here has put you in jeopardy, but knowing you has been the only good thing in my life for a very long time, Kayla. In a world that has been filled with nothing but death and corruption, the life you live here on the mountain and the love you share with your family and friends have given me a reason to believe again. The memory you have of me, of Liberty Starr, is the only thing that I am leaving behind. It's important to me that you know the truth."

Kayla felt a pang in her heart at Liberty's forlorn look. She apparently had no one else in her life that would care if she died, and Liberty was telling her that she wasn't coming back. Her eyes watered when Liberty softly touched her cheek. For a few moments she held Liberty's hand against her face, then her voice broke as she asked, "Is there anyone that you can trust who can help you?"

A single tear in the corner of Kayla's eye threatened to unravel Liberty's resolve to do what had to be done. "Please, don't cry, Kayla."

"Damn it, Liberty, how can I not? We...I...last night was..."

Still kneeling, Liberty turned to Kayla and reached for her hands, then raised them to her lips to kiss her fingers. "I know. It was for me, too."

"What will you do now?"

"This morning I contacted...a friend I believe I can trust. At daybreak he'll be flying into a private airstrip this side of Eureka at

Crystal Lake, and I'll be meeting him." Kayla started to say something, but Liberty gently put a silencing finger on her lips. "No more questions. I'm so sorry to have brought all this trouble into your life." Her eyes searched Kayla's face. "I just...selfishly needed you."

"Isn't there any other way?" Kayla sobbed. "There has to be a way to expose all this without you having to...to get yourself killed. You could testify in front of a special federal grand jury. They could protect you and—"

"Kayla, anyone can be gotten to. No one can be protected if an assassin or a terrorist wants them dead, not Lawrence, or even the President, so how long do you think I'd last? I'd never make it to the courtroom. Even if it were possible, if the world were to find out what has been going on, the aftermath would devastate our country."

Kayla was visibly shaken. "For God's sake, Liberty, what do you think it's going to do to this country when both the President and the President-Elect are...are...mur...killed?"

Liberty flinched. "Our country will survive an assassination; it has before. Kincaide would have been hailed as a hero if his intent and vision to thwart terrorism had succeeded. Now the world will crucify him *and* the United States — and rightfully so — if the murderous activities of the Talons are disclosed. The one bright hope in all this is Brady Lawrence's Vice President-Elect, Ingrid Sheppard. Lawrence was forced to go with her; the party didn't leave him much choice. She's an honest politician with strong ethics, and is more than capable of leading our country out of this tragedy. The country will unite under her direction."

"Are you sure about President Kincaide? Couldn't he truly be reaching out for help by sending you the dollar?"

A pained look on her face, Liberty gripped the silver dollar in her fist. "Kincaide could be sending me a message, or he could be setting me up."

Kayla realized how her words must have sounded. She wrapped Liberty's hands between her own and looked into her eyes. "Please, I'm not doubting you. It's just...all this is so hard to believe." Kayla could see behind the mask Liberty wore. The look — it had been there all along, from the moment she'd first laid eyes on Liberty on Christmas Eve. Liberty was not only prepared to kill two traitors to avenge the Talons and protect the country; she was preparing for her own death as well. Kayla began to pull away. *This can't be happening.*

Surmising what Kayla was thinking, Liberty pulled her gently into her arms and buried her face in her hair. "It has to be this way. I should have stopped this a long time ago."

Tears streamed down Kayla's face onto Liberty's neck. She was angry at the injustice of it all, at the injustice of life. "Fate brought you into my life. You were there when Cassie and I needed you, and now you're just going to walk out of my life and go get yourself killed."

Liberty held Kayla against her and pressed her lips against the softness of her hair. Her voice cracked with emotion. "There is nothing in this world that I would rather do than stay on this mountain with you. My soul aches for what might have been." She wiped the tears from Kayla's cheeks. "There is no atonement for the things I have done. God knows, I will burn in hell, but Kincaide and Lawrence will burn right along with me."

After talking with Kayla, Liberty had called Armanno and again was connected to a secured line. She had to be sure that Kayla and her family would be safe. Armanno agreed to provide protection for Kayla and her family on two conditions: that Liberty meet him face to face, and that she do nothing until then. Liberty agreed, allowing herself enough time to travel to Crystal Lake and to get into position to avoid walking into a trap before she called Armanno with her location.

She traveled in the darkness of night, maneuvering the 4x4 along the logging road Kayla had shown her. It was still dark when she got into position and waited. The hoary light of a full moon framed the silhouette of the Eagle Eye helicopter that came in low over the mountains, then followed along the icy shoreline of Crystal Lake. The modified engine was barely audible as it hovered over the flares Liberty had placed to mark the landing area. The chopper circled once, then put down on the small airstrip that was cut into the side of the mountain.

From her vantage point concealed by the darkness and the dense woods, Liberty scanned the forest around the chopper through the night vision goggles as she waited for the first light of dawn. Everything around her was frozen and dead still, devoid of color except for the white of winter. The only movement was the chimerical fingers cast by the clouds passing in front of a hunter's moon. It would be light soon, and Armanno Santini would step out of the chopper and signal for her to walk out of the cover of the trees and come in from the cold.

Liberty's thoughts were of Kayla as the first hint of light appeared on the cold horizon. Always coldest just before daybreak, the temperature was well below zero. Liberty could feel the stiffness setting in her limbs. She took off her gloves to manipulate the scope of the rifle she had zeroed in on Armanno and the pilot as they stood outside the chopper. It was time. She rose from her position and slung the rifle over her shoulder. As she bent to pick up her duffel, a thud against the tree above her head caused her to dive back into the snow for cover. As she scrambled to throw herself behind a log, two more silent shots kicked up the snow so close that one ripped across her shoulder, tearing her jacket. The shooter was using a silencer; the shots were coming from the forest behind her. She needed to warn Armanno, and the only way was to fire her rifle.

When the two shots rang out, Armanno and his pilot ran toward an abandoned metal hanger off to the side of the runway. They had almost reached the safety of the building when a bullet knocked the pilot to the ground. He went down hard, yelling for Armanno to keep running, just before a second shot silenced him. Armanno could hear the thud of bullets ripping into the pilot's body, then one hit the shed just as he dove into it.

When Liberty saw the pilot go down, she leapt up and ran toward the back of the dilapidated hanger. Hoping she could make it to cover before the sniper had time to adjust targets and draw a bead on her, she zigzagged through the trees. She flung herself through a door that was hanging on one hinge and rolled on the frozen dirt floor, landing at the feet of Armanno. She looked up to see a gun leveled at her head.

"You fire those warning shots?"

Liberty got to her knees and, with two hands, carefully handed the rifle to Armanno. "It was the quickest way to warn you. Check it yourself, two rounds missing. The two I fired into the air."

The shots Armanno heard had been from a high powered rifle, but he wanted to play it safe. Taking the rifle, he said, "Let's have your pistol, as well." Liberty slowly stood and took the gun out of the holster with two fingers, then handed it to Armanno. After he examined Liberty's rifle, he lowered his gun and offered his hand. "I'm sure you still carry that back-up piece in your boot."

Liberty smiled and started to reach for the .25 caliber in her boot when Armanno said, "That won't be necessary." He handed Liberty's weapons back to her. "How do you want to work this to get out of here, Ghost?"

It had been a long time since she had heard Armanno use her code name, one the Pueblo had given her. It brought back the memories of the many missions that she and Armanno had been on together. Her gut instinct told her Armanno Santini was a man that could be trusted. She was just about to say that they would never make it to the chopper when an explosion rocked the building, knocking them both off their feet. Liberty looked at Armanno. "Guess it won't be by helicopter."

In the back of Liberty's mind, the feeling that had begun after she'd fled Denver triggered a flashing red warning that had been her lifesaver many times. This assassin had been one step ahead of her all along, able to anticipate her every move. It was as if a game was being play, a deadly game of chess, and she was the pawn that was being manipulated.

Chapter Nineteen

The shed provided cover and some protection from the extreme cold, but both Liberty and Armanno knew the explosion would draw attention from the small town of Eureka that was close by, as well as the U.S. and Canadian border patrols. They had to risk moving before someone came to investigate. They counted on the freezing temperatures, along with the wind chill, to make it too difficult for the shooter to stay exposed for very long. The smoke from the chopper obscured the shooter's view of the shed, and Armanno improvised a plan. Liberty took up a position to cover Armanno with her rifle and watched the tree line. He went out the back door and crawled to where the pilot lay, then dragged the body as close as he could to what was left of the chopper and the flames. He planned to buy time by making the local authorities think that the explosion had been the result of the plane crashing on landing. Armanno's stomach turned at the sight of his friend's lifeless body; the high-powered rifle had done a lot of damage. It would take time for the body to be recovered and examined, time that would give them a chance to get far away. *Forgive me, Enzo, my friend.*

Armanno covered Liberty as she made her way from the shed to the dense cover of the forest, then he followed. They made their way through the woods to where Liberty had hidden the SUV. She touched him on the arm and pointed. The white SUV was so well concealed that Armanno couldn't see it. Liberty carefully approached the vehicle first, checking the snow to be sure that the only tracks were the ones she had left earlier. She circled the perimeter to make sure that the assassin was not lying in wait, then she signaled for Armanno to approach.

Staying off the main highway, Liberty kept to the logging road that Kayla had drawn on a map for her that would lead them back to Lone Mountain. Waning light lengthened the shadows across the road as Liberty maneuvered the SUV through the deep snow. Armanno took out his cell phone. After a brief conversation, arrangements had been made for them to be picked up at the crack of dawn at the helipad at the lodge. A helicopter landing at that time in the morning would be assumed to be shuttling out-of-state skiers from the airport in Kalispell.

"This assassin was waiting for us. Are you carrying anything that could contain a tracking chip or a chip under your skin?" Armanno asked.

"No, nothing. I went through everything, checked everything. You and I talked on a secure line, so that could only mean I was followed."

"Yes, by someone who is very good. We need to be careful, calculate our every move."

Liberty's thoughts were about what Armanno had told her earlier. "You're positive that Kincaide had no knowledge of what Lawrence was doing?"

"I'm certain. Since before my son was murdered, I had my suspicions about that bastard Lawrence. He knew it, too. Since, I have gathered enough evidence to prove that he was behind it all and that Wade Kincaide knew nothing about what Lawrence was doing. Kincaide thought the Talons had been disbanded right after his first term in office." Armanno's dark eyes narrowed and the lines on his face deepened. "Lawrence is a heartless, greedy son of a bitch. He'll sell this country out, bleed it dry to make himself rich and powerful." Armanno stared straight ahead, his voice low, cold with determination. "He must not be allowed to be sworn in as President. First, we find and take out this assassin, then we go after Lawrence."

Neither spoke for a long while. Liberty knew Armanno was thinking about the man they'd left behind. "Your pilot, was he a friend?"

"Enzo was a good man as well as a good friend. He'd been through much in his life. Enzo was always big and looked older than his years. At sixteen, he lied about his age and joined the Army by using his brother's birth certificate. On his first tour of duty, he was sent to Vietnam. He was captured and taken prisoner and held for four years until the last of the prisoner exchanges. When I met him, we were in Colombia under the guise of being advisors, but we were deep into the CIA and black ops. We teamed up to locate the drug czar, Pablo Escobar, and found ourselves in the middle of the cocaine drug wars. We were sent to take the bastard out, but someone beat us to it. We got into a tight spot and I was wounded, but Enzo wouldn't leave me. He packed my carcass halfway across the damn country, but we both made it out. When my son was killed, I needed a good man to help me protect my family. He left the CIA to join me."

"I'm sorry for the loss of Enzo, and for the death of your son. You've sacrificed a great deal, Armanno."

"Yes, we all have, and it isn't over yet. Your friend, do you think she will mind that you're bringing someone with you?"

Liberty retrieved the cell phone from her jacket, then thought better of it. Kayla's phone line could be monitored. She would explain everything to Kayla when they got there. "I'm sure she won't mind."

Armanno studied Liberty's profile. Even in the dim light he could see the reaction she'd had to the mention of the woman she had asked him to protect. "This woman, she is important to you?"

Liberty kept her eyes on the narrow mountainous road, trying to follow in the tracks she'd made that morning. The snow had drifted, making it hard to see the edge. She gripped the wheel tighter. "Do you think I am incapable of caring about someone enough to want to protect them?" She was silent for a moment as she considered her words. "Well, up until a few days ago, you would have been right. She's an extraordinary woman, and I've brought this trouble to her doorstep. You and I have walked the path to hell, Armanno. I know what an honorable man you are and how much you love your family. You were the only one I could trust."

"I have given you my word, Liberty. I have people in place now that are watching your friend. But I am worried about this rogue. It would be best if your friend came with us to my villa in California until this is over. Can you convince her to do that?"

If only I could. Armanno was right, Kayla could be protected better if she was ensconced within the security of the villa. "I doubt it. She has family on Lone Mountain and won't want to leave her sister right now."

"Understand this, Liberty, until you fired those warning shots today, I wasn't sure that you weren't the one doing Lawrence's bidding. I needed to know about this woman and her family, so I had her investigated. I know about the accident on the mountain, and that her sister is in the hospital. I have people watching your friend's sister, and also at the lodge watching her brother." Armanno's next words reinforced the fear in Liberty's heart. "Lawrence wants you and me dead. He'll not leave one loose end that could connect him to the Talons, including the President of the United States. He will assume that Ms. Sinclair is a lover, and since he can not be sure that you have not told her about the Talons, he will have her eliminated."

Night had fallen by the time they grew close to Lone Mountain, and it was getting more difficult to drive along the logging road without headlights. Liberty pulled the SUV off the road to avoid being seen, and Armanno contacted his people in place on the mountain. He suspected that the assassin would anticipate the surveillance and be long gone, but he would not let his guard down. He was told that the pub had closed early and that there had not been any activity at the pub since, nor had they seen the owner.

They walked the last mile off the road cutting through the woods. When they reached the pub, the lights in the parking lot were off and the pub windows were dark. Heart pounding in alarm, Liberty prayed that Kayla was safe. She set down her duffel and handed the rifle to Armanno, motioning for him to cover her. A lump of fear forming in her throat, she pulled the pistol from her waistband and made her way across a small clearing until she reached the wall, then inched her way along toward the kitchen window.

Liberty could see a soft light edging around the drawn blinds. She signaled to Armanno to flank one side of the door, then when he was in position, she held up three fingers. Armanno nodded and Liberty silently used her fingers to count down three seconds, then turned the doorknob. The door was unlocked. She pushed it open and rolled into the room, landing at Kayla's feet where she was standing at the counter slicing a loaf of bread.

When the door flung open, Kayla jumped and dropped the knife she was holding. "Do you always enter a room by falling through the door with a gun in your hand?" she scolded, but the relief in her eyes at the sight of Liberty was evident.

"I thought you...well when I didn't see a light I..."

Armanno stepped in and closed the door behind him, then extended his hand to Kayla. "Ms. Sinclair, I'm Armanno Santini. It is an honor to meet such a distinguished athlete." He looked at Liberty. "Forgive the unorthodox entry, but when we saw everything dark, we thought you might be in some kind of trouble."

Kayla nodded as she scrutinized the figure of Armanno Santini. He was a distinguished looking man with gray hair and compelling brown eyes, and looked to be in as good shape as a man of younger years. His confident demeanor and charming smile were disarming, and Kayla could see why Liberty trusted him. "Please, come and sit down."

She poured coffee and set about making sandwiches before going upstairs to start a fire in the fireplace in the guestroom. She rejoined Liberty and Armanno at the table while they ate. Her leg brushed against Liberty's thigh, and she felt an instant reaction as Liberty shivered at the contact. She sipped her coffee and made small talk, but she couldn't keep her eyes or thoughts from drifting to Liberty. "I closed the pub after I heard on the radio about a helicopter crash at the airstrip at Crystal Lake. They said that they found a partially burned body that had been thrown from the wreckage."

Armanno saw the lines of worry on Kayla's face and waited for Liberty to answer. When she didn't, he explained. "The man was my friend. A sniper killed him. Under the circumstances, we couldn't bring his body back with us, nor could we afford to be detained, so I did what had to be done. By the time they discover he wasn't killed in the crash, we will be safe at my vineyard in California. In a day or two, I will arrange for his body to be brought home for a proper burial."

Armanno knew that it sounded a bit callus, but there was nothing else that they could have done. "I appreciate you going to the trouble of preparing food, Ms. Sinclair. Is there a place I may rest for a while until we can leave in the morning?"

Kayla stood. "I started a fire in the guestroom. You'll be comfortable there tonight."

Aware of the looks that passed between Liberty and Kayla, Armanno stood. "Thank you for allowing us to stay the night here."

The dim light from the bar was enough to lead Armanno and Liberty up the stairs. When Kayla stopped in front of the door to the guestroom, she turned to Armanno. "I put a few things you might need in the bathroom."

Armanno opened the door and said good night, then went in, closing the door behind him. Neither woman seemed to notice as they stood looking at each other. Liberty's anxious eyes searched Kayla's face. Her senses were acutely aware of everything, like the hitch and increase in Kayla's breathing and the slight elevation of her body heat. She even sensed that Kayla was angry about something, and that the anger was directed toward her. She reached for Kayla and moaned when her fingers touched the softness of Kayla's skin. "Kayla, I...I need...to talk to you and..." Liberty let out the breath she'd been holding and leaned against the wall, pulling Kayla in against her and burying her face in her hair. "I have so much I want to say to you, but right now all I can think of is touching you and feeling you in my arms. I want to lay with you and love you. I—"

Kayla's mouth silenced Liberty, kissing her long and hard until Liberty's knees began to give. When she pulled back, Kayla let loose a barrage of frustration that had been building all day. "I was frantic, imagining all sorts of things when I heard about the helicopter crashing at Crystal Lake. I...damn you, Liberty! I thought it was you they'd found dead!" Liberty opened her mouth to say something, but Kayla stopped her. "Don't, please, not right now. I need to be with you, too. If we have only a few hours, let's not waste them." Kayla took Liberty's hand and led her to her room.

Liberty straddled Kayla's thigh, her hand and hips moving in perfect rhythm with the passion seeking release beneath her. She felt the swell of Kayla's breast sliding against her sweat slick skin, and the intoxicating scent of Kayla's desire fueled her own. She eased deeper into the warm liquid and silken flesh that caressed her fingers. With each thrust she could feel the very beat of Kayla's heart against her fingers as Kayla's hips arched up to meet her. She had learned the places a woman longed to be touched, as well as how to bend a man to her will. It was a necessary skill. Only once before had she felt the emotion and passion she was feeling as she made love to Kayla, and that was with Yancy, so very long ago.

As she moved between Kayla's legs, she used her tongue to caress a throbbing clitoris. The whimpers and sounds of pleasure coming from Kayla left Liberty breathless. She closed her lips around the soft bundle and felt Kayla tremble and swell. As Kayla's hips started to jerk, the essence and taste of her exploded in Liberty's mouth. The exquisite pleasure of Kayla's release caused a raging chain reaction in Liberty that sent impulses to every nerve ending in her body, and an explosion of well-being flooded her brain. Her body shook and she collapsed on top of Kayla. She had given herself permission to feel. *Oh, dear God, I remember. I remember how it feels to be human.*

The firelight glistened off their bodies and Kayla whispered in Liberty's ear and trailed her fingers across her bare buttocks. "Please, I want to make love to you. I need you to give me everything." Kayla's fingers caressed the backs of Liberty's thighs, while at the same time her tongue fondled the fleshy part of her ear lobe. She edged her own thigh between Liberty's legs and easily rolled over so Liberty lay beneath her. Kayla made love to Liberty's body, her soul, and her mind. Her tongue and fingers lingered on every erogenous spot and slowly brought Liberty to orgasm, then she made love to her again.

Liberty felt a physical and emotional intimacy that she'd never before reached, not even with Yancy. When the light of dawn began to brighten the room, they lay in each other's arms, avoiding what had been unspoken through the night: time was running out. The chopper would soon be at the lodge's helipad; it was time to broach the subject of Kayla coming with them. "A helicopter is going to pick us up at the lodge's helipad. Armanno owns a vineyard outside of Santa Barbara. His family lives there, and his security is impenetrable." She hesitated, then said what had to be said. "Armanno and I both feel that your life could be in danger; you must come with us to the villa. It is the only way to insure your safety." Even in the dim light she could see Kayla's face grow pale. "Armanno has people watching Cassie and Nathan. Please come with me, Kayla. You'll be safe there."

Kayla shifted out of Liberty's arms and sat on the side of the bed and ran her fingers through her hair in frustration. "I can't leave my brother and Cassie. My sister has a long road to recovery ahead of her. You know as well as I do, her emotional outlook and the support from her family are what will make the difference. She would never understand. And besides, she would worry if I just up and left and went with you in the middle of the ski season. She'd know something is wrong. They both would. I have to stay here. Our entire future on Lone Mountain depends on this ski season."

Liberty felt the distance creeping in between them, but she had to convince Kayla that her life was in danger, that she had no choice but to go to California. "You don't understand. These people are ruthless. If you don't leave with us, you might not have any future."

Kayla abruptly stood and reached for her robe. She didn't want to hear what Liberty was saying. The stress of the past week caught up with her and she lost her temper. "This is just what we needed on Lone Mountain, what I needed! I'm not going anywhere, so there isn't any point in trying to scare me!"

Unmindful of her naked body, Liberty jumped out of bed and stomped over to where Kayla had turned her back to put on her robe. "Damn it, Kayla, I'm not trying to scare you. I brought this trouble here and I want you and your family to be safe. And the only wa—" A knock on the bedroom door interrupted and Liberty gathered her clothing that was scattered on the floor and stared at Kayla's back. "It must be time to go." She went into the bathroom to dress while Kayla opened the door.

"I am sorry to intrude, but I need to talk to you both." Armanno waited a moment until Liberty joined them. "I was not eavesdropping, but I did overhear your conversation. I'm afraid you will be coming with us, Ms. Sinclair. As long as you are accessible to Lawrence and his assassin, Liberty is vulnerable. We cannot be certain you would not be used to control her. By now the assassin undoubtedly knows all about you and what you mean to her. It's impossible to protect you here. Last night, after you both retired, I was informed that Lawrence has ordered that you and your family are to be—"

Kayla's hands went to her mouth. "Cassie...Nathan?'

Armanno quickly added, "Your sister was taken out of the hospital during the night. Both she and your brother are at La Villa Dell'uva now. You needn't worry about her care, Ms. Sinclair. A specialist will be attending to her treatment and her therapy."

"Nathan agreed to do this? The lodge...we just can't..."

"In the interest of national security, what we could tell your brother and sister was limited, but they did understand the gravity of the situation and they both expressed their concern for your safety. A crew of skilled people is already in place to run the ski resort and the pub. Both will remain open until you all can return home." Armanno's voice softened. "The loans against the ski resort and the pub have been taken care of. I am sorry, Ms. Sinclair, for this disruption in your life." Kayla sat on the edge of the bed in a dazed silence while Armanno looked at his watch. "We will be leaving in less than thirty minutes. The helicopter will take us to Glacier International, where a jet will be waiting for us."

When Armanno left the room, Kayla didn't move or speak. The expression on her face was a mixture of disbelief and anger. Liberty felt as if the light had been taken away, along with the warmth that Kayla had brought into her life. She ached to hold her and to tell her that everything would be all right, but time was not on their side. They had to go. "Is there a bag you want to pack? I could help yo..."

Kayla got up and threw off her robe and began to dress. When she spoke, her voice was distant and cold. "I can pack myself. I'll be ready in a few minutes."

Liberty stood a moment, unable to move her feet. "I'm sorry, Kayla. I'll wait downstairs."

Liberty wasn't surprised when a military helicopter landed at Lone Mountain, or when two F-15 Strike Eagles escorted the chopper to Kalispell, and then stayed with the Santini jet to the NALF airfield on southern California's San Clement Island. Armanno spent most of the flight on the phone in a private section of the plane, and Kayla didn't speak a word to him or Liberty the entire time. She avoided eye contact with Liberty by looking out the window in disbelief at one of the F-15s flying off the wing of the jet. The plane circled out over the blue waters of the Pacific as the pilot prepared to land at the base. When the pilot announced they would be landing, Armanno appeared and buckled himself into one of the leather chairs. "I know it is not easy to be shanghaied, Ms. Sinclair, but it is for your own safety. When this is over, you and your family will be returned to Montana. Meanwhile, you'll all be quite comfortable at the vineyard. My daughter Maggie will enjoy having the company, and so will my granddaughter Tiana."

Kayla diverted her eyes from the window and looked Armanno in the eye. "No, it is not easy; none of this is easy. My sister came close to losing her life just a few days ago. Her recovery is what is important to my brother and me, and yes, I do resent this disruption of our lives. My parents built Lone Mountain with a dream and their own sweat. We live a simple life, Mr. Santini, and Lone Mountain is our home. I would like to ask you a question. Few people can arrange for a military escort for a private jet. My guess is that President Kincaide arranged it. What I don't understand is this: why your vineyard? Wouldn't we all be safer at a more protected place like a military base? And how long is this situation going to go on? I believe my family and I have a right to know."

Armanno's brow furrowed. He contemplated how much more he should say. "I agree with you, you do have a right to know. I will tell you what I can. President Kincaide is planning to expose Lawrence before he is sworn in as President and that's in less than two weeks. The scandal will not only overshadow all the good Kincaide has done while in office, but it will darken his name and ruin his life, as well. He could well go to prison. Liberty and I do not intend for that to happen."

Kayla knew what Armanno meant. They were going to deal with Lawrence in the way of the Talons — assassinate him before the inauguration.

"I will also answer your question concerning La Villa Dell'uva and why we are being escorted by the United States Air Force. My family is the most important thing in my world, Ms. Sinclair, and I trust the lives of my daughter and my granddaughter to the security at the vineyard. You can rest assured that you and your family will be well protected there. The F-15s are here by order of the President to eliminate any risk while we're in the air. Missiles are easy to come by, Ms. Sinclair. A plane can go down very easily. We are being monitored by a satellite tracking system, and the F-15s can also detect and intercept any missile launched at this plane." Armanno saw Kayla blanch. "With the inauguration so close, the stakes are too high for Lawrence to allow Liberty and me to live. The chance to take us both out at the same time would be very tempting, and Lawrence might risk it. Recently I learned he was responsible for my son's death. I also have documents that would expose his involvement in the many murders that he orchestrated by misusing the Talons. This will all be resolved in a short time, and you and your family will return home."

As the wheels of the jet touched down, Kayla feared that it was just the beginning and far from over, and that Liberty Starr would soon be out of her life.

Chapter Twenty

Brady Lawrence held the phone in a death grip. He'd been in a rage since he'd been informed that Liberty Starr had contacted Armanno Santini. Nothing was going to threaten the upcoming eight years he intended to be in the White House and the rewards he would reap. Once he was sworn in, he had planned to deal with Santini, once and for all. Now, the thwarted attempts to be rid of Liberty, and her contacting Santini, were forcing him to deal with the two loose ends before the inauguration. Santini was too keen not to eventually question the timing of the accident that conveniently coincided with the investigation he was covertly conducting into the activities involving the Talons. If Santini discovered that his son's death was no accident, he would leave no stone unturned to get his revenge, and it would be swift. As long as that man and Liberty were alive, they were a threat.

Lawrence yelled into the receiver, "What the fuck is going on with you? Time is running out. This makes three times you missed taking her out, and now she has teamed up with Santini. You know what I think? I think you've been playing cat and mouse with her all along, and now Starr and her little cunt are under Santini's protection. I'm beginning to feel like I should never have trusted you to deal with her at all. Maybe she *is* the best of the Talons. If she comes for you, no — *when* she comes, you can damn well bet *she* won't miss."

A laugh of amusement echoed from the other end of the phone. "Figure all that out by yourself? Well, the game is over. I'll finish Liberty and Santini before you stand before the world and swear to uphold the honor of the office of the President of the United States. Here's something more for you to think about while you're waiting, Brady. Your little suggestion about taking them down while they're in the air won't work. A military chopper picked them up in Kalispell and two F-15s are flying wing off Santini's jet, I presume to California. Someone's damn serious about protecting Liberty and Santini. You would have known this earlier if you had answered my call. Could it be that President Kincaide knows of your little deception with the Talons, and your house of cards is beginning to tumble? You would be better off spending your time thinking about what Kincaide might be up to, rather than wasting it on concern with what I'm doing. Whether you go down or not, rest assured, Lawrence, Liberty Starr is mine. Make sure you have transferred the money to my account in Switzerland by the end of the day."

Lawrence heard a click and the line went dead. The palms of his hands were sweaty and beads of perspiration formed on his brow. *Even if Kincaide knows everything, I still have the upper hand. He would never disgrace his family name or his office by exposing the fact that he was the one who had created the Talons. Or would he?* Lawrence felt the uncertainty pounding against his skull with every heartbeat. If Kincaide had discovered his complicity in the illegal actions of the Talons, he would go to any means to protect Santini and Starr. He had to find out what Kincaide was up to and stop him, before everything he'd worked for unraveled. He picked up the phone and pushed the extension that connected him to Kincaide's secretary.

"Yes, Mr. Vice President."

"Miss Tollefson, put me through to the President."

"I'm sorry. He is unavailable, Mr. Vice President. May I take a message?"

"Interrupt him, I need to speak with him."

"I'm sorry, sir, the President is not taking any calls."

Lawrence slammed down the phone, got up and poured a drink, then went to look out the window of his office in the West Wing. Wade Kincaide had outlived his usefulness. Lawrence raised his glass to the Washington Monument that was visible from his window. "A toast. What better way to be remembered and idolized than as a fallen leader?"

Wade Kincaide sat across from the Attorney General and handed him the statement he had prepared. "I need a promise from you that you will never disclose the true identity of any of the Talons, and that the identities of Armanno Santini and Liberty Starr will be protected. Every Talon died a hero's death. I do not want their families and loved ones to know of this. I want my promise of a new life for the remaining Talons to be honored.

"Please don't do this, Wade. We can find another way."

"There isn't any other way, Mack. I created the Talons. I am responsible for what Lawrence has done by using their skills. The assassinations and cold-blooded murders he has ordered are beyond anyone's imagination. The blood money totals in the millions, and that's just in the bank accounts you were able to trace. His association with militant leaders and factions antagonistic to this country is traitorous. He helped put tyrants in power and has raked off a fortune from the aid he has given to whomever offered him the highest price."

"You didn't know, Wade. Damn it, you didn't know how Lawrence was using the Talons."

"It's no excuse, Mack. I should have been less trusting and more aware of what was going on with my own people. The agents who thought they were following my orders did so thinking it was to fight the war against the enemies of our country. When I gave Lawrence the order to disband the Talons, I signed the documents, as I'd promised, giving each agent a permanent identity and the economic means for a new life. Now they're all dead, except for Liberty Starr, Armanno Santini, and Lawrence's murderous assassin."

"Damn it, Wade, if you do this, you'll not only go to prison, your name will be written in the history books as the most infamous president in the history of our country. Think, Wade, please think what this will do, the enormity of the repercussions."

The agony of his decision was evident in Wade Kincaide's tired eyes and haggard face. "Would you rather see his corruption and evil sitting in this office, Mack? Can you imagine what direction our country, and the world, would take if he were allowed to sit in the Oval Office?"

A look of determination crossed the younger face of the Attorney General. "We could solve the problem another way, Wade. We could—"

Wade Kincaide raised his hand to stop his brother before he could finish what he was going to say. "You are an honest and honorable man, and I don't want to hear what you are about to say. Promise me, brother, that you'll let me handle this my way."

Mack Kincaide sat heavily back in his chair without saying anything. He didn't care what it cost him personally, he was not going to let his brother go down in history as a traitor and a murderer.

Armanno, Liberty, and Kayla exited the Santini jet and were escorted to another military chopper for transport to Armanno's vineyard. As soon as the chopper was in the air, the two F-15s appeared again. A short while later, in a heavy downpour under low hanging storm clouds, they were landing within the walls of the Santini enclave. Two well-armed guards dressed in khaki BDUs appeared out of a Hummer and greeted Armanno, then loaded everyone into the vehicle and started toward the villa.

Liberty had once been to La Villa Dell'uva, the beautiful Villa of the Grapes, when Armanno's daughter Maggie had been kidnapped by a serial killer. Then, the vines were laden with the purple and white grapes, and the sweet smell of orange blossoms hung heavy in the air. Now, the rows of grapevines were barren and dormant, like the feeling in Liberty heart. With Kayla's continued cold silence, Liberty felt the distance growing between them. It pained her that Kayla was so close but she couldn't reach out and touch her, hold her. She couldn't fault Kayla. She had put Kayla and her family in harm's way.

The mood was as dark as the skies overhead as they drove along the vineyard road toward Armanno's villa. Kayla remained quiet, staring out the window of the Hummer. She was distraught about Cassie and her brother, and was anxious to see if they were all right. She had put her family through enough when she'd disappeared after Addie's death. She didn't know how she was going to explain what was going on, much less her relationship with Liberty. So much was at stake: Cassie's recovery, the future of the lodge. Everything was happening so quickly that she hadn't had time to sort out her feelings. Liberty and Armanno Santini were assassins and had killed many people while working for the President of the United States. Now someone was trying to kill them both, as well as her and her family. And the Vice President, President-elect Lawrence, was responsible. The entire story was incredible, impossible to believe.

At the villa, the two guards quickly retrieved the one suitcase Kayla brought and escorted Armanno and his guests across the stone paved driveway into the house. They passed through a heavy iron gate, then through massive stained glass doors into an entryway. The stucco villa was a fortress, but that didn't take away from its charm and architectural harmony. When he created La Villa Dell'uva, Armanno captured the essence of old Italy, with its warm muted colors, fresco panels, and polished terrazzo floors.

"I'm sure you want to see your sister and brother without delay, Ms. Sinclair. My assistant, McKenzie, will show you the way. Liberty, will you join me for a moment in my office?"

Liberty recognized the attractive woman walking toward them. She had been at the Cipriano villa the night Armanno's daughter Maggie was kidnapped. Seeing McKenzie brought back good memories of her best friend, Jake Biscayne, the closest thing Liberty had to family. As Kayla followed McKenzie up the stairs, Liberty thought about the night that Jake had told her about McKenzie Quinn and the woman that she was in love with, Cara Cipriano Vitorre. It was right after Liberty had killed a drug lord and helped to rescue Maggie. She and Jake were on a search and destroy mission of the cocaine fields in Colombia. Liberty remembered the night; it was after several grueling days in the muggy heat of the high country. The liberated villagers, grateful to be free from the drug cartel, had shown the agents where the graves were. Three days later they had dug up and recovered the last of the remains of the brutally slain peasants who had been enslaved to grow and process the white death. The night they'd finished, they had both gotten falling down drunk. She'd held Jake as she cried her heart out over the loss of Cara. Liberty felt Jake's pain and loss that night. It was the last time Liberty had felt a deep connection with another person...until she met Kayla on Christmas Eve.

Chapter Twenty-One

McKenzie Quinn introduced herself to Kayla as she led Kayla through the villa. She'd noticed the obvious tension and Kayla's coolness toward Liberty when they arrived, and with every step, McKenzie could feel Kayla's anxiety building. When they reached Cassie's room, McKenzie stopped, and said in her calm Irish voice, "I don't believe in beatin' around the bush, Ms. Sinclair, so I'll come straight to the point. I know the reason and the circumstances that have brought you all to La Villa Dell'uva. No one but Liberty knows what compelled her to stay on at Lone Mountain to help you find your sister. However, by doing so, she exposed herself, thereby putting her own life in danger. Heaven knows it wasn't the smartest thing she could have done, but Cassie's life was saved. If she hadn't stayed, Cassie might have died. I understand your frustration at being torn away from your life, but you and your family will be safe here, and we will do everything possible to make your stay comfortable and to ensure Cassie's recovery. I'm not sure how much you know, and it isn't important that I do, but the situation is as grave as it can be. The next few days are critical to the future of our country, Ms. Sinclair."

Kayla's temper flared. Both she and her patience were exhausted with all the innuendo and cloak and dagger activities that had disrupted their lives. She was tired, and all she wanted was to see Cassie and Nathan. Her words were sharp, with an edge of agitation. "Excuse me, Ms. Quinn, but what is important to me right now is seeing my family."

McKenzie nodded and opened the door to Cassie's room. The younger Sinclair was lying on a padded table and a woman was stretching the muscles of one of her legs. Another disheveled looking woman sat at a desk jotting down notes, and looked up as they entered. Nathan rushed over to Kayla and pulled her into his arms. His relief upon seeing her was evident on his face.

"We've been so worried about you, Sis. Are you all right?"

Kayla hugged him and looked over his shoulder toward Cassie. "I'm fine. How's Cassie?"

Smiling, Cassie sat up and carefully dangled her sore feet over the edge of the table. "Get on over here and give me a hug, too, and ask me yourself!"

Kayla was pleased at how much Cassie's demeanor had improved since she had seen her last, less than twenty-four hours before. Her eyes went to Cassie's feet, then to her hands. She had seen the look of frostbite many times before, but the sight of the swelling and deep purple color sent a sharp pain straight to her heart.

Cassie wrapped her arms around Kayla's neck. "I won't break. You can hug me, ya know."

Tears formed in Kayla's eyes as she held on to Cassie. When she finally released her clasp, she wiped the tears from her eyes. "Honey, you don't know how worried I've been. I love you, little sister. Do you know that? I know I don't tell you and Nathan that enough, but—"

"Hush, everything is all right. Nathan and I have been just as concerned about you. Can you tell us what's going on here? All we were told is that it was a matter of national security, and that we were brought here by the order of the President of the United States himself. You have some explaining to do, Kayla."

McKenzie stepped forward. "Mr. Santini sends his apology for not being here to brief you all, but he is attending to an important matter that couldn't wait. He has asked me to tell you that he will speak to you all this evening after dinner. Meanwhile, I'm sure Kayla would like to meet your therapist and your doctor, Cassie."

Cassie smiled at the therapist who had been working on the circulation in her legs. "Sis, this is Lynne, my therapist, and Doctor Avril Bagenstos."

Doctor Bagenstos brushed a strand of hair out of her eyes, then pushed her glasses up on top of her head. She had closely watched the interaction between Cassie and her family. The support of the siblings would certainly help her patient's recovery. She approached Kayla and extended her hand. "Your sister has been anxious for you to arrive, Ms. Sinclair. I have examined her, and I've reviewed the progress notes from Dr. Mican. The quick response and treatment Cassie received when she was brought in not only saved her life, but most likely her fingers and her toes. I believe we can save them. We have already started Cassie on a therapy plan that has had great success with victims of frostbite in Canada." The doctor turned and gathered the papers off the desk. "I am sure you would like to talk to your family, so Lynne and I will give you some privacy." The disheveled doctor searched through her pockets, then absently reached into her hair and slipped her glasses back down on her nose, spilling the papers she was holding onto the floor.

Lynne and Nathan bent to pick them up. After the rumpled doctor and the therapist left the room, Kayla asked. "Does this doctor know what the hell she's doing?" Both Nathan and Cassie burst into laughter at the look on Kayla's face. "What? Did I say something?"

Cassie was trying to hold back the giggles. "I know she doesn't look it, but Doctor Bagenstos is not only a medical doctor, she is a leading scientist with the agency of Defense Research and Development of Canada. Among other things, she helped to develop the frostbite protocols that have been adopted by many governments for their military personnel. I know she's a bit...well...unusual, but she does know her business. Mr. Santini has her flown in every few weeks. She has been directing the care and therapy of Maggie Santini. Seems Mr. Santini is connected in high places."

Kayla's face brightened. "And she really thinks your fingers and toes will be all right?"

"She's sure of it. I was taken for a technetium scan as soon as we arrived. Dr. Bagenstos met me there and was quite encouraged at the results."

Kayla cringed as she looked at Cassie's toes and fingers. "Are you in a lot of pain?"

"More like a throbbing and an ache deep in the bone, but the pain medication the doctor is giving me takes the edge off. Now, can you tell us why we're here, and what Liberty Starr has to do with all this? And please, if you hadn't noticed, I'm all grown up now, Kayla, and don't need to be protected. Give, what's the story?"

When Kayla had finished telling what she knew, Cassie and Nathan sat looking at her. Nathan managed to swallow, then uttered, "You're kidding, right?"

"I wish I was, Nathan, but everything I've told you is true, and yes, it is hard to believe. I...I didn't know...about the Talons or President Kincaide and Lawrence's involvement until last night. Liberty—"

Cassie interrupted, "How awful for Liberty. To give up who you are, your very life, thinking that you're doing it for your country, and then to find out that you're being used for someone's personal agenda. Are we in danger from this person who is trying to kill her? Is that why we're here?"

Kayla knew by the look in both Cassie and Nathan's eyes that there was no point in denying it. "Brady Lawrence would not take the chance that Liberty had told me anything. He had given his assassin a directive to kill us to erase all doubt."

Before anyone could say anything, the door opened and a young girl burst into the room. "Cassie, Mom wants to know if you're coming to the pool."

Cassie laughed. "Yes, Tiana, I'm coming. First, come here and meet my sister Kayla."

Barely able to contain her excitement, Tiana stood in front of

Kayla. "Are you the one that won all the gold medals in the Olympics? Cassie told me about you. She said that you are the best ever. Could you teach me to ski?"

Kayla smiled for the first time that day. "It's nice to meet you, too, Tiana. And Cassie is a much better skier than I am. If you come to Montana, I'm sure she would be glad to teach you."

"Avril says Cassie won't be skiing for a while, but maybe next year I can come to Montana and she can teach me?"

"What about it, Cassie? Think you can teach Tiana to navigate those moguls?"

"You bet I will. She'll be a natural on the mountain. Tiana, how about if you help me into that wheelchair and then you can push me to the pool?" Cassie looked at Kayla and saw the exhaustion. "Why don't you go find your room and rest, Sis? You look tired. We'll meet up later for dinner."

Kayla nodded. She did feel fatigued and a hot shower sounded like just what she needed to take some time to put things into perspective. Cassie's thoughtful comments about Liberty were gnawing at her. She'd been selfish, thinking only of how all this was affecting her and her family and not about how hard it must be for Liberty. Her conscience pricked her because of her unkind behavior toward Liberty all day.

Surprisingly, Kayla's room was almost as big as the entire second floor of the pub. The bathing area had several showerheads, and a marble whirlpool tub was elevated and surrounded on three sides by smoked glass. The view was spectacular — looking out over the vineyards to the blue hazy mountains off in the distance in one direction, and to the Pacific Ocean in the other. Kayla had intended to take a quick shower, then go find Cassie and observe her therapy. Instead she eyed the whirlpool tub and the breathtaking view, and decided to indulge herself. She undressed and turned on the jets, then eased her weary body down into the soothing water. The rhythmic motion of the water pounding against her body relaxed her, but the hint of soreness between her legs, that she'd ignored all day, reminded her of the night before and making love with Liberty. Images of Liberty lying between her thighs, and the memory of the feel of her mouth, had her heart fluttering and her body aching with desire. She'd taken the passion offered, and in return, gave what she thought she could never give to a woman again — her own passion. Without thought to Liberty's feelings, she'd selfishly blamed her for all that was happening, when Liberty had risked her own life by staying. That realization clouded Kayla's thoughts with guilt.

She must have dozed off, for when she woke, the light was

fading and the shadows had grown long across the vineyard. She was drying off when the phone rang. It was Nathan telling her to come down for dinner. After she dressed, Kayla found her way through the wing of the villa toward the stairs. The walls absorbed the warmth from the ceiling apertures that radiated soft hues of natural light. Everywhere she looked was a statement in architectural resplendence, a perfect blend of old and new. Kayla stopped to look at a painting on the wall. It was Armanno Santini and what was apparently his family. The young man standing next to Armanno was handsome, a younger version of his father. The older woman was elegant, aristocratic looking, with beautiful blue eyes. Kayla was drawn to the younger woman in the picture. She was tall and slender, and had the same gorgeous eyes and was every bit as exquisite as the older woman. Kayla could see the resemblance to the little girl she'd met earlier.

"That's Maggie, Tiana's mother."

Kayla turned to see Liberty looking at the painting on the wall as if she could read her mind.

"Maggie is a special lady and very stunning. You'll meet her at dinner."

Kayla felt an irrational twinge of jealousy and stormed past Liberty down the stairs with Liberty following, trying to catch up to her.

"Damn it, Kayla, wait, I need to talk to you."

Kayla stopped abruptly and turned to face Liberty, who almost ran into her. Liberty instinctively put her arms around Kayla to prevent her from falling. Kayla didn't try to push her away, her body responding before her mind could censor the action. "You're right, I'm acting childishly, taking all of this out on you. They're waiting dinner for us. Can we talk later?"

"You have every right to be upset, Kayla. You and your family are only in this predicament because of me. I want to talk to you before I...I leave. Can you come to my room after dinner?"

Kayla's heart started to pound. "You're leaving? When?"

Liberty could see the concern in Kayla's eyes...and something else — desire. Kayla didn't mind being in her arms. Liberty's voice was husky with emotion. "Soon. I need to see you before I go." Her lips were on Kayla's and Kayla's arms had just circled her neck when they heard a slight cough as Nathan appeared at the bottom of the steps.

Kayla reluctantly pulled away and whispered, "I'll come to your room after Cassie is settled in."

They joined Nathan at the foot of the stairs. "Sorry. I was just coming to find you for dinner."

"It's okay, Nathan. I'm sorry to have kept everyone waiting. I fell asleep."

When they entered the dining room, Armanno stood and seated Kayla, then Liberty. He smiled and took Maggie's hand. "Ms. Sinclair, I think the only one you haven't met is my daughter Maggie."

Kayla looked at the woman from the family portrait. She was a bit older and, if anything, even more beautiful than she was in the picture. Kayla's eyes went to the wheelchair, and she felt guilty for her jealous thoughts on the stairs. Liberty was right — Maggie Santini was striking.

When she smiled and spoke, she radiated charm and friendliness. "Welcome to our home, Kayla. I am a big fan of yours. It was so exciting to watch you ski in the Olympics, and an even bigger thrill watching you win." Maggie smiled at her daughter who was hanging on every word.

It was impossible not to be captivated by Maggie's eyes. The artist who had painted the picture hanging in the stairway had captured the color, and her loveliness. "Please, call me Kayla."

"Tiana says you've invited her to come to Lone Mountain next year to learn how to ski." Maggie laughed, "We just might take you up on that. If you can rig up a pair of skis for me."

Kayla knew that Maggie was trying to make her feel comfortable. It was easy to understand what Liberty meant when she said that Maggie Santini was a special person. Kayla looked at Cassie and smiled, saying a silent prayer that Doctor Bagenstos was right and that next winter Cassie would be out of her wheelchair and back on the slopes.

Chapter Twenty-Two

After dinner, Armanno excused himself and went to his den to take a phone call. When he returned, he requested that everyone gather in the living room. His voice was serious, and an edge of uncertainty filled the air as they waited for McKenzie to return from putting Tiana down for the night. Maggie spoke quietly to her father, while Cassie and Nathan talked with Lynne and Dr. Bagenstos.

Kayla's thoughts kept wandering across the room to where Liberty stood at the window, looking out into the darkness. She'd been quiet through dinner, only speaking when Tiana asked her a question. Kayla couldn't imagine the isolated life that Liberty had lived, but she was familiar with the lonely, solitary look she saw in Liberty's eyes. She couldn't accept that Liberty was leaving, that she would never see her again. Liberty had made her feel things that she hadn't felt in a long time, things that she was afraid to feel and never thought she would again. She had just decided to go talk to Liberty when one of the guards entered the room and approached Armanno.

As the guard quietly said something to him, a subtle look of concern crossed Armanno's face. Armanno stood. "Excuse me, please. This will only take a moment."

A few minutes later, McKenzie returned and sat beside Maggie, taking her hand and leaning in to brush her lips against Maggie's cheek. "Your father won't be long; he'll explain everything when he returns. Then, my love, we'll go upstairs and I'll help you into the whirlpool. Afterwards, I'll give you a good massage before we go to bed. Would you like that, darling?"

Maggie smiled at McKenzie and whispered something in her ear. McKenzie blushed as a salacious twinkle brightened her green eyes. Kayla was taken aback for a moment as she realized Maggie and McKenzie were lovers. She'd been so absorbed in her own thoughts, she'd failed to see the loving touches and adoration the two women had for one another. Maggie's eyes worshiped McKenzie and McKenzie glowed in the light of Maggie's affection.

"You do know the way to my heart, Kenzie. Just the mention of a massage sounds heavenly. I am a bit sore tonight, and I'm going to blame it all on Lynne and Avril. They really worked me out in the pool today. Actually, all of their hard work has strengthened my arms. Today I was able to swim the entire length of the pool and back."

McKenzie beamed with excitement as she threw her arms around Maggie's neck and hugged her. "Love, that's the best news ever. I'm so proud of you!"

Maggie stroked McKenzie face. "You are my inspiration, sweetheart. Your faith makes me believe anything is possible."

Kayla felt like she was intruding on a very private moment between the two women and was about to give them some privacy when Maggie turned to her. Maggie's gaze followed to where Kayla's eyes were fixed on Liberty across the room. "She's quite the enigma, as well as beautiful. Even before she joined the Bureau, she was a loner. She grew up in New Mexico with the Pueblo Indians, never knowing who her parents were. With her blonde hair and hazel eyes, it's doubtful that they were Pueblo. Looking at her, it's hard to believe what she's been through, especially these past eight years."

Kayla nodded. The more she learned about Liberty, the less a mystery she seemed. "She'd been wounded the day I met her. She sat most of the day in my pub and never said a word. Just sat there looking at the door, as if she was waiting for something or someone. I've seen the scars on her body and I can hardly imagine what emotional scars she carries. She was the last person I expected to see on the mountain the day of the avalanche, but there she was."

Maggie could see the struggle going on in Kayla's mind behind the look in her eyes. "Are you lovers?" Kayla didn't answer and Maggie retreated. "That's too personal. I'm sorry."

"Don't be sorry; I just don't know how to answer that. Are we lovers? Yes, one could say that we are. To be honest, the first time we were together, love had nothing to do with it. We were drawn to each other out of need, each driven by our own ghosts. After my partner died in an avalanche, I drowned my grief in a bottle. When Cassie was buried in the avalanche, it was as if I were reliving my nightmare all over again. I wanted a drink, and that need was more powerful than staying sober for Cassie and Nathan, or for myself. One night, if Liberty hadn't intervened, I would have given up my sobriety."

Kayla thought for a moment before continuing. "Love has many faces and touches a heart in different ways. From the first moment I laid my five-year-old eyes on Addie, I think I knew that I loved her and would forever. That will never change. At the risk of sounding sappy, it was as if we were meant to be together. When she died, I died too. Death leaves a heartache that needs to heal in its own time and in its own way. If I had met Liberty under different circumstances, if she wasn't who she is, who knows? Maybe we could have fallen in love. I haven't been...kind to her since my family and I were forced to come here. Now, watching her standing there alone, she seems distant, and I can't blame her."

McKenzie, who had been quiet during the conversation between

Kayla and Maggie, spoke up. "She is in a place right now that we can only imagine, Kayla. As far-fetched, as all this seems, Liberty and Armanno may be the only ones who can save our country from the dark days ahead if Brady Lawrence is allowed to become President. They're both preparing to do battle with very some very powerful, corrupt people."

Kayla knew what McKenzie was saying was true, but she didn't want to face it. "Can I ask you a question about your father, Maggie?"

"If I can answer, I will. We're all in this together."

"All of the others gave up their identities when they joined the Talons. Why did your father keep his?"

Maggie looked at McKenzie and McKenzie nodded. "My father is a wealthy man and has business interests in every corner of the world, Kayla. He can move about in most countries without suspicion, and he can use his connections and his name to gather information without drawing attention. In one capacity or another, he's worked for the government in covert operations since he was a young man. When President Kincaide approached him about the Talons, he felt the cause was just and agreed to take command of the unit."

"Your father left the Talons?"

Maggie looked down at her legs; McKenzie squeezed her hand and answered for her. "Armanno suspected something unauthorized was going on with the Talons and started to investigate. Lawrence got nervous and arranged an accident for him. It put Maggie in this chair and killed her brother Robert."

Maggie's eyes misted over as McKenzie continued. "It was a hard time for all of us. Armanno came home to grieve. He devoted all of his resources and attention to Maggie's recovery and to Tiana. He had begun to make the villa a secure place for his family long before the accident. When Robert and Maggie were growing up here at the vineyards, he wanted them to live their lives as normally as possible, safe from the threats that a man in his position fears. After the accident, he turned it into a virtual fortress to protect Maggie and Tiana."

Maggie gripped McKenzie's hand. "My father always suspected the crash that killed my brother and paralyzed me was not an accident. He has worked unrelentingly to gather the evidence needed to prove Lawrence was responsible. At the same time, he documented that Lawrence had been using the Talons for his own corrupt agenda."

The narrative stopped as Armanno entered the room and walked over to Liberty. After a few words, he turned to face everyone in the room. "You are my guests and my family. You are all here because of your connection to either me or to Liberty. I want to assure you that your safety is being taken care of. President Kincaide has ordered military protection for the villa. A Delta Force unit is taking up positions around the perimeter, and another unit is being positioned inside on the grounds and around the house."

Armanno's eyes went from one person to the next, trying to judge their reactions. "Right now, this is the safest place you could be in the world. La Villa Dell'uva is your home until you can resume your lives. From this point on, you will not have knowledge of anything other than what I have just told you. That includes my family, with the exception of McKenzie, who is also my lawyer. It is better for you this way. When this is finished, you will not be culpable for anything that has transpired. If we do not succeed in stopping Brady Lawrence, the evidence that will put him away for a very long time is in the hands of the Attorney General, Matthew Kincaide, and will be turned over to several major newspapers as well as the Justice Department."

Armanno went over to Maggie and kissed her on the cheek. "This will be over soon. I love you, Magdalene." He turned to McKenzie. "You have completed everything I have asked of you?"

"Yes, sir. I have handled everything personally."

"Good, now you take care of my daughter and my granddaughter until I return." Armanno turned toward the gathering in the room. His tired, dark eyes made contact with each person. "I bid you all a good night. For now, this is your home; please make yourselves comfortable. If there is anything you need, the staff will provide it. Now, please excuse me."

The mood was somber as everyone absorbed Armanno's words. Still holding tight to McKenzie's hand, Maggie sat straight in her wheelchair and graciously said, "I too will say good night. Please, try to get some rest." Then she looked lovingly at McKenzie, "Darling, I would like to check on Tiana. Will you come?" McKenzie nodded and said good night, then pushed Maggie toward the lift.

Lynne and Avril were too keyed up to sleep and decided to take a swim, then go to the small theater off the therapy wing to watch a movie. Lynne's voice shook a bit as she offered, "Hey, if anyone wants to join me and the doc for a swim, you're welcome."

Cassie looked at Kayla, who seemed in deep thought, then she looked at Nathan who was standing behind her wheelchair. "I think I will turn in, too. It's been a long day and I'm a bit tired. Nathan, do you mind helping me upstairs?"

"Sure, Cassie, Kayla, do you want to go up with us?"

Kayla looked across the room to where Liberty had been standing, but she was gone. She hoped that Liberty hadn't left the villa. "You two go ahead. I'll be up in a minute."

When everyone had left the room, Kayla went to the window. Beams of white light searched the grounds; shadows dressed in dark fatigues moved quickly about, blending in with the darkness. A sense of loss filled her as she watched the scene playing out. McKenzie was right — it was hard to imagine the life of the Talons, the life that Liberty had lived. She recalled the frightened look in Liberty's eyes as she'd traced the scars on her body with her fingertips after they had made love. She knew now that the fear she'd seen in Liberty's eyes was because her soul was struggling to give her permission to feel and to accept the honest touch of another human being. Kayla closed her eyes and held back the tears that threatened. *Liberty, I need to see you. Please don't be gone.*

Armanno had gone upstairs to check on Tiana and to say good night to Maggie and McKenzie. As he walked downstairs toward his office, he saw Kayla standing by the window in the living room and went to speak to her. "I appreciate what an ordeal this had been for you, Ms. Sinclair. What you see out there has to be upsetting for you. I am sorry for that."

Kayla turned to face him. "You have gone out of your way to be kind and to protect my family and me, Mr. Santini, and I appreciate it. I would like it if you would call me Kayla." With a troubled look in her eyes, Kayla asked, "Can you tell me if she's still here?"

Armanno crossed the room and stood next to her. "She's briefing the commander of the Delta team, then she'll check the security. The Talons went through Delta Force training, but the Talon training went far beyond. If anyone can find a weak spot where an assassin could penetrate, it will be Liberty." Armanno paused, debating how much to say, then continued. "Liberty hasn't known a lot of affection in her life. I believe that she cares for you, perhaps even more than she realizes. She's trying to find a place in her heart that will give her purpose and peace before we go after the assassin. Knowing you are safe will help her to do that."

Kayla face paled. She fought to keep in the fears that were tearing at her. "No matter what happens, there's no way in hell Liberty can come out of this, is there?"

Armanno knew that giving Kayla false hope would be wrong. "No...no way in hell."

Chapter Twenty-Three

Wade Kincaide's concentration was off as he sat in the Oval Office reviewing a list of pardons he was considering. Also awaiting his attention was a sheaf of laws that had been passed by Congress before the Christmas adjournment. He had to decide which ones he might have to veto, but his thoughts were on the meeting that he'd had earlier with his brother. Mack had confronted Brady Lawrence with the evidence he'd compiled proving Lawrence's corruption of the Talons. The President-Elect was given an ultimatum: resign, citing a health problem that would prevent him from performing his presidential duties, or have the evidence of his treason turned over to the Justice Department.

Kincaide was troubled but not surprised by Mack's description of Lawrence's violent outburst when he learned that all of his ill-gotten accounts had been traced and frozen. Lawrence lost control and started yelling threats loud enough to bring the Secret Service agents running. Kincaide looked at the picture of his family on his desk, relieved that Lawrence had taken to using the Vice President's office in the Executive Office Building more often than his office in the West Wing. There was little doubt in his mind that Lawrence would resort to anything, even to threatening the lives of his family.

Anxious to finish for the night and go upstairs to spend with his wife what was left of a very trying day, Kincaide put aside the papers that he'd been reading. In just a few days they would be moving out of the White House into a future that was uncertain. With a heavy heart, he picked up the picture of his family. He would not be able to protect them from the disgrace and pain that would come if Lawrence didn't see reason and step down. If the evidence was turned over to the Justice Department, would his children understand why he had created the Talons? How would they cope with their father being portrayed as a traitor? The Kincaide name would be tainted for generations to come.

Flanked by his Secret Service agents, Brady Lawrence arrogantly stomped down the hall of the White House toward the Oval Office. When he reached the door to the office of the President's secretary, he didn't bother to stop but barged right past the Secret Service detail. Face contorted with rage, Lawrence clenched his fists and pounded on the secretary's desk. "Tell him I want to see him, now!"

Alarmed, and ready to protect the President, the Secret Service agents inside the secretary's office put their hands on their weapons. Hearing the commotion, President Kincaide got up from his desk, crossed the room, and opened the door. When he saw Lawrence's state of agitation and growing aggression, he waved off the agents and stepped aside. Lawrence was about to enter the President's office when the agent in charge stepped in front of him to prevent his entrance.

"Sir, given your emotional state, I will ask you to go away and calm down before talking to the President, or I will ask that you submit to a search before I can allow you to enter the Oval Office."

"Like hell, I will! Do you know who you're talking to? Get out of my way!"

Lawrence attempted to push past the agent and the President's Secret Service agents pulled their weapons, stunning the agents that had accompanied Lawrence. The agent standing in front of Lawrence spoke calmly and clearly. "The duty of everyone in this room is to protect the President against all threats, and that includes you and your security detail, Mr. Vice President. I'm afraid we have a situation here."

Lawrence shook with rage. He looked to his Secret Service agents as if he expected them to intercede. When they didn't, he unwillingly stepped back and jerked open his suit jacket so he could be searched. One of the agents stepped forward and waved a wand over Lawrence's body, then patted him down and stepped back.

"Thank you, Mr. Vice President."

Lawrence's pupils were dilated, his eyes glazed over and filled with hatred as he pushed past the agent into the Oval Office. Kincaide waved everyone off and closed the door. The President's secretary, the Marine guards, and the agents stood uneasily outside the door, looking at one another and wondering what the hell was going on. A few minutes later, the sound of angry voices, scuffling, and a crash had everyone converging on the Oval Office. President Kincaide stood over a prone Brady Lawrence, pounding his fist repeatedly into his face.

Everyone stood awkwardly watching, at a loss as to what to do. Nervously, the senior agent stepped forward. "Sir, do you need any assistance?"

Kincaide grabbed Lawrence by the lapels of his suit and jerked him up off the floor, then threw him toward one of the agents. "Get this slimy bastard out of my sight and out of the White House. Escort him off the property, with orders not to allow him anywhere near here as long as I am still the President! If he tries to return, shoot him!"

"You can't do that, you son of a bitch." Lawrence wildly pushed away from the agent and lunged at Kincaide, only to be stopped by a well-placed uppercut. Lawrence went down again, bleeding from cuts on his face and from his nose.

"No? Just watch me. You dare threaten my family!" Shaking with fury, Kincaide grabbed Lawrence, dragged him along the floor, and flung him out the door of the Oval Office and into his secretary's office. "Remember what I said, you murderous bastard. Call off your assassin. If anything happens to my family or the remaining Talons or their families, you'll not only go down hard, I'll kill you myself!" The President looked at the dumbfounded agents standing with their mouths agape. "Now, pick up this trash and get him out of here!"

As two of the agents holstered their weapons and went to assist Lawrence up from the floor, Kincaide turned his back to go into his office. A split second later, there was a flash and the deafening roar of the agent's gun that somehow appeared in Lawrence's hand. Bodies moved in slow motion and disbelief seized the hearts of those who watched as President Kincaide went down. Before Lawrence could fire a second shot, he was hit, his body ripped with bullets, his blood spattering the cream colored walls.

All hell broke loose. People were running and shouting. The senior agent yelled into the mic on his lapel as he knelt on the floor pressing his hands against the flow of blood coming from the President's back. "Grey Hawk is down! I repeat, Grey Hawk is down!"

The President's body lay in a growing pool of blood as the Secret Service agent tried frantically to find a pulse and to determine if Kincaide was still breathing. Another agent quickly regained his composure and began giving orders. "Get everyone out of here and follow the procedure to secure the White House! Move! Move!"

The Secret Service and the Marine guards pushed everyone out of the secretary's office and cleared the West Wing. Minutes later, surrounded by an army of Secret Service agents, Wade Kincaide was being rushed on a gurney toward the helipad.

Wailing sirens tore through the night, and the throbbing streets of DC could feel the urgency in the air. The protocol adopted after September 11, 2001 put the capital under the strictest security measures. A flurry of activity at Bethesda Navel Hospital began within minutes of the shooting at the White House, following well-planned emergency response procedures. The response team, including the specially trained trauma surgeons, were alerted and ready to react. The instant that Marine One set down, the teams were rushing toward it. It didn't take long for the activity around the White House and Bethesda to alert every Federal agency, as well as every television network and reporter in the city. All rushed frenziedly to both scenes.

A light in the upstairs bedroom of the brownstone home of Ingrid Sheppard came on. A few minutes later the Vice President-Elect, dressed in a robe, was answering her door. Scott Elliot, the Secret Service agent in charge of the Vice Present-Elect's security detail, was standing on her step, along with several others. "Ma'am, I'm sorry to wake you. May we come in?"

Over the agent's shoulder, Ingrid could see the heightened activity in front of her house. She shook off the remaining grogginess of sleep and stepped back into the entryway. "Yes, please come in. Something has happened."

"Yes, Ma'am."

Ingrid led the way into the entry hall, then saw her partner standing on the stairs, tying her robe. Their eyes locked for a moment, each silently acknowledging that something monumental was going on. Ingrid's housekeeper entered the room, apparently also awakened by the knocking. "Mrs. Garast, would you please make some coffee? You know how bad mine tastes, and something tells me we're going to need plenty of it." Mrs. Garast hurried toward the kitchen and Ingrid directed her attention back to the agents. "Please, let's go into the living room." Ingrid held out her hand to the woman standing on the stairs. "Marty."

Ingrid took her partner's hand and together they joined the agents in their living room. Agent Elliot turned on the television. Every station had interrupted their regular programming with a special report. Those in the room watched the unfolding scene.

An out of breath reporter pushed a receiver into her ear as she stood some distance away from Bethesda Naval Hospital waiting for her cue. A telephoto lens panned to a shot of the helipad at Bethesda. "Behind me, you see Marine One. It arrived at Bethesda Naval Hospital about fifteen minutes ago, reportedly carrying the President of the United States. Our sources say that Wade Kincaide has been shot. At this time, we cannot confirm the President's condition, or the extent of his wounds. Another unsubstantiated report out of the White House indicates that President-Elect Brady Lawrence has been fatally shot, and his body is en route to Bethesda. The White House has not released an official statement, but moments ago, a spokesperson announced that a news conference is imminent. Station

WUSA-9 will stay on this story throughout the night to bring you more breaking news as it develops. This is Lee Stressenger, reporting for WUSA."

No one in the room moved. Everyone stared at the television screen in disbelief. Ingrid Sheppard finally broke the silence. "Has the Speaker of the House been relocated to a safe house?"

The agent looked at the woman who, if the reports about Brady Lawrence's death were accurate, would be the next President of the United States. "Yes, Ma'am, he has."

Marty held tight to Ingrid's hand. Unashamed tears fell down her cheek. "I'm right beside you, darling. We'll pray that President Kincaide is alive."

Chapter Twenty-Four

Maggie sat in the dark, watching Tiana sleep. She was afraid to go to bed and sleep because of the fear that gripped her soul. Fear for her daughter's safety. Long before the accident that took the use of her legs, she'd lay awake at night, listening to every sound, too afraid to close her eyes. Her kidnapper's leering face came to her in her dreams, and his words haunted her. It was Tiana that the serial killer, Sandro, had wanted as a hostage, not her. Tiana had slept in the nanny's room that night, and Sandro's men took Maggie instead to use as a bargaining chip against Cara Cipriano, her best friend. McKenzie knelt alongside Maggie's wheelchair. "Honey, she's asleep. We'll leave the door open. Let's get you into the whirlpool, and then I'll give you that massage."

Maggie kissed McKenzie lightly on the lips. "What would I ever do without you, my love?"

"You'll never have to find out."

"Will you join me? Your day hasn't been any better. The water will feel good, and I need to feel you close to me right now."

McKenzie's eyes softened, filled with the love she felt for Maggie. Then, in her thickest Irish brogue, she said, "Now, how could a warm blooded Irish woman refuse an offer like that?" She gathered Maggie's face between her hands. "I love you so, Maggie."

After bathing, McKenzie turned on the whirlpool and helped Maggie in, then joined her, positioning Maggie between her legs. Maggie leaned her head back against McKenzie's breast and McKenzie wrapped her arms around her. Soon, McKenzie could feel Maggie's tension begin to ease. They sat quietly for a long while, enjoying the comfort each derived from the other, then McKenzie kissed along Maggie's neck and whispered into her ear, "Are you ready to get out, love?"

Enjoying the attention and the sensation of McKenzie's lips as they caressed her neck, Maggie groaned. "Hmm, I think that might be a good idea."

Love shone in McKenzie's eyes as she gently helped Maggie from the whirlpool and wrapped a towel around her. Tonight, she sensed that Maggie was troubled and needed a loving touch. She took her time and fussed, pleased that Maggie let her help her to dry off. She always took special care when inspecting Maggie's skin, and tonight even more so. She gently massaged Maggie's muscles as she went. Love for Maggie filled her heart as her fingers touched and caressed the softness of her skin. She knew that she had never loved anyone as much.

Maggie was lying on her stomach watching a naked McKenzie standing next to the bed, drying her hair. She could feel the warmth spreading throughout her body. She loved the feeling. It made her feel alive. The frustration of not being able to use her legs was always there, but because of McKenzie's gentle patience and love, their sex life was pleasurable for them both.

She trailed her fingers up McKenzie's thigh and McKenzie chuckled and dropped the towel, then straddled the back of Maggie's legs. She poured the heated essential oil into her palms and rubbed her hands together. The oil made her hands tingle and, when she massaged it into Maggie's thighs and hips, Maggie groaned.

"It's not my imagination, Kenzie. I swear I can feel a warmth on my upper legs and thighs when you rub on the oil."

McKenzie loved the feel of Maggie's skin under her hands, and she gave thanks every day that this wonderful woman chose to love her. She worked her way up Maggie's spine, taking time to massage and stimulate around every muscle and each vertebra. "How does this feel, love?"

"Hmm...I'm enjoying this too much to answer. Just keep doing what you're doing."

"Oh, you are, are you?" McKenzie nibbled along Maggie's spine to the back of her neck. "Tell me, my love, what else would make you feel good?"

Maggie tilted her head. "Let me turn over. It would be more effective if I show you."

It broke McKenzie's heart to see Maggie's effort as she positioned her legs so she could turn over, but she didn't offer to help. It would undermine the independence and confidence Maggie worked so hard to accomplish. Once Maggie was on her back, McKenzie, as always, was stunned by Maggie's beauty. Maggie was the woman that songs were written about. Her long slender legs and perfect breasts drove McKenzie wild with desire. Maggie had inherited her olive skin and brown hair from her father's side of the family, but her unusual light blue eyes and lovely smile came from her mother. McKenzie looked into those eyes and her heart did a stutter step when Maggie winked.

"Now quit gawking and come here; let me show you what would feel good."

McKenzie leaned over and kissed the inside of one thigh, then the other. She used her shoulders to position Maggie's legs so she could settle between them. Maggie's nipples grew hard as McKenzie's tongue teased and formed around each one. "Now tell me, Maggie, my love, just what you have in mind?"

Before Maggie could answer, McKenzie slid down and her tongue tasted the sweetness that was only one woman, Maggie.

A feeling of euphoria filled both women as they lay spent in each other's arms. Maggie brushed the damp red hair from McKenzie's forehead. "I love you, McKenzie Quinn. The day you came into my life was the luckiest day of my life. I hope to spend the rest of my life giving you the same joy and love you've given to me. Oh, I do love you, my dear McKenzie, with all my heart."

McKenzie's eyes filled with tears of happiness; Maggie's words cradled her heart. "Maggie, my love, with the sweetness that rolls off your blessed tongue, I would surely swear that you were a true Irish lass. You mean everything to me. I love you too, my darling, so very, very much, and I'll spend the rest of my life telling you that."

Maggie lay in McKenzie's arms thinking how very blessed she was to still have McKenzie in her life. Maggie had met McKenzie when she came to Cipriano for a Santa Barbara Vintner Festival. When McKenzie decided to move from Tucson and buy into a law firm in Santa Barbara, Maggie had offered to acquaint her with the Santa Barbara area. Both had lost at love and when their hearts began to heal, they found that they had a growing attraction for one another. They fell in love and built a home on Santini property that overlooked the Pacific Ocean. They were raising Tiana together, and they were in love. Life was perfect. Until the accident that had almost killed Maggie.

Days later when Maggie woke in the hospital, the last thing she remembered was laughing and telling her brother how happy she was and how much she had grown to love the spirited McKenzie Quinn. After the accident, Maggie's relationship with McKenzie suffered. In her grief, she tried to drive McKenzie away. She wasn't going to tie McKenzie to a woman who was a paraplegic. But McKenzie's love for her and her stubborn Irish nature wouldn't budge, and their love survived and grew stronger.

Maggie shivered and McKenzie's arms tightened around her. McKenzie's love surrounded her and she felt safe, but she could not eradicate her fears. At times, she would still wake at night seeing the face of her kidnapper. She had always been an independent woman, strong mentally, as well as physically. After the kidnapping she had lost her balance for a while, but had regained it before the accident.

"You're thinking too much, love. Can you try to go to sleep or do you want to talk?"

"It's times like this when I feel so helpless, so inadequate. Since the accident, I have to depend on you and others to do so much for me. This threat and the uncertainty of what is going to happen to all of us, especially to my father and Liberty, as well as to our country, has me on edge and frustrated. I'm not of much use tied to a wheelchair."

"I can't say I know how you feel, love. No one can, except someone who has experienced what you have. I can tell you this — I will protect you and Tiana with my life. We'll get through this, and when it's over, we are going to move back into our own home. We'll raise Tiana, and grow old watching our grandchildren grow and the sun rise and set on every day, lying in each other's arms. I promise you, Maggie, for the rest of our lives, I will fill each day with as much joy and love as you can possibly stand. I also promise you that we will do everything it takes to get back the use of your legs. It will happen, I just know it."

Tears rolled down Maggie's cheek. McKenzie held her until she felt Maggie relax against her. She kissed her lips softly and pulled the sheet and blanket up so Maggie wouldn't feel cold. "Honey, you didn't eat much tonight. How about if I go and fix something for us to snack on while we watch the news?"

Maggie turned on the television as McKenzie slipped out from under the covers and put on her robe to go downstairs. When McKenzie returned, carrying a tray of food, Maggie was staring at the television in disbelief. McKenzie took one look at Maggie and then at the television. "What's wrong, Maggie!"

"Oh my God, McKenzie, President Kincaide has been shot!"

Armanno sat at his desk drinking a bottomless cup of strong, black coffee, hoping that it would ease the cold feeling he had in his gut. He'd been making phone calls throughout the night, ever since Mack Kincaide had called him and filled him in on what had happened — how Lawrence grabbed an agent's gun and shot the President, and how the Secret Service agents then shot and killed Lawrence. The news reports had not yet reported that Brady Lawrence had done the shooting, but had confirmed that Brady Lawrence had died of gunshot wounds he had suffered at the same time President Kincaide was shot. Wade Kincaide had been in surgery for hours, and the world was holding its breath waiting. Armanno had spoken to Mack several times during the long night, and had been kept informed about Wade's condition.

Armanno took his coffee and went out the doors to the veranda, where he stood looking out over the fog-shrouded vineyards in the dim gray light of morning. He was thinking about Mack Kincaide, who was hell bent on not allowing his brother to sacrifice his career, his reputation, by trying to atone for the heinous deeds for which Brady Lawrence was responsible. Mack had asked Armanno and Liberty to meet with him. They had been scheduled to fly to DC that morning to meet with the Attorney General to go over a plan to neutralize Lawrence and find the assassin who did his bidding. If the traitor hadn't died at the hands of the Secret Service, the two remaining Talons would have eliminated him.

Out of the fog came the vision of a dark day in Dallas and the days that followed. The world wept as a little boy stood bravely and saluted a goodbye to his father. The words Robert Kennedy spoke years later, only months before his own assassination, echoed in Armanno's mind. "We've had difficult times in the past. We will have difficult times in the future. It is not the end of violence; it is not the end of lawlessness; it is not the end of disorder." Robert Kennedy had known that the world would all too soon forget the lessons taught by our violent history.

Armanno said a silent prayer for Wade Kincaide and grieved for mankind, because he knew that the infection and corruption of a Brady Lawrence would rise again. There would always be those who feared the dream in the eyes of leaders like John and Robert Kennedy and Martin Luther King, Jr.

He stared into the fog. Lawrence's death at the hands of the Secret Service solved many problems. The medical records were already in place to support the story that Brady Lawrence's bizarre behavior had been the result of a brain tumor. As deceptive as that would be, Wade Kincaide, whether he lived or died, would then rightfully be remembered for his distinguished career and all the things he had accomplished while in office. In a few days, a new president would be sworn in — the first woman president, and a lesbian. But first and foremost, the country would have the leadership of Ingrid Sheppard. He was contemplating his future, as well as Liberty's, when he heard a noise behind him. He turned to see Liberty standing in the doorway.

"It isn't over. Lawrence's assassin is still out there. There's no reason now for the assassin to be concerned with Kayla and her family. It doesn't matter that they know about Lawrence or the Talons. Now, many others know. Whoever it is out there is too smart to take any unnecessary risks by killing them." Liberty stood next to Armanno looking out. "It's you and me that the assassin wants. This traitor will know that we will never stop until we find him. It's time I stop being a pawn in this game. We make too easy a target if we stay together here. If I leave, the assassin will follow me."

Armanno agreed. He'd anticipated Liberty's plan to lead the assassin away, but he didn't know where she would choose to fight this battle. "Where will you go and how can I help?"

"To Chimayó, the little village where I was raised in the Sangre de Cristo Mountains. It's the only place I guess I can call home. It's isolated and the Pueblo will not interfere. I need to go alone, Armanno."

"I understand. If you succeed, will you contact me?"

Liberty's eyes saddened and turned the color of the storm clouds gathering overhead. "I hope, my friend, that you never hear from either one of us again."

Armanno nodded. "When will you leave?"

"As soon as I... I should..."

Armanno wondered what in life was fair. The good guys didn't always win and ride off into the sunset, and the corrupt ones in the world didn't always pay for the wrong they did. Liberty was one of the good guys who had been betrayed, just as the rest of the Talons had. She'd lived her life with little love, and when she finally found it, it was too late.

"After you left last night, Kayla went to your room looking for you. I could see the disappointment in her eyes when she came back downstairs. She didn't sleep, no one did. Everyone stayed up waiting to hear any news about Kincaide. She asked me this morning if you would return to the villa and if you were all right. She cares for you, Liberty. It is your decision whether you speak with her before you go."

Two old friends, who had fought many a battle together, stood side by side, each fearing that it would be for the last time. No more words were needed. The fog rolled across the veranda and when Armanno turned to where Liberty had been standing, she had slipped away, leaving him alone in the cold light of dawn.

Chapter Twenty-Five

Everyone was still gathered in the great room in front of the television, listening to an update on President Kincaide's condition. He had made it through the surgery and was holding his own, but his condition was still critical. Reports remained sketchy about how Lawrence had been killed, but the intrigue was building. Rumor and speculation were running wild, fueling the hysteria. Until Ingrid Sheppard could be sworn in, the Speaker of the House had his hands full coordinating the security of the United States. The country was in shock, and might be viewed by terrorists as vulnerable to attack. The focus of the world was now on Ingrid Sheppard, the first woman to become President of the United States. The opposing party was already rushing frantically to exert its influence to prevent her from nominating the person who would likely be her choice for Vice President — the moderate Democratic senator from New York, Dean Rodney.

When Liberty entered the room, she caught Kayla's eye, then with a heavy heart, she climbed the stairs and walked toward her room. One thing lay easy on her mind, the fact that Lawrence was dead. Kayla and her family would be safe now. No doubt Kayla and Nathan would want to return to Lone Mountain as soon as possible. Armanno had said that he was going to encourage Cassie to stay at the villa and continue her recovery under the supervision of Dr. Bagenstos.

Liberty stood looking out the window at the rain that had begun to fall. If Kayla did come to her room, she wondered what she should say to her. Hearing the door open, she turned. Anything either might have wanted to say was left unspoken as they stood facing each other. Liberty hesitantly opened her arms and Kayla walked into them and wrapped her arms around Liberty's waist.

"Please, just hold me."

The only sound in the room was the rain beating against the window as they undressed and crawled between the sheets and into each other's arms. Liberty knew it would be for the last time. "Kayla, you know that I have to—" Soft lips stopped the words that neither wanted to hear. They made love, and after, when Kayla had dozed off, Liberty slipped quietly out of the room and out of Kayla's life.

Liberty flew from Santa Barbara to Albuquerque on a commercial flight and rented a car in her own name, making it easy for anyone to follow her. She didn't bother to look over her shoulder. The assassin would come; it was only a matter of when. She would be ready. The sun was beginning to set when she check into a motel for a few hours of sleep before driving to Santa Fe, New Mexico, then north to Chimayó on the High Road to Taos. She felt at peace as she passed the rolling mesas and copper colored hills toward the sacred piece of land known for its healing powers. It seemed appropriate to return to the place where so many pilgrims sought healing and spiritual penance. As the apple orchards and tin-roofed adobe homes disappeared into the rear view mirror, Liberty's thoughts were of the woman she had left behind. *I didn't tell you that I love you, Kayla, but I do.*

She reached Chimayó just as the sun was beginning to crest over the Sangre de Cristo Mountains. It was the first time since she had left for college that she had returned to the tiny village where she'd grown up. She pulled over in front of a restaurant, stepped out of the car, and inhaled a deep breath. The air at 6200 feet was invigorating and cool. It soothed her soul as well as her senses. Rays of gold from the morning sun broke through the gray clouds as she walked up onto the screened porch that was covered with woody bougainvillea vines. The aroma of fresh coffee brewing greeted her when she opened the door and walked into the café. As she took a seat at the counter, memories of her childhood washed over her. An old woman, face wrinkled from years of the sun and hard work, placed a mug in front of her and poured coffee.

"Do you want breakfast?"

Doroteia Naha's dark eyes seemed to stare into Liberty's soul. A hint of a smile formed around Liberty's eyes. "All depends. Do you still make those apple filled sweet cakes?"

"I see you still have that sweet tooth, Starr."

Liberty chuckled. Doroteia had always called her Starr. "I'll have one of your special sweet cakes and a cup of coffee."

"Humph...you're still as thin as a rail. A good wind would blow you away as easy as the tumbleweed."

The old woman came back with the sweet cakes and two bacon and egg burritos. As tempting as Doroteia's cooking was, Liberty didn't have an appetite, but she knew she would need her strength. She finished one of the burritos, then took out a bill and set it on the counter as the woman poured her another cup of coffee. "Can a person buy some hiking gear around here?"

"If you remember where the general store is, you can get what you need there. Just follow the creek that runs past the church. You won't miss it. You planning on staying a while, Starr?" The sadness in Liberty's eyes didn't escape Doroteia's sharp eye.

"They still rent rooms across the street?"

"They do, and this time of year you will have your pick, especially of ones facing the street." The old woman hesitated a moment. "They came and told us you were dead. Said you got killed in some foreign place." She shrugged. "Didn't surprise me when you walked in. You always came and went like a ghost. The government sent us a medal. It's hanging in the Santuario."

A sardonic look crossed Liberty's face. A medal in return for a wasted life; somehow it didn't seem like a very good trade. "Doroteia, is that old cabin on the mountain overlooking the lake still standing?"

Doroteia nodded. "It will be cold out there this time of year, but there's plenty of firewood and provisions. Just replace what you use."

Liberty stood up and the old woman's eyes followed her. "If anyone comes looking for me, tell them where I can be found."

The old woman went to the window and watched as Liberty strode down the street toward the church. She wasn't the same person as the young woman who had left Chimayó. Her soul had aged and the light had left her eyes. Doroteia sensed a dark sadness in Liberty's heart. She had seen it before in the eyes of those who were preparing for their final journey. Liberty Starr had come home to die.

Doroteia looked at her husband who had appeared beside her. He shook his head and said solemnly, "She's a strange one, that Starr. Even when she was a small child, she would look at you with those eyes as if she could see into your soul. Now she has come home, and she has brought the devil with her."

"Old man, I feel that you are right, but she did not bring the devil. The devil is yet to come."

There was a light covering of snow on the road Liberty walked along. When she came to El Santuario, she stopped. The Pueblo held twin beliefs — Christianity, and the ways of their ancestors. Honoring those beliefs was why the Pueblo had accepted Liberty: she was found abandoned in a basket beside the altar, lying on sacred ground in the Santuario. Why she had been left did not matter. The Pueblo believed it was an omen, that their ancestors had sent Liberty to them for a reason. Now she stood outside the arched entrance looking at the crosses on top of the twin bell towers. The adobe church held the powers of the sacred earth, Tierra Bendita. It was where her life with the Pueblo had started. She took a step toward the entrance, then determinedly continued toward the general store.

In her rented room later, Liberty packed the supplies and gear she'd bought, including a few bottles of water, into a backpack. If she needed more water, she would melt snow on the potbellied stove in the cabin. She estimated it would take the assassin no more than two days, possibly less, to figure out where she was. In the morning, when the package arrived containing the weapons that Armanno was sending, she would drive to Taos and leave the car, then hike in to Wheeler's Peak and the cabin on Blue Lake.

Liberty looked around the room. It was comfortable enough and had a kiva fireplace with plenty of wood piled beside it. She crumpled up a newspaper and used a few pieces of kindling to light a fire to chase away the chill. She checked out the bath, then stripped. She usually showered, but tonight she turned on the faucets in the tub and eased down into the hot water. She couldn't fend off the loneliness she felt deep in her heart. Closing her eyes, she leaned her head back against the tub and thought about Kayla. She treasured every touch and each memory, telling herself that it was enough. It wasn't. She needed Kayla, needed to feel the warmth of her smile and her touch. Her heart ached for what would never be.

Morning found Liberty lying awake, staring at the ceiling. She knew that she had made the right decision by coming to Chimayó. The old cabin on the lake was isolated, and the area was restricted to the Pueblo. She dressed in jeans and a sweater and pulled on her boots, then went across the street to Doroteia's and sat in a seat by the window. She sipped her coffee and looked out at the main street of Chimayó. Everything in her life had changed, she had changed, but the small community of Chimayó had stayed the same. When the package from Armanno was delivered, she took it back to her room. Her rifle had been broken down and placed in a pack, along with her scope and her SIG. He had taken care of everything, including ammunition for both weapons.

It was still early when she drove on to Taos and parked the car she'd rented, then began her hike in to the lake and the cabin. The old log dwelling had been built as a lookout by the forest service when the federal government placed the land under the control of that agency in 1906. In 1970, the land and lake were returned to the Pueblo. The transfer of the land made the sacred lake and mountains off-limits to all but the Taos Pueblo.

It had been a long time since Liberty had trekked in to the cabin, but she knew the trail well. Growing up, she'd made the hike many times, spending as much time as she could there. She took it slowly, adjusting easily to the higher elevation, and had just topped a pinon-studded hill when the cabin came into view through the trees. This place that had been her shelter from the world now would be where she would make her last stand.

Chapter Twenty-Six

Liberty made her way along a deer path that brought her to the back of the cabin, then trenched her way around to the front porch through the knee-high snow that had piled up alongside. She cleared the snow away from the door and tried the knob, knowing that she would find it unlocked. Once inside, she lit the oil lamp and built a fire in the fireplace, then stood in the middle of the room and looked around. The cabin was just as she remembered. She lifted her pack onto the wooden table into which she had carved her initials a long time ago, and unpacked her weapons. She cleaned and assembled the rifle and attached the scope, then cleaned the SIG and laid it on the table along with the extra ammo for both weapons. She gathered and stacked firewood in the bin next to the fireplace, and put snow in a pot to melt for wash water. After taking out a bottle of water to make coffee with, she checked the supplies in the cabin. Before long, the small cabin started to warm and the smell of burning wood and boiling coffee filled the room. She poured herself a mug full and took the napkin-wrapped sweet cake out of her pack, then went out to stand on the porch. The sun was just beginning to go down behind the Sangre de Cristo Mountains, and the serene lake shimmered as it reflected the golden color of the setting sun. Its beauty only accentuated the melancholy in Liberty's heart. *Oh, Kayla, I miss you.*

It had grown dark, and the darkness brought the chill of night. Liberty emptied the coffee grounds from her cup and stared out into the blackness. Tonight she would rest; tomorrow she would prepare her mind for what was to come, for what she had not wanted to face.

Sleep did not come, and dawn found Liberty sitting on the top of a high peak overlooking the rugged canyon and the lake below. Even without her scope, she could see for miles in all directions. She spotted movement on the eastern side of the lake among the juniper and pinon pine and brought the rifle up so she could get a better view through the scope. A herd of mule deer was making its way down to the water. As the day passed, the memories of her childhood growing up amongst the Pueblo people flooded her thoughts. The Pueblo were a simple people, honest and hard working. They had taught her honor and respect for the land and all living things. Ancient cries and drums from the past carried on the wind and echoed through the canyon below. The sacred ground beneath her feet remembered the heartbeat of the Pueblo. A lone tear slid down Liberty's cheek. She had fallen so far from grace.

Shadows were beginning to grow long when Liberty decided to head back down the trail to the cabin. No one would try hiking the rugged terrain around the lake in the dark. She'd made her way down the trail to within a few yards of the cabin when she heard what sounded like the crunch of a pine nut behind her. She slipped into a crouching position and froze. The pounding of her heart was a deafening roar in her ears. A full moon crept in and out of the clouds, playing tricks in Liberty's mind as her eyes scanned for the danger lurking in the shadows.

Liberty closed her eyes and allowed all of her senses to feel what was around her. She could hear the howl of a coyote off in the distance and the shuffling of an owl along a tree branch. The wind brought the smell of mule deer bedded down in pine needles. She caught the familiar scent before she heard the rustle of something that did not belong in the forest. There in the place that she longed to leave as a child, it became crystal clear. It had been there all along, hidden in the part of her mind that refused to believe. Her head dropped to her chest as she fell to her knees. *Oh God, I know.*

She stood up with the rifle in one hand by her side and raised her eyes as if she could see through the darkness and into of the soul of the person that waited there. She spoke as she turned and walked toward the cabin. "You're here, make your move."

Liberty sat in front of the fire, but the flames couldn't chase away the cold hand that held her heart. She was numb. How could she not have known, not seen it from the beginning? She covered her face with her hands and forced her mind to think of Kayla. After a while, she got up and emptied her pack and put the replacement supplies she'd brought on the shelves, then she doused the fire and made sure it was out. She reached into her pocket and placed her silver Peace Dollar on the table, on top of the letter that she'd written and addressed to Kayla, then she picked up her rifle and went out the door. She started toward Blue Lake. It was as if a hand was guiding her along, protecting her from the perils of the night. She hiked along the tree line toward the same peak she had sat on the morning before. When she reached the top, she calmly stood and looked out into the blackness where the moonlight reflected off the water. As the darkness began to wane into the grayness of dawn, Liberty gathered dry wood to start a fire. She sat with her back to the lake, facing the trees with the rifle across her lap. She knew that the assassin was close. Her breathing slowed as she heard a breath being taken, and against her chest she could feel the heartbeat of the person watching her. Her eyes lowered and she stared into the flames. When she heard the voice that spoke from the grave, she set the rifle down beside her on the ground and continued to stare into the fire as the figure slowly approached. Liberty never looked up, nor did she speak.

"It doesn't surprise me that you know, that you've been expecting me. I know this has to be hard for you to accept. I never meant for it to go this way. It wasn't easy for me to leave you that day the way I did, but it had to look convincing."

The reflection of the flames flashed in Liberty's eyes and anger flashed in her heart. "Was it easy for you to take the lives of the Talons, Yancy? What was it that you valued so much that you sold us all out, the money? You killed them! The men and woman who would have laid down their lives for you, you murdered in cold blood." Yancy didn't answer and neither woman moved. "Did you ever love me, or was I just a pawn that you and Lawrence could mold into the perfect assassin?"

Yancy approached, then stood still on the other side of the fire. Liberty finally looked up into the face of the woman she'd loved and had grieved for, into the eyes of the woman that had betrayed her. Yancy still took her breath away. She was older, and the hardness that etched Liberty's own face was there, but Yancy was still as beautiful as she remembered. She had looked up at Yancy with the same wounded expression the day she'd gotten her nose broken at the Academy. That day Yancy had come to her rescue; today, she had come to take her life. Liberty's eyes went to the ring hanging around Yancy neck — cascading diamonds and sapphires set in white gold. The gift she was going to give Yancy for their anniversary.

"I couldn't leave it behind. I've worn it every day since I left you."

As she looked at the woman she'd once loved, Liberty fought to keep control, to hold back the resentment. "What now, Yancy?"

The voice that she had longed to hear for so many years told her, "If I had wanted to kill you, I could have done that at anytime. I only meant to wing you in Denver to convince Lawrence I tried, but he was getting suspicious. That day on the mountain in Montana, when the agent reached into his pocket, I thought he was going for a weapon. Lawrence had a tail on me, hoping that I would lead him to you. I didn't know until later that the one I shot was Kincaide's man. I had you dead in my sights when you went down that mountain. I had to make that look good, too. I didn't want to tip my hand, so I aimed at the rocks until you were out of sight."

Liberty stood up. "You know Lawrence is dead. Why are you here?"

Yancy didn't answer right away and she never moved a muscle. Finally she said, "Because I knew that you wouldn't give up looking until you found me, and neither would Santini."

Liberty's face darkened. "You always were savvy. You're right, we wouldn't have. I imagine Armanno already suspects that you are the assassin. I knew that you wouldn't leave it to chance that Armanno or I wouldn't come for you one day, just as I knew you would follow me here. Last night I could feel your eyes on me; I could smell your sweat, yes, and your fear."

Yancy slowly walked around the fire until she was standing so close that Liberty could feel her breath on her skin. Yancy slipped her hand to the back of Liberty's head and pulled her close, then kissed her. The taste of Yancy was imbedded in Liberty's memory. Without thinking, she responded, taking Yancy's tongue into her mouth. But it wasn't Yancy's face that flashed in Liberty's mind; it was Kayla's. She broke the kiss and reached up and removed Yancy's hand from behind her head.

Yancy put her hands on Liberty's chest. "It doesn't have to end this way for us, Liberty. We could leave here and go someplace and be together." When Liberty didn't respond, Yancy stepped back, and in a split second, a knife appeared in her hand. She lunged. Liberty deflected the sharp blade, but it caught her, slicing deep into her arm just above the wrist. The blood was running down Liberty's hand, staining the snow-covered ground red as she circled the fire and backed away from Yancy. The knife had sliced through the muscle, rendering her arm useless. "Is this what you want, Liberty? Do you want me to kill you?"

"How did you kill the rest of the Talons? Did you even give them a chance, or did you make them suffer? Did they see it coming? Did they know it was you?" Liberty cautiously took another step back toward the granite edge of the peak as Yancy continued to stalk her.

"I've watched you through the years, Liberty. You condemn me, but you all killed without conscience, just as I have. You're no different than I am. Your price was just different. Tell me, is there a difference between money and a cause, Liberty? The act of killing is the same." Yancy moved closer, but not close enough for Liberty to use her long legs to defend herself. "You never stayed with anyone longer than was necessary to complete your mission. It's that bartender, isn't it? I could have killed her, you know. Lawrence wanted her dead. He wanted her whole family dead."

Liberty stiffened at the mention of Kayla, but it displaced the passive acceptance of her fate with anger.

Yancy sensed it and acted, thrusting the knife at Liberty's heart. Liberty stumbled as she felt the cool blade tearing through the skin beneath her jacket. It sunk deep into her chest. She gasped as she felt the air sucked from her lungs and the taste of blood in her mouth. Her good hand moved up and gripped Yancy's wrist. Her only thought was that she couldn't let Yancy extract the knife out and sink it again. The heel of her boot was over the edge of the rocky peak as her other arm went around Yancy's waist, pulling her as close as she could. She was falling backward off the cliff, and she wasn't going alone.

Yancy's eyes widened in disbelief as they grappled and went over the edge. They hit something and Liberty felt as if she had broken every bone in her body. She let go of Yancy and somehow managed to grab at a tangle of roots growing out of the side of the mountain. Her body jerked to a stop and she felt Yancy grab onto her boot. The pain was excruciating as they hung together, dangling from the side of the mountain. Desperately, Liberty gripped the vines with her one hand. She heard a scream echo across the canyon. Was it her own or was it Yancy's? The knife was still protruding from her chest and blood was pumping from the wound on her arm. She couldn't get any air into her lungs. She knew that it was over. Kayla and Armanno would be safe.

The weight of both of them was too much, and Liberty's hand slipped along the root. She could feel the burning pain in her palm as she desparately tried to hold on. Dangling above the jagged rocks, Liberty gasped for air as she looked down at Yancy who was still clutching her leg. It was the face she'd once loved. Their eyes locked just before Yancy released her leg and Liberty's hand slipped from the roots. Liberty's boot caught in a tangle of exposed roots and she was propelled headfirst. The sound of the bones of her leg breaking echoed across the valley below before her body impacted against the ragged rocks on the side of the mountain.

Chapter Twenty-Seven

Cassie trailed behind Tiana as she traversed down the bunny slope.

"You're doing great, Tiana! Step into the turn. Good!"

When they got closer to the bottom of the hill, Tiana was picking up speed a little too quickly. "Snowplow, Tiana, snowplow!"

Tiana and Cassie reached the bottom of the bunny slope at the same time. Tiana was excited that she'd made it down without falling for the first time. She hugged Cassie and turned to wave enthusiastically at her mother and McKenzie who were watching from the deck of Lone Mountain Ski Lodge.

"Can we go down one more time, Cassie? I won't ask to go again. Please!"

Cassie laughed. "That's what you said the last two times, Tiana. I have to help get things ready for the torchlight parade tonight. Come on. If you'd like, you can ask your mom if we can come out after you open your presents in the morning."

Tiana hurried and took off her skis and ran toward the deck, Cassie on her heels. "Mom, can me and Cassie come out skiing tomorrow?"

Maggie and McKenzie burst out laughing at Tiana's eagerness. "Cassie and *I*. I take it that you like to ski, Tiana."

"Mom, I love it! Can we come back one more time this year? Pretty please!"

"We'll see. Now go change and get ready for dinner so you can eat and rest a while. You don't want to be too tired to watch the festivities later."

McKenzie got up and kissed Maggie on the top of her head. "Come on, Tiana, I'll go with you. I still have a few presents to wrap that one nosy someone has been trying to see. Darling, I would ask you if you want to come in, but I want to finish wrapping your gifts."

"As if I'm the one who shakes a box to death, asking every minute if she can open just one." Maggie laughed. "You go ahead. I want to visit with Cassie a bit, then I'll be along."

Cassie wheeled Maggie into the lodge and found a table by the fire, then went and fetched two cups of hot chocolate. "I'm so glad you all came up for the holiday. I've missed you. I will never be able to thank you all for what you did for me. You shared your beautiful home, and doctor, with me for weeks. For a while there I thought I would never walk again, let alone ski." Cassie realized how that might have sounded to Maggie. "Oh, Maggie, I'm sorry...that must have..."

True to her good nature, Maggie immediately put Cassie at ease. "It's all right, Cassie. Nothing pleases me more than to see you up out of that wheelchair. You know we're back in our own home now, and, as much as we love La Villa Dell'uva, it's good to be home. We expect you all to come and visit so Tiana can show you her California girl skills and teach you how to snorkel and surf."

"Maggie, I think Tiana would be great at any sport she chooses to participate in. She really is a natural athlete."

"I haven't told you this yet — I guess we were afraid it wasn't real — but I have feeling in my thighs, and Avril believes I will regain even more in my lower legs."

Cassie jumped up off the chair and threw her arms around Maggie's neck. "Oh, Maggie, that is the best present anyone could have given me! Can we tell Kayla?"

"I knew you would be as excited as we are. We planned to tell you all tonight, but I thought the moment called for it now." Maggie sipped her chocolate. "Cassie, how is Kayla? Is she doing all right? At times, I think so, but it's hard to tell."

Cassie looked out at the mountain. "She's been through a rough patch, but she's doing okay. She's still sober; she's faced her feeling for the mountain, and is actually skiing again. Sometimes I think she has finally laid Addie to rest, then I see her looking at the mountain with sadness in her eyes, and I wonder how much of that sadness is for Liberty Starr. It's hard to believe that it was a year ago tonight that Liberty walked into the pub, and our lives, and touched us all. She saved my life, and, in many ways, gave Kayla's life back to her."

Maggie thought about the night on Sandro's boat when Liberty took the shot that killed Sandro, saving her life as well as Cara's. "I know. Liberty saved my life, too, a long time ago."

"Your father has never heard anything from her?"

"No, he never has. Nothing since the letter and silver dollar for Kayla were delivered to him."

Both women sat quietly for a few minutes, each lost in their own memories of Liberty Starr. Finally, Maggie broke the silence. "Where ever she is, I hope she has found the peace and forgiveness her soul was looking for."

Kayla closed the pub early, loaded her skis onto the snowmobile, and headed for the chair lift. She wanted to spend some time alone on the mountain before the crowds showed up for the Christmas Eve torch procession. She loved being on top of the mountain, looking out at the beauty of Montana that surrounded her. It was her way of praying. By the time she reached the lift, it had started to snow, just like it had the last Christmas Eve. She leaned against the snowmobile and looked out across the snow-covered mountains. She thought about Addie and about Liberty, the two women she had loved. Each held a special place in her heart. The ache for both would always be there, but she was learning to live one day at a time.

Mike had shut the lift down until the skiers arrived for the evening festivities. He was surprised when he saw Kayla unload her skis from the snowmobile. "Hey, Kayla, what brings you up here so early? The procession doesn't start for a couple of hours."

"I'm not skiing tonight, Mike. I'd like a little time alone up on the mountain."

"Sure, Kayla. By the time you get to the lift, I'll have it up and running."

Kayla put her skis down, slipped her boots into the bindings, and picked up her poles. "Is Nathan going to run the lift tonight so you and Anne can go into Kalispell to spend Christmas Eve with your son?"

"He is running the lift, but my family is spending tonight and Christmas here with us on Lone Mountain. The grandkids are all into skiing now since their parents gave them skis last year. Can't keep 'em off the mountain. I'll sign you in and put the time you went up in the log book."

"Thanks, Mike. I'll see you later. Enjoy the festivities, and Merry Christmas!"

It had started to snow lightly and snowflakes landed gently on Kayla's hair and shoulders as she rode the chair lift up the mountain. The big sky of Montana was brilliantly lit by what seemed like an endless parade of stars. Kayla could feel the subtle change in temperature and looked toward the sky at the snow clouds that were beginning to gather. She felt at peace. The anger for the mountain that she'd held in her heart for so long was no longer there. She had loved two extraordinary women, each as different as night from day, and each had touched her soul.

Kayla reached into her pocket and took out the silver dollar. She held it in her hand and ran her thumb across the image of the eagle. The words from Liberty's note echoed in her heart. *I never told you, but I love you, Kayla. My heart had turned to stone until you gave it wings. Keep this dollar close. It will always bring you good luck.* Kayla put the silver dollar back into her pocket and looked toward the heavens and smiled. "I hope you soar forever, my sweet Liberty." Kayla pushed off down the mountain, toward the pub and home.

Daybreak early that same morning, Christmas Eve, Chimayó, New Mexico

The woman leaned on the old wooden cane and bent to remove a piece of brush that had blown onto the unmarked grave in the cemetery behind the tiny adobe church in Chimayó. She shoved her hands deep into the pockets of her coat and stood for a while, looking down at the grave. She felt the cold seeping deep into her bones.

She had hung from the sacred mountain, near death, but somehow the Pueblo had known, and came and took her down. Her leg had tangled in a small tree that was growing out of the solid rock, breaking her fall. The cold had slowed the loss of blood from her wounds, and the Pueblo and the healing powers of the sacred ground nursed her broken body, and her soul, back to health. She picked up the old duffel and flung it over her shoulder. She had a plane to catch and somewhere to be for Christmas Eve.

Kayla hooked her skis on the rack outside and entered the pub through the kitchen door. She filled the kettle with water and put her favorite mint tea leaves into the teapot, then reached for a mug out of the cabinet. The pub was quiet, so quiet she could hear the ticking of the clock on the wall and the sound of the water as it started to boil. She poured the water into the teapot and leaned against the counter to let the tea steep for a bit. Rue Mican had invited her to dinner at the lodge to meet the new woman in her life. She was happy that Rue had found someone, but she'd graciously declined. She would see her family and friends at the lodge in the morning. Tonight, she planned to watch the torch light procession alone from the deck outside her bedroom with a good cup of tea.

As she climbed the stairs, she remembered having led Liberty up them the previous Christmas Eve. It was the night Lone Mountain was snowed in and a quiet blonde with sad eyes spent the night in her guestroom, the beginning of an implausible sequence of events that had changed the lives of many.

What a year it had been! President Sheppard and Vice President Rodney were leading the United States along a positive path, carving the way past the antiquated leadership that had stifled the growth of the country for so long. Cassie made a full recovery, and they had all become very good friends. Maggie, McKenzie, and Tiana had come to visit and invited Lynne to come along. And Lone Mountain had become Avril Bagenstos' favorite place to ski. Armanno was growing grapes and making the finest wine in California, and Wade Kincaide had survived and was encouraging his brother Matthew Kincaide to run for President following the Sheppard administration.

Kayla set her cup of tea down on the nightstand and grabbed the throw off the foot of the bed. She wrapped it around her shoulders and picked up her cup, then opened the doors to the deck. She sipped the tea as she stood at the railing watching the first of the skiers light their torches and start down the mountain.

"It's quite inspiring, isn't it? Do they do this every year?"

Kayla's breath caught as she turned to see a figure standing there in the shadows on the deck. Her voice shook as she answered, "Yes, ever since I was a little girl." The wraith hesitantly took a step closer and Kayla noticed the limp and the cane.

"I've...been waiting a while...I..."

Kayla trembled as she took a step closer. "You should have come in from the cold."

"I did, a year ago tonight, and it was the best thing I've ever done."

Moonlight reflected off the tears that gathered in Kayla's eyes. She took a step closer. "Do...you plan to stay...in out of the cold?"

"If the woman I love will have me." Liberty's arms went around Kayla and her mouth hungrily found that which had given her the will to survive. The throw slid from Kayla's shoulders as her arms tightened around Liberty's neck. Snowflakes fell softly around them as they held each other. The North Star seemed to wink from behind scattered snowclouds. As a brilliant shower of shooting stars raced across the Montana sky, Liberty whispered in Kayla's ear. "Make a wish."

Kayla's heart was bursting as she trailed kisses on Liberty's face and lips. "I already did. What took you so long?"

J.P. Mercer is a native of Big Sky Country, Montana. She moved to the Valley of the Sun in the Sonoran Desert of southwestern Arizona twenty years ago.

"I never planned to stay, but when I turned around, twenty years had gone by. A native Hawaiian once told me that if a gecko entered your home it meant that good luck would follow. The first living thing that graced my doorstep when I arrived in Arizona was a gecko and good fortune and health did follow.

"As splendid as Arizona is, I am looking forward to going home one day to the mountains of Montana."

J.P.'s interests are as diverse as the ever-changing landscape of the beautiful Sonoran Desert. Writing being on top of that list.

"I believe in friendship, the kind that nurtures and transcends all other frail human emotions. I believe in living each day to the fullest and opening one's heart and mind to the incredible goodness and beauty of all people...regardless."

Contact J.P. Mercer at jpmercerauthor@aol.com.
www.jpmercer.com
www.pdpublishing.com